The road had not been shelled. It had been left open by the Germans, whose guns were trained on its three-mile stretch, waiting for the next column of tanks to advance. By night, dust drifted from the city and from the battlefield to the north of it, and the light of fires turned it orange, and tinged the smoke that crawled from the red horizon. It was not possible to watch the city from the battalion line and believe that men still lived in it.

Falaise was burning, but from the bombed and fire-gutted heart of the city, the Germans still kept up their murderous fire. Now it was to be captured, and the tanks of "C" Squadron were to be part of the assault . . . .

THE KILLING GROUND *is a novel of the great tank battle that smashed the German armored divisions in France. This is war as it was lived by the men who fought in tanks—a man-made inferno, mechanistic, ruthless, reeking of cordite and blood.*

New Ballantine War Books
You Will Enjoy

THE
KILLING GROUND

by

ELLESTON TREVOR

BALLANTINE BOOKS   **NEW YORK**

To
KENNETH AND PEGGY WALLIS

Library of Congress Catalog Card Number: 57-5209

This edition printed by arrangement with the Macmillan Company

First printing   July 1965

Printed in the United States of America

Ballantine Books, Inc., 101 Fifth Avenue,
New York, N.Y. 10003

CONTENTS

GLOSSARY

A.R.V.—Armoured Recovery Vehicle used for recovering bogged-down and crippled tanks.

A.V.R.E.—Armoured Vehicle, Royal Engineers.

Besa—Birmingham and Enfield Small Arms. A machine-gun.

Brew-up—The term has two very different meanings. 'To have a brew-up,' or 'to brew-up' means to make tea. A tank brews-up, however, when it is hit and starts blazing.

Coaxial—Machine-gun that turns with the turret.

D.D.—Dual-drive tank—amphibious.

Echelon lorries—Each squadron has echelons, units for its maintenance and supply. At nightfall after a day's march, echelon lorries come up to the harbour with fuel, supplies and ammunition.

Harbour—Where a tank lies up, usually under a hedge or in some kind of shelter that will help to camouflage it.

Horns—of a tank. The forward ends of the tracks where they run round the leading wheels. They are the first part of a tank to meet obstructions, except where a tank has its gun projecting past them.

LcT—Landing-craft, Tank.

On net—With wirelesses tuned-in to Battalion or other tanks.

Soft vehicles—Those other than armoured vehicles.

S.P.—Self-propelled gun—a very heavy mobile weapon.

Special devices—Armoured and armed vehicles fitted with special equipment for detonating land-mines (with flails, ploughs, etc.), for laying small bridges across gaps, for filling in ditches with 'chespale' (chestnut paling) fascines, for bull-dozing, laying tracks and throwing flame (the crocodiles). These vehicles usually break open the route and clear it of mines and obstructions, giving the fighting-tanks a clear run through.

Start-line—Where the squadron waits, in one of several patterns of formation, to be ordered away on an attack—much like competitors in a motor-race awaiting the flag to start them.

Swan—A long clear run through easy country and little opposition, usually after a bitter attack has given them this momentum.

THE SEA

I

A FEW of the men were standing by the rails, towards the stern. As the light failed, minute by minute, sounds died away too, as if the day were for noise and the night for silence. Across the water, shapes were humped, making a wall against the horizon to the east. They were the main bulk of the convoy, and soon, as night came down, they were blotted out.

LcT 39 became an island, now, in the sea and in the night. On board were six fighting-tanks and forty men, and as the short sea came chopping along the water-line it drove wedge-like waves under the landing-craft, and slipped them out, and drove them in again, so that the thirty-ton tanks moved slowly, bowing and shifting on their suspension in a quiet elephant dance; and more of the men came up from below, to lean over the rails and stay there with their slack bodies hooked over the metal piping, half-asleep with sickness, retching automatically, long past hoping to die. For these men, LcT 39 was not like an island in the sea and in the night; it was a little district of purgatory, a torture-place that rose and fell, lifting them and dropping them until their heads became full of their own moaning and their stomachs empty even of bile.

A dozen of them were untouched, even by the sound of their friends' misery. These chosen ones had nothing physically in common, except the balance mechanism that allowed them to sniff the salt air happily and tune their bodies to the easy rhythm of the ship. Sergeant Goodall was one of them, Trooper Cox another. Lieutenant Pope was up on the bridge, talking to the captain, blessing his luck whenever he heard vomiting from below. Four men were playing cards, crouched on a hatchway amidships.

7

Trooper Adams was leaning his arms, doubled in front of him, against one of the tanks. He was praying, and Sergeant Goodall was listening. Taffy Adams was not praying for any sickness of his own: he was one of the chosen here. He was praying for his friends, and for the future of them all. He was not kneeling, because he knew that humility of the mind was more real than humility of the knees; he was leaning like this, his bent arms against the tank, in a kind of unconscious communion with the tank and therefore with the future. Where it would go, he would go, because this tank was Moby Dick of Two Troop, and he was its driver.

Against the rail, Sergeant Goodall listened to Taffy's prayers. Goodall was not religious; he thought there was a God, and once or twice a year he went to church, and he knew most of the names of the Apostles; but he was not a religious man, in his own mind. He would never do a thing like this: prop himself against Moby Dick and ask the good Lord to deliver his friends and his officers and his generals from death and destruction. Moby Dick had a good straight seventy-five-m.m. gun and a stack of ammunition, and the sergeant would put his faith in that, when the time came to ward off death and destruction. But he liked listening to Taffy's voice; it was a clear Welsh voice, warm and melodious, and the sergeant would have stayed here listening even if Taffy had been reading out the trains from a time-table. The words came fluting softly away from the big hump of the tank, as light and as quick as birds flying up in the gloom. Another thing that Sergeant Goodall enjoyed was Adams's approach to his Lord. He wasn't begging, nor pleading. There was a good deal of diplomacy in this prayer, and persuasion, and even craftiness. Taffy was arguing for the defence, and doing it well. What was the use, he was asking the Lord, in putting the Army to sea, and letting it get smashed up against those beaches on the far side of the Channel? There'd have to be fighting, and they'd fight well enough for the Lord, because they were all good men and the enemy was evil. Some would be weak, and some too rash, and some just plain unlucky they'd be, and these would pass over in all their glory and in the name of God; but the rest must go on, and slash down the enemy and send him running with swords at his back, the bright strong swords of the Lord in all His mighty anger. (Sergeant Goodall felt that Taffy had got a bit on the romantic side in this part, and had forgotten he'd be grinding up the beach in a thirty-ton tank without so much as a pen-knife in his hand, let alone a sword. But the sense was right; he knew what Taffy meant.)

When the prayer had finished, Adams remembered to add a few words on behalf of his mother and his three sisters. In his family there were no men to be blessed; his father had gone, and no brothers had ever come. At eighteen, Taffy had seen himself to be the only Adam among these Adamses, and he had packed his things for the Army. Nothing but frills and fancy things in the whole house, there'd been, making up silly faces, and no room for a man to move in the kitchen but for stockings all hanging round to dry like seaweed, and such a nice fuss if ever he brought a friend to the house, a man, either because he wasn't handsome enough for the girls, or because they wanted him, or some did and some didn't, until Taffy had packed and gone, and glad still. But they weren't beyond praying for. Nobody was beyond that.

He lowered his arms. He had meant every word he had been saying in the prayer, and so he felt better for getting out with it. Evil and sin were like being down the mine among the hard dark coal, and praying was like letting the cold sting of the shower go rushing down you at the day's end. A prayer, like a good wash, was for the day's end, for there was more time, and the little fears of the night were creeping in, and wanted kicking. Higher than where Taff stood, Sergeant Goodall looked down at him, feeling the same benefit from the prayer although he was not a religious man. You can feel almost the same thrill when you watch a good goal scored as when your own boot does it. He said quietly:

"Taff."

Adams looked up, squinting in the gloom. "Who's that, then?"

"Clear off the tank deck, Taffy, it's out of bounds."

"You, is it, Sergeant?"

"You're out of bounds. Clear off before I see you there."

Taffy said confidently, "I been with God, here."

"Then the both of you should know better. Orders are to keep off the tank deck."

Adams said he would go, in a tone of agreement rather than obedience. The sergeant watched him, the small head bobbing as Taffy climbed the ladder rungs, the thin straight limbs of the man loping along the rails towards the stern. If being with God made Taff Adams as good a man as he was, and as good a driver, then the sergeant would keep his blind eye turned, and the Lord was a welcome stowaway.

The landing-craft rocked more slowly soon, but each time it rose it covered more of the sky, and each time it fell it showed more of the faint white sea. The short waves were drawing out, and the ship was meeting with trough and crest in a longer rhythm, so that the men whose bodies were hooked across the rails began retching again, and those below went rolling from side to side, unable to steady themselves with their sweat-softened hands, able only to go on thinking, over and over again, that the pills were no good, the pills were no good against this filthy rotten heaving wreck of a hellish bloody ship.

Taffy lit a cigarette, leaning with his back to a bulk-head, next to Sam Cox. Cox said: "Christ, it's quiet."

"It is."

"What've we stopped for?"

"We been stopped an hour," Adams said.

"What for, then?"

"It's not for us to know, man."

Cox dug his hands deeper into his pockets, his whole body shrinking away from the quietness. It wasn't peace. He was a city boy, but he didn't mind a bit of peace. This was just quietness, the kind that is full of shocks that are holding off until you turn your back, before they come cracking down at you, when you're only half listening and half ready for them. It had been like this in the desert, just before the barrage, many a time; and even if it was your own barrage going up, it was frightening, just the noise, and the awful suddenness of it. He said:

"It's too quiet, Taff."

"It'll start, soon enough."

"Then why doesn't it?"

Adams smoked his cigarette in silence, wondering at the night, what he could see of it, the sky and the sea and the red glow of his cigarette. The Lord God made them all. It was a wonderful thing, just to be here, to be anywhere at all.

"Listen," said Cox. They waited. In a minute he said: "There's planes up."

"Never."

"There's sirens going."

Taffy went on listening, and at last heard the faint far note from northwards over the sea. The sirens were going, along the coast of England, miles away. It was a sound as thin as a thread, taut in the darkness, trembling against the ear, making its tenuous contact between this ship and that land, so fine that a gull's wing, in swooping, might snap it clean.

"I can't hear planes," said Taffy.

"I can, then."

"Never."

"You jus' listen."

"I been listening, man."

The thin far note went drawing out across the night until it snapped, cut through by a voice from above them.

"Put that cigarette out."

Taffy's fingers moved, expertly nipping the end of his cigarette, saving the rest for next time. Another voice sounded, so faintly that they knew it was from another ship, somewhere along the convoy. Sam Cox said: "There's a raid on."

Thinking in terms of a raid, he did not, in his mind's

eye, see wings or bombs; he saw his wife, standing by the bedroom window, watching the sky. She would be there now, looking upwards, her hands on the window-sill. 'Keep away from the window,' he said in his mind, calling all the way across the sea to her; but she said: 'I like watching,' just as she always said, when he was really there with her, on leave, sitting upright in the bed and trying to make her come away from the window. He never knew why she did it; not from bravado, nor because it thrilled her. He never knew so many things about Grace; she was the cool, quiet type, with a slow smile that had to serve as an answer to so many questions. Not that she was secretive, or had anything much to hide: he had made sure about that before they were married, and if her past had been a bit hectic, at least he *knew* about it, and that was all he cared. But why stand near the window, every time Jerry came over? 'Why d'you have to stand near the damn' window?' he asked her again, all the way over the sea. She half-turned and smiled, so he had to prop another pillow up and light a cigarette and sit there trying not to think of her cool, fair face cut suddenly to pieces by the flying glass, with blood where the smile had been. One day, he'd drag her away and back to bed. On his next leave. He had said that, three years ago, and there'd been a lot of leave since, and he'd never done it. But he would, next time, by God he would.

He stood with his hands shrunk into his pockets, listening to the distant sirens, while Adams said:

" 'Tis marvellous, the way you can hear them, over these many miles."

"Bloody marvellous," he grunted.

A man came padding along the iron walkway, one of the naval crew, a petty officer. "You boys okay?"

"We're okay," Cox answered. "When are we moving on?"

"Any time, mate. You the eager type, eh?"

Cox moved his shoulder-blades against the bulkhead, straightening his back. "We just want to get started. The sooner we start, the sooner we finish, is how I see it."

The petty officer put his hands on the rail, facing

north. He was chewing a piece of gum; they watched his jaw-line moving, silhouetted against the glow of the water. He said after a long time: "It's gettin' up."

"What is?"

"Eh? The sea."

"How the hell," Cox said, "are we going to put ashore in France, with the sea rough and most of our blokes down with seasickness?"

The strong dark jaw-line went on moving rhythmically. "We'll put you ashore all right, mate."

Taffy Adams moved across to the rail and stood beside him. He liked the aura of strength that surrounded this sailor. Taffy sought out strong men all his life, men strong in their mind and in the way they lived, whether or not they were big or small in their body. When he was with strong men he was beside his brothers who had never come, and his father who had gone.

He said: "Listen, how many ships in this convoy?"

After a moment the petty officer said: "Twenty-eight."

"All LcTs, are they?"

"Ay."

Adams worked it out. Six times twenty-eight was a hundred and sixty-eight fighting tanks, with their crews alone making eight or nine hundred men. And most of them seasick, if this ship was anything to go on. Five or six hundred men prone in their bunks or draped over the rail, feeling like death.

"That's bad," he said.

"What's bad? Twenty-eight in convoy?"

"No. The sickness. Like a plague, it is."

"Oh, ay."

Taffy Adams half turned, appealing also to Sam Cox. "An invadin' army we are, an' only a few of us can stand up."

Cox grunted. "Can't you think o' something more cheerful?"

Taffy put out a quick hand, grabbing the rail as the big square craft pitched up again. "An' there's all the other convoys, man. Hundreds an' thousan's of ships." He tried to think what they would be carrying, all those ships; but the khaki world outside his mechanised home was unfamiliar to him. Only one other contingent came to mind. "There's the infantry, hundreds an' thousan's of them. I tell you, it's like a plague."

The petty officer chewed his piece of gum, watching the rise and dip of a chance light as the convoy wallowed in the swell. Cox said, keeping his control: "All right, Taff, it's like a plague."

"An' who's goin' to feel like fightin', then?"

"I am, for one," said Cox.

"But we're not sick, man."

Cox stood away from the bulkhead, and let his feet ride up and down with the swinging deck. "There's nothing we can do about it. Let's just forget it, eh?"

"But I been prayin' for us all."

"Then let's hope it'll do some good."

The petty officer said: "They've stopped."

"What have, mate?"

He jerked his head. "Sirens."

"Oh-ah." Cox looked northwards, where the land would be. He could see her cool fair face at the window, smiling to him. He loved her very much. When he got back there on leave again, he'd always make her come away from the window; or maybe when his next leave came round, there wouldn't be any more planes over; maybe people could go to their windows and look out at the sky and the trees and flowers without risking a face full of flying glass.

His feet tilted with the deck. "This festering war," he said. Taffy said:

"The trouble with the war is that nobody wants it, an' everybody's got it." Then a bell sounded aft.

The petty officer left them. Adams crouched down low, and lit his cigarette-stub, cupping it carefully so that no one should see the glow of it. Cox said:

"What's the panic, then?"

"I don' know, Sam."

A voice called, and another answered. Within a minute the LcT was trembling to the pulse of her engines. A lamp was flashing, from among the shadows of the convoy. A voice came again, and then for minutes there was no sound but for the sea, but Cox felt the air moving against his face, and heard the engines steady, and felt the swing of the ship die away as the stern came down and the wake went gleaming out behind.

Taffy said: "We're moving."

Cox nodded. "Yes."

"The whole lot of us, goin' off." Twenty-eight of them; a hundred and sixty-eight fighting tanks; eight or nine hundred men. "There wasn't much fuss, was there now?"

Cox said: "No." He leaned with his back to the wind, his face to the north. All through this war, in the idle hours when there was time to think, his face had turned like a compass needle, looking home.

II

A WAVE, four feet high, hit the bows of the leading LcT with the blunt force of a hammer, and drove on towards the next. The flotilla kept station fifteen miles from shore, lying back while the minesweepers worked in the last dark hour before dawn. An onshore wind, rising Force 4, swept over the mounting sea and sent spindrift stinging across the rails. Three assault-craft had turned back an hour ago; another twenty were wallowing on the east fringe of the Juno convoy, struggling to nose into the waves while the waves came beating each as strongly as the next and with no sign of abating. Some of these craft were drawing off north, leaving the big ships to ride it out.

The Navy was working without pause and without humour. Through the long night, ships had come south, gathering. They were assembled now, keeping station in the areas allotted to them; and they could stay here for as long as the orders demanded, whatever the sea; or they could cross the Channel again and again come back; they could sail wherever the signals sent them, and if needs be ride out a storm. But their job was landwards. They had to put an army on to that hidden shore, where the waves raced with a high white malevolence, dashing against the sands; and most of the army was sick. The army was lying down. If it could have chosen, it would have ordered the ships for home, not because these men were afraid of the beaches or the mines or the guns that were there for them, but because a man cannot think about picking up his rifle and running to attack when he is sprawled on the swaying boards of a ship that has never been still, nor is still now, nor will ever be still, because the sea goes on for ever. This feeling, among many of these men, was strong. There would never be a time when they were not lying here in hell, retching their hearts out, with nothing but the stink of their sickness in the air, and nothing but the rise and fall of whatever they lay on or rolled against or pitched into while the whole world rose and fell, rose and fell, and their friends' white faces went floating past them under the lamp, and the lamp swung up, swung down, and another man spewed, and another man spewed, and his face went swaying past in the glare of the swinging lamp.

The invading army was sprawled on its back, long past hoping to die. The attack was scheduled for dawn, in an hour from now.

Lieutenant Pope had come down to the wardroom, where a last conference was in session. In the cramped space, officers in khaki were standing or squashed together on seats, a few of them fit, the rest with white faces and dull eyes, their hands limp, elbows on their knees. Lieutenant Ashton was clutching his greaseproof paper bag, fighting his sickness out and holding on. The Colonel was on his feet, with the maps spread out in front of him. As Lieutenant Pope came in, a medical officer grinned at him and said in an undertone:

"You still all right?"

"I'm all right," Pope said. He swayed to the lift of the ship. "But what about all these other poor bastards? Can't you chaps do anything for them at all?"

"Not a thing, old boy. They'll be okay when the time comes."

"There's another hour, and most of them are half-dead." Pope's throat was tight. He was worried stiff, and furious with the sea, pinning his worry to anger, and pinning his anger to any man who could be blamed: the ship's captain for not handling his ship in some way that would lessen the roll, the R.A.M.C. officer for not producing a pill that would stop the sickness, his own Colonel for standing there as fit as he was with three-quarters of his men knocked out.

"Take it easy," said the M.O., and gave him a cigarette.

"We shall have to do something, you know. We can't start an attack in this state."

"We can, old boy. As soon as we strike the land, and there's something to do, they'll be okay."

Pope left him, squeezing past some of the others until he was next to Major Knowles. "What the hell are we going to do?" he asked him briefly.

Knowles turned his head. "Do?" His round face was placid.

"We're not fit."

Knowles looked surprised, playing on Pope's worry. "I don't see any sick parade."

Lieutenant Pope could look down three inches at this man's eyes, but he felt inferior, and it had nothing to do with the difference in their rank. He was younger than Knowles, and less experienced; this he knew. He was also less subtle, and less patient; this he sensed vaguely. He was, finally, a more honest man, and had a wider mind; but of this he was not aware. Knowles looked up at him complacently, waiting for a retort to his deliberate remark about the sick parade. But Pope, remembering how well this man could goad another, said nothing. He edged away, towards the table, and stood with his back half turned. The men were sick; the M.O. didn't care; the

Squadron commander was a bastard; and H-hour was in fifty minutes. Perhaps he was taking too much on himself. Perhaps he had read too many treatises on the maintenance of morale in an armed unit, and the brotherhood of officers, and their sacred responsibility to the men. Perhaps he was just too young, too soft. Twenty-one years, six months. Was that too young?

"Gentlemen." Colonel Rawlings looked up from the maps. Lieutenant Ashton, suddenly aware that the conference was on, and that the last chance of rushing out to be sick had gone, rushed out to be sick. Pope heard the door slam, and went on watching the Colonel.

"There is nothing to add," Rawlings said, "that will make any change in our plans. I think you're too well briefed by now to go over it all again." Knowles thought he looked tired, or anxious. Rawlings was too old for this job, by ten years. "But there's one thing that needs pointing out. When this operation was planned, it was hoped that the weather would at least be neutral. As you know, the most diligent attention has been given to this factor. Unfortunately we've been obliged to press on with this plan despite the change in the weather, rather than postpone it for some weeks." He wiped his nose with a khaki handkerchief, gazed for half a minute at the maps, and said finally: "The wind is rising to Force 5. On paper, the operation we are about to carry out is, in these conditions, impossible. We must therefore see to it that we perform it carefully."

Lieutenant Ashton came back, trying to close the door quietly, catching his foot in it and knocking into Sergeant Goodall. While someone was asking the Colonel a question, Ashton quietly asked Goodall:

"What's been said?"

"Colonel says we've got a job on, sir."

Ashton wiped his face. His handkerchief was dark with sweat. "We knew that, didn't we?"

"I s'ppose it was just a reminder, sir."

"Any change of plan?"

"No, sir."

Ashton leaned against the door, the weight going on to his shoulders as the ship rolled. It rolled slowly, taking a second or two, and then held it, so that Ashton could see deep green water and fish picking at skeletons with Army boots on. When the door came up slowly against his back, he murmured: "Jesus, I thought we weren't coming up again, that time."

"She always seems to," said Goodall. They squeezed aside as someone came scrambling, uphill across the tilting floor, towards the door. He opened it and went pitching out. Ashton and Goodall braced themselves, leaning forward now against the others as the ship went dipping to the other beam. Ashton said in a stifled voice:

"Sergeant, how are the boys getting on?"

"Oh, they'll be okay, sir."

Ashton got his balance. "Jesus!" he said, and pushed his way to the door again, slamming it behind him.

On deck, Corporal Pike put the cards away.

"One more round," said Burrage.

"That's the lot for now, Charlie."

"Ah, come on, there's nothin' doin' yet."

"You heard what I said." Pike stood up, catching a gust of wind past the hatch where they were sheltering. Trooper Levy stood up too, sniffing the salt wind suspiciously.

"I can hear something," he said.

Pike went on watching the sky. "I'll say you can 'ear somethin'." The wind brought gusts of sound. Aircraft were in the sky. Their drone had reached his ears while the cards were still in his hands; now it was louder, and rising. They were above a thick blanket of cloud that in the east was beginning to show ragged edges.

"Struth," said Trooper Burrage. "Listen at 'em!"

"I'm listenin'," said Pike. To the dark sky he said: "Go on then, boys, get at 'em."

Levy stood beside him. "What's that lot then, Corp?"

"Eh? Paratroops."

"That's the third shower, then."

" 'Sright. Bless 'em all." He looked around as Watkins-Price came up. "Does you good, er, Watty, listenin' to that lot?"

Watkins-Price cocked his head up, getting one ear clear of the wind. "So it's really on," he said.

"On? What's on?"

"The whole thing. The invasion."

Pike popped his eyes open. "O' course it's bloody well on. What you think us lot're muckin' about 'ere for like flippin' lemons?"

"I thought they might have called it off."

"What the 'ell for?"

"Well, it's not quite the weather for it."

"Weather? This? 'Aven't you ever fetched yourself an earful of ozone before?"

Watkins-Price shrugged in the gloom. "It doesn't worry me, but you should go and take a look below."

"Wha's wrong, then?"

Patiently Watkins-Price said: "They're all flat on their backs."

"Oh-ah. Pukin'. I 'eard 'em, yes." Pike dismissed them. He was too excited to worry about a lot of pig-sicks below. The airborne lot were going over, sounding like the thunder of doom, and there was dawn coming, in the east, and he was itching for his first sight of the coast-line. "You see anythin' yet, Watty?"

"Not yet."

"Ain't you excited?"

"Very."

"Well, you don't sound like you was."

"What d'you want me to do: scream like an Indian?"

Burrage said: "Watty, you got any cards, mate?"

"Sorry."

"There'll be no more flippin' cards, Charlie, you 'eard me the firs' time."

"Jus' because you've got yourself all excited," said Burrage.

Corporal Pike grinned, catching the wind in his teeth. "You'll get yourself bloody excited, too, soon as you find one or two o' them little Nazzies up your jacksie on that there beach, mate. No error."

The great drone went on.

" 'Ow many of 'em are there, d'you think?"

"God knows."

" 'Undreds."

"See any?"

"Fat chance, wi' that cloud."

"Poor bastards."

"We're poor bastards too, ain't we?"

"Who is?"

"We are."

"Well you c'n speak for yourself, Charlie. I'm all right."

"I know, you're fireproof."

"Ain't you got no asbestos drawers, then?"

The drone went on, high above the cloud; and the light strengthened in the east. Shapes darkened against the sea, and Pike took his little body of men to the starboard rails, where they leaned in the wind and picked out two destroyers, a capital ship and a fleet of smaller craft. They each felt reassured. They had known, in the long night, that their convoy was not alone; but it was good to see the horizon dark with ships. The sea was high and the wind was enough to choke a man, but the Navy was here, and it knew about these things, and could deal with them.

"Are you chaps all right?"

"Eh?" said Corporal Pike. He turned and saw Lieutenant Pope, his battledress flattened against his body as he leaned towards the group against the wind. "Yes, sir."

"None of you sick?"

"Not 'ere, sir."

Pope's voice was caught by the gusts, some of the words whirling away, lost. "You—any—to eat?"

"We've grubbed up, sir."

Pope nodded and went down towards the hatch, steeling himself to the hot sickly smell as he went down the rungs and tripped over a prone man. He asked him if he were all right, but had no answer but a moan. The man was moaning in his sleep, his hands moving limply across his chest. Pope went on, finding the boards treacherous with vomit as the landing-craft pitched, sliding him against the bulkheads until Sergeant Liefe stopped him and asked:

"Have you seen Mr. Ashton, sir?"

"What? No." He braced himself to the roll. "How are the blokes down here?"

"Bit rough."

"You look a bit rough yourself."

Liefe grinned horribly with his wet white face. "Bit of terra firma's all we want, sir. Any hopes?"

"We'll be cracking off on schedule, and you know when that is." He wanted to stay with this man for a minute. Liefe had come from Africa and then Sicily. He had spent a lot of his time under fire. Pope had not. He had never fired a gun at an enemy nor put his tank across country any more dangerous than Salisbury Plain. He had never been fired on. It was going to happen soon, now. In about forty minutes. He said, swaying: "How d'you feel, about the beach?"

"Me, sir?" The sickly white grin came again. "It'll be firm ground, won't it?"

"It'll need to be. We'll have a bit to do."

Liefe watched him in the wan yellow light of the guide-lamps. "Oh, I dunno about that. The barrage ought to flatten a lot of the lumps out. There's been heavies goin' over, half the night. Remember what we was told? Six thousand tons of bombs on the coastal defences before dawn. Ask me, there won't be much of the beach left, sir."

Pope nodded. He tried to think of a final word, by which he could excuse himself from the man's presence. He felt, again, inferior. His lack of battle experience itched on his face like a birthmark; he was ashamed of it, in a way.

He looked at his watch, as a gesture, and staggered past Sergeant Liefe to go and look at the men. Some were still in their bunks, but many were up and checking their equipment. There was very little talking. They had come through the night, and were getting ready for the day quietly, as if they must not disturb those who still slept or lay weakly on the bunks with no sleep in them, and seemingly no life.

"How's it going, sir?"

He looked at Corporal Todd.

"Very well. We're standing off the coast."

Todd straightened his webbing. "What's it look like, sir? Any tea-gardens open?"

"You can't see the coastline yet. Is your troop all right, Corporal?"

"Rarin' to go, sir."

The lieutenant went on, climbing to the tank-deck and looking east. He stood for minutes, alone, drawing the wind into his lungs, letting it cuff his face, leaning himself against it as gust followed gust. Then he looked at his watch again, this time to know the hour. In thirty-five minutes the second wave of LcTs would be moving in, behind the special-device armour that would clear the way for them. Before that, there would be the barrage.

"Sir."

He turned. "Yes?"

"We got a man bad, sir. It's Woods."

He looked at Lance-Corporal Munro in the strengthening light. "Where is he?"

"Down there, sir. Delirious."

"Seasick?"

"Yes, sir; but bad."

"Get him to the sick-bay. Have you told Mr. Hallett?"

"I can't find 'im, sir."

"Woods is in your troop, isn't he?"

"Yessir."

"Get him to the sick-bay, and then find Mr. Hallett or Sergeant Verity. You'd better double—there's not much time."

Munro dodged off. Pope walked slowly along the rails past groups of men. He mustn't worry himself about Knowles or Woods or anyone at all. Colonel Rawlings was the one to take all the troubles on; that was what a colonel was for. His own job was quite enough to handle.

He had to get Bloody Mary across the beach to number three exit and then push on to the first village, La Hermielle; and he had to take Moby Dick and Top Dog with him. He could forget everything else, and concentrate on that.

"About time, isn't it, sir?"

Sergeant Goodall was pacing beside him, his face newly shaved and his boots bright.

"Time?"

"The shooting, sir."

Pope stared across the sea. "Yes. Any minute now." He was aware suddenly that the rails were crowded with men who had come up from below, sensing the dawn. One or two looked very smart, parade-ground standard; most were a little creased-looking; a few were still white-gilled and slack, moving about uncertainly, grabbing at anything firm when the next wave came and the craft went rolling beneath their feet. The wind was still hard, but Pope thought it had shifted a few points. Except for the wind, there was no sound, either from the ships or the shore. The light, seeping wanly across the Channel, had not yet penetrated the south haze; the coastline was still unseen. Above the fleet there was low cloud. He said:

"I'm surprised to see them up here."

"The men, sir? They'll be all right now. With a lot of 'em, it was more claustrophobia than seasickness, I reckon. Cooped up, they were, down there." They stood together for minutes, their heads turned sideways to the wind so that it shouldn't deafen them. Goodall said: "There she is, then."

"What?"

"France." The sergeant pointed.

In a moment, Pope said: "Yes." It didn't look like France, or any country. It was a thin line between the sea and sky, that might have been the horizon, or watermarking, or a rope between the huddled assault-craft carriers to the east and the big capital ship on the other side.

"What's your French like, sir?"

It surprised the lieutenant to find that his mouth was

dry. He had to unstick the words, and make them sound light.

"It'll get by. How's yours?"

"I've been brushin' up, sir; but you can't get it right, from just books, can you?"

The thin line was darkening. The land looked very flat. From here, it looked as if you could free-wheel a Mark 7 right across to the Rhine.

Goodall was turning his head an inch, to say something to Pope, when the whole sea exploded with noise. Pope grabbed his arm, shocked into instinctive movement, and then they laughed together, stupidly and soundlessly as the barrage kept on, pressing a physical weight of air waves against their ears. The grey of sea and cloud was being ripped with colour, orange and white and flaring yellow as the sixteen-inch guns of the capital ship hurled their shells skyward and southward, beating out a gigantic rhythm amid the sharper cannonade of the smaller guns as the barrage was taken up from horizon to coast and sent its shock waves running across and back, compressing the air against men's ears and drumming along the decks under their feet. Even in this welter of sound, a long-held drone came lifting overhead as bomber squadrons went in from the north towards the coast.

Sergeant Goodall stood with his ears clamped and his stomach tight, watching the line of land for answering fire. So far there was none. Pope, with his tongue curled in a dry mouth, was thinking of what the Colonel had told them, in his slow, vague monotones . . . "at dawn, in our sector, the preliminary softening-up barrage will comprise thirty minutes' bombardment from one battleship, thirty minutes' simultaneous fire from four destroyers, totalling sixteen five-inch guns, and from twenty-four twenty-five-pounders firing from a field regiment landingcraft. There will also be two thousand fifty-pound rockets going up from a rocket ship, and bombs from six squadrons of Flying Fortresses going down. During the night the enemy battery at Mont Fleury will have received three hundred tons of bombs from R.A.F. Lancasters. We shall then follow the special armoured devices on to the beaches."

The drawn-out bomber drone was an audible ceiling above the din of the guns. At intervals the sea to the east was riven with light that streamed up from the rocket ship that was putting up its projectiles in a massed volley from barrels as close packed as organ pipes. Their smoke-stream, torn away on the wind, joined the thickening pall from the rest of the armament, until the northern horizon was blotted out. But no one was looking in that direction. Southwards the bombs were going down, and the shells were in. The dark line of the land was blossoming redly with the blooms of high explosive; smoke came drifting heavily on the cross-wind, tangling among the ships as they stood off in perfect station with their gun-crews working without a pause. Even the memory of silence was gone, just as the memory of firm land had gone from the minds of the seasick. This unrelenting din had the quality of a fifth dimension, and the men learned, in minutes, to live with it.

A lone Spitfire, attracted moth-like by the dawn inferno, came darting through cloud, and vanished beyond the ships, a silent winged thing with its own sound too feeble to be heard. Another followed, vanishing after it. There could only have been one reason for their presence here: there was a party on, and no one was watching the door.

Along the rails of LcT 39 the men stood with their hands covering their ears. One of them was trying to shout a word to his friend, but it was lost, and his friend shook his head and laughed, excited by the thundering of the guns. Many of them, after the first shock was over, felt this excitement going through them; each was forming his own estimate of the damage that was being wrought along the coast-line, each feeling that surely the tanks could go ashore and make their free way through nothing more difficult than a rubbish-heap, when this mighty barrage stopped. Only a few had doubts; they were the men from the desert and from Sicily; they reserved their optimism. The West Wall had been built to withstand a massed invasion, and account would have been taken of preliminary bombardment. There might be cracks in the wall, perhaps some sizeable breaches; more than that could not be counted on.

Lieutenant Pope had reckoned twenty minutes on his wrist-watch. It was almost full daylight now, but a smoke-screen spreading from the west shore was slowly engulfing the sector; he was not able to judge whether it came from the land defences or from a naval ship, put out to shield the fleet from the batteries at Le Havre. It gave a strange twilight as its fringe encroached, merging with the low-lying cloud. He checked his watch at minute intervals, waiting for the din to die away. His head was throbbing with it and his stomach ached with the tension; a man standing here, in the midst of this great percussion storm, felt that if he relaxed his stomach muscles it would be ripped open like a bladder.

The deck of the LcT lost movement, and the men looked round them, surprised. The stern was down, and the bow-wave was drawing out, streaming to join the wake. Corporal Pike saw Burrage form words with his lips.

"We're movin'."

He nodded. Faintly he could feel the vibration beneath his feet, and the thud of the wave series as they smacked past the blunted bows. The faces around him were questioning; he had no answer. They were running south, under the arch of the barrage. They were going in.

At 5.40 hours the capital ship ceased fire. The main tension left the air; the snatch of the wind and the pummel of the lighter guns remained. It was possible to breathe, consciously, to free the ears. It was even possible to shout and to be heard.

"We goin' in?"

"Reckon we are!"

"What's orders?"

"We got 'em already. Don't panic!"

A sailor came running aft at a loping trot, stopping to push his way through a group and going on, vanishing down a hatch. Then the barrage died, within seconds. Far

to the east an artillery craft was running its Bofors on,
but the sound was feeble in this new, strange silence.
Even the wind seemed dead, as the ears expanded, losing
their numbness. The vast weight of that thirty-minute
sound shock was lifted from the men, so that their heads
cleared and their muscles relaxed, bringing a lightness of
heart. A new sound came across the water now in a soft
rising wave. It was a cheer. It had started from one of the
landing-craft and had gathered voices from the rest. The
Navy had hit a high top note and had held it for half an
hour; and this was the applause.

Lieutenant Ashton looked at the M.O., beside him.

"Jesus!" he said.

Spray came across the bows, lying over them as they
ducked sideways. The landing-craft drove on against the
waves with the dogged persistence of a water buffalo, and
with as little grace. Men staggered as they moved amidships, where Sergeant Verity and Sergeant Goodall were
standing. When the men were gathered, Verity shouted
against the wind: "Have you got any questions?"

He was a middle-sized man with a big head, out of
which the face was chiselled crudely. If you hit this face
with a hammer, the hammer would bounce. He waited;
no one had any questions. He called: "Keep your eyes on
Major Knowles. You know the signal."

They turned away, when it was clear that Verity had
no more to say. They waited round the edge of the sunken
tank deck, facing the bows, waiting for a sight of
Major Knowles. One or two were trying to smoke a cigarette, shielding the tip from the wind. Trooper Burrage
was going over in his mind a horse-racing system that
someone had told him about last evening. So far, he
couldn't see anything wrong with it. It seemed foolproof.
But it would have to be Burrage-proof too, because he
was the all-time world champion loser; so he went over
its mathematical intricacies again, slowly and thoughtfully
as the LcT ploughed on through the tilting sea. Beside
him was Taffy Adams, saying in his mind: 'We shall be
fighting Your fight, O Lord, and therefore we shall need
Your help, as much of it as You can spare us on a day as

busy as this one.' Trooper Steiner, just behind Taffy, was watching the coast of France as it swung up from the bows and then dipped out of sight, swung up again as the bows dropped into the next trough; he watched it without any expression at all. He had come a long way to France, starting out from Austria and fleeing to Hungary, thence to Switzerland, and finally England, his mother now murdered, his father missing among the millions, believed hanged, his sister mercifully in London, where he had left her. Now he was coming to France, where the jack-boot was lording it. To look at Steiner's expression at this moment, it would not seem that there was any hate in the man at all. He looked a neat, dark soldier, waiting for the order to move.

Corporal Pike steadied his feet, getting his balance, fretting over the wording in the will he had made. It had sounded so off-hand, the way he'd been told to word it, as if he had said: 'There's a bit of Spam left on the shelf, and if I'm not back by eleven, don't forget where to leave the key.' He had wanted to put a farewell message of some kind, mention something about what a good wife Sophie had been to him, say how sorry he was about not getting the garden finished on his last leave, instead of being so much with the boys down at the 'Angel.' He felt that a proper will should give a lot of things, apart from the bit of goods. He watched, with his brow puckered in thought, the coast-line ahead.

"They're goin' in, Corp."

"Eh?"

Sam Cox pointed. The corporal saw the white froth of the surf making a lacy line five miles in front of them. Between here and the surf, the sea was a-swarm with craft milling about in the sector approaches. At intervals the white surf was broken up by small dark shapes, and there were gun-flashes peppering the haze. Pike said:

"Special devices."

"Ye'. And there's bloody Jerry firing."

"What you expect 'im to do, mate? Sit back an' look silly?"

"After that pasting, I wonder he's still alive."

Pike said: "Well, let 'im enjoy 'is little self. 'E 'asn't got long, the bleeder."

Spray came stinging across them and they turned, catching it on their backs. From somewhere on the sea there came a dull boom, reverberating.

"Christ, what was that?" said Burrage.

"Somethink 'it somethink."

"E-boats," said Watkins-Price.

"Sod 'em," said Pike.

"It was a mine, goin' up." Cox was shielding his eyes against the spray. A few miles eastwards, flame was on the sea, torn to an orange banner by the wind. Trooper Woods, crouched against the tank deck rails, watched the ship burn, his face grey. In a moment he turned his back. Corporal Pike said:

"What you doin' up 'ere, Woody?"

Woods was a thin, bony boy with a quiet face. He had said he was nineteen. "I'm better now, Corp."

"You don't look it, kid. You seen Mr. 'Allett?"

"Yes."

"You're a liar. 'E's still lookin' for you."

"I'm better now."

Pike said no more. That poor little perisher wasn't going to last a minute, on the beach. He was ready for the chopper, that kid was. You could knock him down with your little finger. Thin as a reed, sick as a dog, and scared. It was a shame to take him along on this trip.

The beach neared slowly. A long cross-current was at odds with the wind, bringing the waves slanting against the landing-craft. It shuddered, lifting and dropping, while the six big Churchills swayed on their springs like troubled elephants. A gun was pulsing, south-east, somewhere beyond the ridge of the land; it was answered by two of the destroyers. It was now possible to make out a row of houses, or the shells of houses, along the sand-dunes. They were burning well, and their smoke came down across the beach and then spread out, flattening. Bright flashes were popping on the sands, as mines went up. The special devices were ashore, with the Crabs and Bullshorns flailing and ploughing through the mine-fields, clearing their lanes. Two more guns were thudding, joining the first that was not yet located by the destroyers.

On LcT 39 the men began super-imposing the scene on the pictures they had been shown of it in England. Not much of it fitted. On the plans and maps, markings had been clear; but with the sea haze and the smoke and the motion of the ship, it was hard to make out any pattern. The scene was more nearly like the mock invasions along the Essex coast; but the great difference remained, changing it: the difference between the sham and the reality, in the mind.

"How far now?" someone said.

"Couple o' mile."

"Looks like we're goin' to get a bit of action."

"What did you expect, a flippin' picnic?"

A fourth gun had opened up, sending cross-fire along the beaches. Cox said: "Eighty-eights."

"I'll give 'em eighty-eights," the corporal grunted. He spoke with his head turned towards Woods, because Woods needed encouragement, and no mistake. "You wait til I get me 'an's on one o' them flippin' eighty-eights."

"What you goin' to do then?" piped up Burrage.

"I'm goin' to knot it roun' their bleedin' necks an' pull it tight till they shout out: 'Mother, I'm chokin'.' "

"You've got a hope, you have, Alf."

"We've all got 'opes, mate. It's all we want, that an' the flippin' ammunition."

The beach neared. LcT 39 was running into ploughed water as the craft alongside broke up the waves. A party of men were singing at the stern of the LcT ahead. The wind carried the strange forced sound of their lonely voices; in a little while the song fluttered away. Corporal Pike edged nearer the inboard rails, and said to Woods:

"Okay, mate?"

"I'm okay." The boy's face was tight; it looked as if a knuckle would crack it like a shell. Under the drawn lines

of the mouth the teeth were chattering. He clenched them
hard, but they wouldn't stop.

"Cold, are you?" said Pike. He got his flask out. "Drop
o' this'll set you up, boy."

"What is it?"

"Rum. Go on."

Woods took the flask and swigged from it while the
corporal watched him. "Tha's it. Warms your cockles."
He took the flask back and slipped it into a pocket. Spray
came across the bows and they ducked most of it. Pike
gave a wink to the boy and left him. The four big eighty-
eights were thudding across the shore-line, and there was
the smell of the wind, of high explosive. Corporal Pike
knew the smell intimately; it was exciting, and frightening, and deathly. Soon they would cease to notice it and
would breathe it as naturally as the smell of sweet grass
in a field. This was their browsing-ground.

The beach neared. They could see assault-craft going
in, tipping out men. They could see from the shore-waves
to the dunes, from the gun emplacement at the east end
of the sector to the knot of struggling tanks that were
forming their own bottleneck as they tried to clear a lane
to number one beach exit. They were half a dozen big
A.V.R.E.s, two carrying chespale fascines, two more
carrying bridges, the others working alongside, widening
the lane. From here on the water they looked like ants
toiling; soon they would be monsters. Tracers were picking at them now, curving across from a pill-box and
bouncing off.

Sam Cox looked down at the sea, bunched with his
equipment against the rails. There was scum on the lift
and fall of the waves, and oily rainbows. Cardboard
boxes were floating by, small square ones, fruit-pie con-
tainers; he could almost read the lettering on them. A
body surfaced and turned over slowly, passing beyond the
stern, boots and khaki and a face, all nameless now. He
looked upwards at the shore. The LcT was heading for a
gangway between three abandoned assault-craft and a
gun-barge that was stuck beam-on and taking in water.
The sand was nearer now than five hundred yards.

"All right, you lot!"

He turned round and saw one of the sergeants shaping up the crews. His mob was near the midship ladder, and he clumped quickly to join it, weighted under his equipment. Major Knowles was up for'ard, watching the shore through his field-glasses. Colonel Rawlings was beside him. Corporal Pike was nudging Woods again, giving him the flask, watching him swig, taking it back. Taffy Adams stood like a stick, head level, watching the Major, waiting. Sergeant Goodall was nearest the middle ladder, and had his left hand on the rail; his tin-hat sloped to one side; he tilted it straight; it sloped again; he left it alone. Lieutenant Pope was farther forward, abreast of the front two tanks, facing the bows, watching Rawlings and Knowles; Hallett had joined them. Sergeant Liefe was hitching his equipment straight, and a man was helping him while a burst of spray came up and spattered them, hissing on to the deck. Watkins-Price munched an apple, his lop-sided face screwed up against the wind and the flying salt; once he glanced at Woods and then away. A stupid smile was on Wood's young face, fixed, white and bright-eyed; three long swigs of rum on an emptied stomach had left him with a drunk's bravado that distorted his whole appearance, giving Corporal Pike the impression of an apprentice clown in a lion's den. He'd give this kid half a minute on the beach. Joseph Steiner, neat and dark with his equipment straight and his feet together, stood behind Corporal Todd. Lance-Corporal Munro came jerking heavily across from a hatchway, picked his crew and joined it, his water-bottle clouting the iron rail and ringing with a dull bell's note.

The beach neared. There were men in the water. Two assault-craft were sinking, cocked against submerged obstacles and settling as the waves came in. Gun-fire was spreading from all quarters, with the rattle of small-arms fire quickening amid the cannonade and the burst of shells. Sand flew up, clouding away in the wind. The waves threw their whites against the beach, sending small craft askew and men overboard as the line of LcTs drew inshore with the naval crews ready at the ramps.

Major Knowles turned round and raised his arm.

The signal was passed along by the sergeants.

"Get down there an' start up!"

The men moved, jostling. One fell and was helped up. A tin mug dropped and was forgotten, rattling overboard. The chocks were coming away from the tracks; the chains were off. An engine started up, and two more, sending out gas, throbbing steadily, warming up. The wireless-operators pulled on their gear, netting their dials, remote and alone inside the walls of their earphones, seeking only the company of voices in the drumming air.

Six engines were running; the drivers were in. One by one the sets came on to net, with signals testing. The gunners were settling, squeezing a space for their bodies among the cramped equipment and the iron walls of Moby Dick, Top Dog and Bloody Mary, Dumbo, Phart-arce and Balham Belle. The long seventy-five-millimetre barrels poked stiffly out, trained forward, fingering the air with their breeches charged. Above the big shapes of the tanks the commanders were ready, Lieutenant Pope leading Two Troop, Lieutenant Ashton leading Three. The pennants were up, stiff in the wind, crackling.

LcT 39 ran on through the waves, hit an obstacle twenty yards from the shore, broke clear and wallowed forward until the bell rang in the engine-room and the megaphone sounded from the bridge:

"Down ramp!"

The chains ran through. The ramp hit the shallows and Moby Dick gunned-up, grinding its way to the slope and going down, hitting the surf and churning through the clay strip and floundering on with its tracks buried, but driving hard until the forward horns were over a tangle of matting and the power found something to bite on. The thirty tons of steel were dragged to the firmer shore and the last of the water streamed away and then broke into violent mist as the Cordtex fuse was blown, exploding the water-proof seals.

Tracer was streaking across from a pillbox in the dunes and Sergeant Goodall ducked for cover while his gunner brought the slim, cold seventy-five to bear on the target. Two Troop, thirty seconds landborne, was answering enemy fire.

THE BEACH

I

IN THIS SECTOR the beach was two hundred yards deep and a mile wide. The sand was soft. It ran upwards to the dunes and to the sea walls. On the dunes the dry grass was alight, and smoke drifted thickly along the upper ridge. Beyond the ridge a row of houses burned. Beyond the houses ran the lateral road, between marshes. Craters were already harassing the forward flail-tanks along the road, and three stood immobile, half blocking the fourth beach exit. Two more had bogged in the ooze and an A.V.R.E. bulldozer was struggling to drag them out. A big Crab, its jib and flails shot away, stood burning, and sometimes it shuddered as its own ammunition blew up inside it. There was no sign of the crew.

'C' Squadron, with a full complement of eighteen fighting-tanks, was coming off the ramps of three landing-craft, guided to dropping-points opposite numbers one, two and three beach exits. The clack of the beach-masters' Aldis lamps broke off as they left the three LcTs and went on to bring in the cluttered flotilla of landing-ships, assault-craft and barges. The three tanks of Two Troop, 'C' Squadron, were roughly together: Moby Dick, Top Dog and Bloody Mary. In Moby Dick, the first seventy-five-m.m. shell sent out by the gunner, Watkins-Price, still deafened the crew. The shell struck the sea-wall ten yards to the left of the German eighty-eight-m.m. gun that was commanding most of the sector with accurate observed fire. The wireless-operator, Trooper Woods, was reloading as the spent case came cracking back against the deflector-scoop. The second shell hit the emplacement squarely below the gun's casemate, doing no damage, but indicating fair aim. As Woods reloaded he was swearing aloud but unheard. The rum that Corporal

Pike had given him had not made him drunk; it had
stopped his teeth chattering and had cast a haze over his
senses, so that he worked automatically, and swore automatically, realising only dimly that the big gun was firing
at an enemy. Unworried by his half-drugged nerves, he
brought something of a rhythm to his work, and five
shells went out before a yelling M.P. persuaded Sergeant
Goodall to shift his tank another fifty yards up the sand
as a group of soft vehicles began gathering behind it,
frantic for gangway.

Between Moby Dick and Bloody Mary was a bullet-
swept area where men were lying, some quiet, others
trying to move. As they lifted their awkward bodies,
dragging a leg or keeping a crimsoned arm clear of their
own weight, the stutter of Spandau fire broke out again,
and again they dropped, beginning now to gouge at the
sand with their hands, seeking shelter. In Bloody Mary,
which was number one tank of Two Troop, Lieutenant
Pope was standing on his iron pedestal, guiding his
driver, watching the signals of the two M.P.s who were
working to organise the beach traffic. His wireless-operator was still on net with the battalion, but the few signals were confused and halting. Pope was shouting in
exhilaration, because he was under fire and he was attacking. This was his baptism, dreadful and magnificent;
after this, he could shed his inferiority; he had come of
age, in war.

In Three Troop, Lieutenant Ashton was not exhilarated.
His tank, Balham Belle, was a dozen yards up the
beach and coming under direct fire from an eighty-eight
gun positioned just beyond number two beach exit;
through this exit Balham Belle had to move inland. Ashton's hatch closed down, because a stray bullet had
grazed across his tin hat and he was having a look at the
damage, running his fingers through his hair and finding
nothing to alarm him. The percussion had dizzied him,
but now that he knew he was not hurt, he slammed the
hatch open and half crouched, sending orders down to
Trooper Burrage, bringing the gun to bear on the eighty-
eight emplacement. Burrage was calm, sitting at the

sights. He put the first shell against the corner of the emplacement and took away a hundredweight of concrete. The second shot went wide because the tank slewed badly, cocking against an abandoned truck and righting slowly. Burrage waited, and then sat in a sweat of hope with the German casemate dead in his sights. If the tank moved now, it would be a waste. If it didn't, it would be a beauty. He kept steady, and fired. It was a beauty. It was like posting a letter. The shell screamed into the dark slit and exploded. He could see the flash. He watched the smoke billow out. Someone near him was yelling, thumping his shoulder, and he nodded again and again, grinning like a fool. The eighty-eight had ceased fire; its crew would be dead.

Lieutenant Ashton was shouting in his ear: *"Jesus, that was a smacker! Jesus!"* He was laughing as he shouted. The wireless-operator, little Levy, was reloading, smacking a kiss on the shell and slamming it in, slapping the gunner's arm. Burrage waited while Balham Belle moved up the beach, veering towards number two exit. A Spandau was spraying the turret and Ashton was down again, cursing. The driver, closed down and, steering on periscope, kept on a straight course and hoped for new orders. The left track hit an obstacle and the tank reared on that side, swinging down and finding soft sand. For a minute it churned for grip, while two eighty-eight shells tore into the beach within yards of it. The third hit the fuel-tanks and they blew apart.

Lieutenant Ashton pushed with his feet, scrambled over the rim and leaned forward into the turret, getting a grip on the gunner's harness and pulling hard. A Spandau stream veered towards him and ripped along his spine. He hung down, his dead hands loosening. Burrage and Levy were pulling at the escape door and Levy was shouting something about getting out or roasting in here, but Burrage didn't want telling. The fuel-tanks had gone up and they were trapped.

The turret was at ninety degrees, blocking off the hatch over the driving compartment, so the driver and co-driver squeezed through the gap into the turret while Levy went

on shouting at Burrage, and Burrage at last dragged him
upwards. Flame was touching the ammunition racks, and
he threw himself across the turret rim and dropped across
the lieutenant's body on the sand. As Levy came down,
Burrage shouted to him that Ashton was dead. Levy spun
round, falling, as bullets clipped into him. He fell with
one boot across Ashton's face and his mouth in the
sand.

A mortar bomb exploded against the other side of the
tank as Burrage got to his feet and climbed, drawing
himself over the turret rim and looking for the others.
The driver was crumpled against a jagged hole in the
armour, unrecognisable as a man. The co-driver, blinded
by the smoke, was still dragging at him. Burrage hit him
on the shoulder with force enough to stun him, but he
kept on dragging while Burrage yelled: *"Get out, he's
dead, get out, you bloody fool!"* He went on dragging
until Burrage came over the turret rim and jerked a blow
at the side of his face. It sent him against the breech of
the gun, but as he collapsed Burrage got a hand on him
and yanked upwards, pulling him clear across the rim as
the first ammunition started firing off, roasting on the
racks. Burrage got the man over and they both dropped.
He crawled a yard, taking the other with him, then dropped
his head as a bullet stream crossed them, leaving
them alive, but with a pain shooting up one leg as he
crawled on again. His eyes stung, but they were watering,
and he had a blurred view of the sand and a big shadow
ahead of him; it was a derelict tank, and it might shelter
them. The co-driver was unconscious still, and a dead
weight; but the sand made the journey less hard. Burrage
moved them both, by driving his elbows into the sand,
reaching back for the other man, then crawling on again,
and reaching back, and crawling on until a machine-gun
found them there, half-way between the burning tank and
the derelict, and left them there, with Burrage humped
against the co-driver, their brows resting on the sand,
their last blood mingling.

An armoured bulldozer, lumbering down the beach,
stopped at the rear of the derelict, and an R.E. jumped

down, fixing a cable. The derelict was in the pathway between the shore and number two exit, and it must be shifted. Nearer the sea, a platoon of infantry was huddled, lying flat under the smoke from Balham Belle, using it as cover. Assault-craft were still coming in, and as men came overboard into deep water, life-lines went out. Others reached the shallows, wading in, their boots leaden under ninety pounds of kit. One fell forward, and was not seen; the water swirled, and later a note-book floated, the pages opening slowly like a flower. Three tanks lay drowned, their turrets breaking surface and then, minute by minute, submerging as the tide came in. Shells hit the water, ploughing it into fountains, and bullets from Spandaus and snipers went flashing against the waves as quick as minnows, and the men swam through them, some of them reaching the sand. Smoke from fires on the left flank of the sector was darkening the beach, giving cover, but increasing confusion as bulldozers strained to clear the bottleneck at number four beach exit, and the M.P.s ran down to drive the diversion onwards to number five. Sappers were still at work, disarming the Teller mines, with their sweat blinding them and their hands raw as they rooted and then dropped for cover, rising to root again while the tanks came lumbering by along the flailed lanes. The last Crab had gone, crossing the lateral road and clearing a lane towards La Hermielle. Many of the fighting-tanks had followed; others rested at strange angles, with a track gone, a hole ripped out of the steel flank, the gun jammed, or flame still licking from the turret rim.

Down by the sea, Balham Belle stood gutted. In the water, the notebook had floated away. The bulldozers had dragged the derelict half a dozen yards and had moved on to other work. Levy's boot lay across Ashton's bloodless face. Below the shapes of Burrage and the co-driver the sand was dark, draining the crimson away. On the dunes, the eighty-eight gun was still silent; sappers had gone in there, and found nothing alive. Two pillboxes, near the row of smouldering houses, were putting out sporadic fire as the landing-craft came in, jostling for room. A party of infantry was crawling down the landward face of the ridge towards these active posts; the men carried grenades. The smoke thickened from the east, muffling the distant throb of the big guns at Le Havre.

An A.V.R.E. had breached the sea wall with a flying dustbin from its Petard, and the diversion from number four exit was moving across, easing the pressure of traffic towards the road. An M.P., who had been working for three hours to keep the exits clear, dodged back from the path of a half-track, and was pinned between two tanks. His scream was cut short; the half-track swung wide, hitting the front horn of the tank and then clearing, leading the way to the exit, the driver's red eyes squinting painfully for direction through the dust.

The sergeant's tank of Two Troop, 'C' Squadron, was at rest on the right edge of the traffic to number three exit, its two Besas firing on to a sniper's post in the dunes. Woods, clamped in his ear-phones, had reloaded the seventy-five and was getting signals on the A set from battalion. Two Troop was to stay where it was until ordered to move on. To move on, in any case, was not possible. The traffic was solid, and number three exit was blocked by a burning A.R.V. Sergeant Goodall was standing, directing his Besa fire towards the dunes, ducking as the air hummed and bullets fluted past. Again he shouted, *"Can we shift?"* Woods shook his head, looking up at him white-faced but alert as a monkey. The sergeant reached down for a couple of hand-grenades and swung himself over the turret rim and dropped and lay flat with his tin hat covering his head. They had seen him, but he had been quick. The bullets came snicking against the tank, humming as their flight was turned by the impact. Some came spitting into the sand near where he lay, slanting down heavily, reminding him of summer raindrops on a paving-stone.

He rolled over as soon as there was a chance and crawled towards a big concrete dragon's-tooth that stood between the tank and the snipers' nest. By the time he had reached the bastion there was sand in his eyes and mouth, and he was drenched in sweat. A shell, coming in from one of the heavy batteries inland, had fallen not far away. He felt nothing but the blast, and a cloud of driving sand that piled against one side of his prone body. He crawled round the base of the concrete and reached a gully, making a detour past the ragged remains of the M.P. who had screamed. He was no longer within sight of the snipers; but they would know that he was coming.

A dark wing of smoke, folding down from the burning A.R.V. at four exit, gave him sudden cover and he stood up, jogging over the sand until he reached the last ridge of grass that stretched below the snipers' nest. The smoke was bringing tears from his eyes and he lay prone again, letting them stream until the wind shifted and the light seeped through. He lay for another minute, his hands cupped downwards over the two grenades, as if he had come upon two ostriches' eggs in the hollowed sand. He judged the distance to be short enough for throwing, but there was the risk that when he stood up he would expose himself to the snipers and to his own Besa fire, because he was hidden, just here, from both. If he stood up at the wrong moment he would drop immediately, riddled.

Bullets were passing above him with intervals of no longer than a few seconds. He brought one grenade back, drew breath into his lungs, held it, and threw, and waited, and heard the thing coughing beyond the grassy ridge; then he scrambled round and raised himself until he could see Moby Dick. The boys were wise to him: the turret had swung away, taking the coaxial Besa with it; there was no fire from the other one. Turning again, he picked up the second grenade and went up the ridge at a run, seeing a Jerry helmet dodging beyond the gap in a shattered wall. He steadied, and aimed with care, dropping to wait. Fragments went singing past, after the explosion. He got up and climbed slowly, with his revolver ready. A German was stumbling down towards the ridge, but his hands were in the air, fingers spread open to shield his face. Before Goodall had reached him he fell forward and went rolling to the bottom of the ridge. Goodall went on to the wall. There were three bodies and a man staggering about clutching his groin with bright red hands, his mouth open

but silent. The sergeant gave him a wrist blow behind the
knees and caught him as he crumpled.

He carried him as carefully as he could. He was light,
a boy as fragile as little Woods. The breath was choking
in and out of him and he had begun muttering. Goodall
said: "*Doktor. Doktor.*" The muttering stopped, and the
boy stared at him, his head lolling. Blood was soaking
into the field-grey lap, but it was not pumping out fast.
When they reached the other one, who lay at the bottom
of the ridge, Goodall saw that he was clutching a revolver, steadying his right hand with his left, so Goodall
took the last few yards at a bumping trot and kicked him
in the mouth as the revolver fired. It spun away as the
man rolled back. Goodall watched him, swaying with the
boy in his arms, and was aware suddenly that the boy's
breath was no longer rasping in and out. A thin line of
blood was tracing down from the side of his face; the
bullet had gone into his head. The sergeant lowered him,
felt for heart-beat and stood upright, looking down at the
other one. His teeth had been kicked inwards and there
was a red hole for a mouth. He was grunting out a word,
repeating it as each breath gave him the strength. It
sounded like *Kamerad*. Sergeant Goodall watched him for
a few seconds, trying to think of some German, but he
knew only those few words that sounded English, and he
was too angry to care. He pointed to the dead boy and
said: "I hope you're satisfied." Then he went down to the
flat sand, dropped, and began crawling towards the tank.
He was angry about the dead boy because he had reminded him of Woods. The groin wound might not have
been bad; he was meaning to take him as far as the field
dressing-station by number one exit, not far away. There
had been no need for the bullet. The other man had been
a fool, and a criminal, because to raise the hands in
surrender and then, later, shoot to kill, is a criminal act
of war. The shot had not killed him, the enemy, but it
had caused a death during the commission of a felony,
and was therefore murder. Sergeant Goodall was very
particular about these things, and so he was angry. Be-
sides, the boy had been frail and ashen-faced and should

not have been in uniform under fire, any more than Woods should be. That was how Woods was going to look when his crotch was bloodied or his head was lolling with a bullet in the brain.

A group of mortar-bombs, sailing together in a focus from three emplacements beyond the dunes, exploded in front of him, and he lay on the fringe of the blast. Fragments sang over him and sand pattered down, softly caressing his neck. He began crawling again and then dropped as a shell landed. His face was resting against the sand; his right hand was under one cheek so that the fingers could filter the air past his nostrils. The shock of the shell left him deafened, and it was five minutes before he moved again, coming upon a man's hand and then a boot stuffed with red and white. He passed by these things and did not think about them, because he had been in this long war from the beginning, and he had seen the severed parts of men lying upon earth or floating in water or stuck to a wall, many times, until now they reminded him of nothing more horrible than a kicked over doll's house. Man was the king of beasts, and these were his tracks, and he must crawl among them.

Rapid fire was sweeping down from a gunpost near the sea-wall, but it passed him by as he groped flat-bodied towards the tank. It was looming in the smoke-haze, the long gun now forward. Before he reached it he could hear voices, singing. Adams and Cox, cooped in the driving compartment, were singing 'Why Are We Wai-ting?', the old cook-house question. He lay flat for minutes, checking on sniper and Spandau fire before he got up with a spring's quickness and bundled into the turret.

Watkins-Price was munching an apple.

"You got 'em, didn't you, Sarge?"

"Ay."

"You all right?"

"Of course I'm all right." He looked at Woods. "Haven't we got any bloody orders through, kid?"

"Not yet, Sarge." He looked ashamed of his Number 19 set, as if it had broken. Goodall said:

"You still on net, are you?"

"Oh yes, we're on."

"Well, ask 'em again, go on."

Woods put the message out, received a curt order to keep the air clear, and switched to his B set. After five minutes of interference he heard Lieutenant Pope calling: *"Moby, get into line. Get into line, blast your eyes."*

Woods looked up in alarm at Goodall.

"We're to get into line, Sarge."

"Into what, for God's sake?"

"I got Mr. Pope. Says get into line."

Goodall stuck his head out of the turret and used his field-glasses, searching for Bloody Mary. It was packed among a group of 'C' Squadron's tanks, boring into the traffic of number one exit. He bobbed down and shouted orders to the driver. Moby Dick shuddered as the tracks rolled, turning in first gear towards the traffic. A spatter of bullets hit the plates as the tank moved off, and the sergeant kept low.

He asked Watty: "Where d'you get those apples?"

"I brought 'em along."

"You'll pee cider, boy."

"You want one, Sarge?"

"No." They lumbered past a dragon's-tooth with a foot to spare, and he looked at Woods. "Are they closed down in there?"

"No, Sarge."

Goodall straightened up as they lurched through a shell-hollow, and for a moment gave himself to the luxury of feeling content. Moby Dick was in good form. Down in front, Taffy and Sam were opened up, not giving a cuss for the bullet drizzle. Watty was munching apples, waiting to shoot, and little Woods looked as fit as an underfed schoolboy could ever look in the front line of a war. As soon as the traffic worked through the exit, they could be on the road and start work. He wanted to hear this pregnant elephant go trumpeting down the road, free of this poxy sand.

A stray bullet came in through the half-raised hatch and flicked round the plates, dropping on to Watty's lap. He picked it up and tucked it behind his ear. Woods's white face began to crack in a laugh when Watkins-Price snatched the bullet away and clapped a hand to the skin.

"Christ, it was still hot!"

Woods was laughing silently now, and Goodall watched him, proud as a father. The kid was coming on. Thin as a pull-through and with not enough length of gut inside him to string a tennis racket, he was sitting here laughing, under fire. It was one of the million little wonders of a war, and for an instant Goodall was touched by it, and his contentment swelled. His confidence was such that he slung the hatch fully open and leaned there with his field-glasses raised.

He was in time to see a shell hit the beach-marker wind-sock; it vanished, a shrivelled balloon, and half the post went whirling away. Two of the 'C' Squadron tanks were drawing eighty-eight-m.m. fire from half a mile away; one of them had a track shattered but its gun pulsed at regular intervals. It was Steamboat Bill, of Number One Troop. The other was moving off, nudging its way into the traffic. The sergeant could see Top Dog and Bloody Mary, and two of Three Troop's machines. He could not find the third, among the swirl of smoke. He dodged down and said to Woods:

"What's happened to Balham Belle, d'you know?"

The boy looked up. "She went up, Sarge."

Goodall tightened his mouth. Woods said: "It was a long time ago." He meant half an hour. That was a long time, on this beach.

Goodall asked: "What about the boys?"

"It was an eighty-eight, Sarge. She's burnt out. I don't know about them. I heard Mr. Pope tellin' Battalion. They claimed an eighty-eight. It couldn't've been the one that hit them."

The sergeant nodded. "Keep your ears open, kid." He stood up straight again, going over their names: Ashton, Burrage, Levy, Scott and Thompson, remembering their faces, hoping they had baled out in time. Balham Belle would be that smoke-black shell down there, then, half sunk in the sand. He was not surprised about their claim. Burrage was the third top gunner in the Squadron.

The tank jerked under the clutches and moved forward again, bouncing him against the rim. They halted on the tail of Bloody Mary. There was Mr. Pope, waving his arms at an M.P. who was running up the dunes, burdened under makeshift signposts and marker flags. He tripped on a man's body, dropped half the signs, picked them up and went on, with the soft sand flying up from behind his boots. A German plane was over, suddenly, an M.E. 109, strafing infantry. A Bofors rattled up a shot, but the plane was too low; it left thunder in the air and vanished behind the dunes. Goodall saw someone loosing off a Bren from a turret; it was Corporal Pike, on his feet in Top Dog. He caught sight of Goodall and waved two fingers in the plane's direction.

Top Dog was on the left of the Troop-leader, with one of its tracks on the edge of a Somerfield strip and the other in the sand. In the driving compartment Luff sat happily, waiting to move off. His co-driver, Soaper, was lolling with his head rocking between his hands; the heat inside the tank, and the acrid stench of the smoke were prolonging his seasickness. It was only when he had been forced to fire the Besa that he had forgotten his stomach, but now the queasiness was back again. Twice Luff had grinned at him and said: "Go out an' 'ave a good spew," but Soaper hadn't answered. He was sick in his stomach, sick of the sea and the tank and the war. He was making a vow, as his head rocked slowly in his hands. As soon as leave for Blighty came round, he'd be off out of this lot; and he wasn't coming back. He would have done his bit by that time, and they could stuff their war. "Go out an' get it up," grinned Luff, with a stomach as strong as a barrel; but Soaper went on rocking in the fumes.

Lance-Corporal Munro was fiddling with his set. He was getting signals from the Troop but he'd lost the Battalion. He went on fiddling until Corporal Pike shouted: "What's your trouble, Gutsy?"

"Gone off bloody net, mate."

"You don' wanner worry, time like this. You think we

got a battalion 'eadquarters in this flippin' shambles?"
He came crashing down as a hail of small-arms fire
caught the turret base. Munro said:

"Where the hell did that lot come from, Alf?"

"Where the 'ell d'you think? This is the front line, ain'
it?" He poked his tin hat up an inch, and fetched a rattle
of shot. "Well, this is a stuffin' game, this is. Every time
you try to sniff a bit o' fresh air you get shot at or shat
on."

Weston, sitting at the gun, said: "Give 'em a dose o'
Besa, eh, Corp?"

"Don' be daft, you'll 'ave Mr. Pope's bloody 'ead off
if you fire that thing. We got to wait."

A shell sang down and hit ground near the gutted
A.R.V., splitting the plates open. It rolled drunkenly
into the hollow, and two soft vehicles banged their gears
in and backed, butting into the stuff behind. Lieutenant
Pope reappeared in his turret and began shouting again as
an M.P. captain ran past. Pope wanted to know what the
hold-up meant: was there a counter-attack, close inland?
The M.P. ran on without answering. Two men followed
him, bumping a stretcher along to the field dressing-station, a limp arm dangling from the canvas and a white
face turned to the sky. Pope felt a tug at his legs and bent
down. O'Hagan had got a signal through.

"One, Two an' Three Troops to number five exit,
sir!"

"Well, God almighty!"

He caught his elbow as the tank began turning out of
line, to lurch across the shell hollow and squeeze its way
through a gap in the soft vehicles. The signal had reached
Moby Dick, and it followed, scraping a track on a dragon's-tooth and losing the Somerfield strip until it was
closing on the Troop-leader. In Top Dog, Corporal Pike
was shouting:

"Where're them flippers goin' now?" He bent down.
"Gutsy! Whasser signal, eh?"

"I got nothing, ain't a squeak." He fiddled violently,
thumping the set until Pike got through to Luff and told
him to follow the others down the beach. Luff brought his

clutch in and made a neat right turn, and Soaper raised his head and lolled about, fumbling for the grease-proof bag he had brought with him, not finding it; he forced the bile back as the tank lurched badly and one track screamed against metal and then tore clear. Two Troop was in line astern, crossing the open beach and driving through a storm of Spandau fire towards five exit, half a mile away.

On their left a group of infantry was being pinned to the sand by machine-gun fire; in ones and twos they were loping for cover behind knocked-out tanks, some of them running to a shelter that had been roughly thrown up by the sappers. They were exposed to a drenching fire as a Spandau nest worked without pause, until one of the 'C' Squadron seventy-fives made a direct hit; there was peace, of a sort, after the insistent chatter of the gun. Within minutes, a bunch of prisoners came hobbling down the dunes, and Corporal Pike watched them as they passed. Their faces were grey and their uniforms ragged; two of them dragged their feet and were helped on by the rest. Their eyes flickered, all the time, as they stumbled across the littered sand. They had been here, at first light, under the bombardment; probably they had been here under the night bombers; in a few hours they had been subjected to the sum total of war, and were old nervy men with their youth gone and their minds turned. They passed beyond the corporal's sight. His voice was inaudible. "You shouldn't have started it, you cocky bastards."

Top Dog passed an armoured recovery vehicle that had put two chains on to a Churchill that leaned empty with one track torn off. The crew of the A.R.V. was sweating, two men lugging planks and dumping them on the soft sand, kicking them under the wheels as the trackless side came up, shouting for more pull and standing back, watching the tug-of-war, hearing Pike shout: "Garn, yer not even tryin', mateys!"

"It's all right for you!" called one of them, and slung a fistful of sand at Top Dog and went back to watching his planks.

Two Troop broke up as mortar-fire reached them from the east of the sector, and Moby Dick halted, with its big gun swinging as Goodall ordered: "Gunner traverse left . . . left . . . steady. . . . Ruined villa. . . . On!" Below him, Watkins-Price checked his sights, waited, and fired. The villa, at the end of the row of burning houses, had been broken up by bombs, but the skeleton of rafters remained, supporting the remnants of walls and the staircase. Goodall had sensed that an observer was there, directing the mortar-fire on to beach objectives. There was no other vantage point commanding so large an area.

Watty's shell hit the ruin in the centre. Already poised at the point of collapse, the structure caved lazily inwards, and white dust rose and was caught by the wind and drawn downwards across the dunes. A dark doll's shape went flying among the débris, jumping and then curving down to the ground; and the sergeant lowered his field-glasses.

"Watty, you're a very good boy, you are."

"I could've spat as far as that, Sergeant."

"But it wouldn't have been quite so effective."

Moby Dick started off again with the turret traversing right. Twenty yards ahead of them was Bloody Mary, pounding through the haze, with Top Dog following both. Mortar-bombs fell short, bursting among three shattered trucks that had been bulldozed into a heap, clear of the traffic lines. When the sand haze cleared, pieces were still falling and a sapper went running across the foreground, holding his face.

Within fifty yards of number five exit, Two Troop halted again, with Battalion orders to wait. The congestion was worse in this area because the beach was almost flat, and the tide was coming in fast, covering the litter of débris and driving a light scum of timber towards the idling tanks. A medical half-track was swerving along the water's edge, picking up half-drowned men and the remnant of an infantry platoon that had formed up behind an obstacle for shelter half a minute before a stray shell had landed, blasting it apart. Two men were limping, arm in arm, towards the nearest dressing-station; as one stumbled, the other dragged him up. They ran for a dozen yards in a shambling lope and then dropped flat as mortar-fire ploughed up the wet sand at the edge of the sea. When they got up again, one was shouting and hitting out at his mate, trying to make him go on alone, but his mate pulled one arm round his shoulders and half-carried him along until the medical half-track saw them and stopped, waiting. They began climbing aboard as a hail of Spandau shot came whipping through the haze; they dropped and did not move. An R.A.M.C. orderly came out of the truck and grabbed one of them and lugged him aboard, coming back for the other. Something fell from his hand. Corporal Pike, watching from Top Dog, put his field-glasses up and saw it was a concertina. It lay on the wet sand as the half-track moved off.

Corporal Pike took a look at his Troop-leader and at the traffic strung out towards the beach exit. The Spandau fire had stopped. Sporadic shelling was making a mess of inshore shipping as fresh assault-craft were brought in, but the immediate area was quiet. He hit his gunner on the shoulder.

"Back in five minutes."

Mortaring began again as he dropped over the turret-rim and he had to lie flat on the lee side of the tank while the sand-cloud drifted away. He got up and ran, stopping half-way to the water's edge and waiting until a group of infantry had gone up at the double towards the exit. While he waited he poked a dog-end out of his pocket and lit it, choking as he inhaled too greedily. The Spandau had started again, picking on the infantry group and sending it to scatter for cover behind obstacles higher up.

He could still see the concertina, but he would have to be quick about it, because the water was rushing over the flat sand, drawing white foam across the débris and leaving it scummed. He took another drag at the dog-end and then started to run again, dodging for the nearest cover, an overturned trailer with boots poking out from beneath it. He broke away some of the timber to check on the man; there was nothing he could do for him now, so he straightened up in the lee of the wreckage and looked along the water line for the concertina. He could not see it. Empty boxes were skating in on the foam, some sticking, some drawing back as the wave receded. The hulk of a fighting-tank wallowed farther out, with the sea breaking over the turret and swirling round.

When he saw the concertina at last it was turning over in the foam. He began trotting down the wet sand, and little clods of it flew up behind his boots. Débris was drifting in round the concertina, but he picked out its shape between a log and the upturned canvas hood of a soft vehicle that was lying on its side, awash in deeper water. A shell hit the water a yard from it, and he dropped prone, covering his head and waiting. The shock flattened his battle blouse and blocked his ears; then water came down in a slanting sheet and left him drenched. He crouched and shook himself. Lying on the sand a yard from him, brought in by the waves, was a shred of battle rubbish that sickened him; he stood upright and stepped over it, walking on along the line of foam until he passed the canvas hood. He picked up the concertina, turning it to let the water run off; none seemed to have gone inside. He gave it a squeeze, and it worked well. A bullet cluster fluted past him, so he sat down and squeezed the concertina again, trying some of the notes. A long time ago, he had played one of these things in a party at the Angel, when Billy Lee had won the football pool. Sophie had been there, in a dress she had altered for the occasion, and Billy had made eyes at her, and said how he'd take her twice round the world in a big white yacht with a solid gold anchor, and they'd drop Alf Pike off at Egypt with a season ticket for the most expensive harem in the place, so as he wouldn't be lonely and miss his Sophie. By ten o'clock, Billy was as drunk as a skunk, and Sophie made him go home. It had been Jeff Carter's concertina, and Alf had played it till it bust.

He sat on the sand, remembering Sophie's dress, and how smashing she'd looked in it. He'd played her favourite tune, *La Cumparsita,* three or four times. He could hear it now. His hands jerked to a stop. Flippin' 'ell, he was *playing* it now! Sitting here with a wet bum and his back to an active Spandau, playing a concertina! Alf Pike, he said, you want somethin' tested, don' you? Your flippin' loaf, don' you?

He got up and fixed the elastic band round the bellows, so that they wouldn't dangle and break. He'd look after this, he would, and they'd all have a sing-song, soon as there was the chance. He walked on to the dry sand and then stopped, hearing someone laugh. There was nobody near him. A naval beach-master, fifty yards off, was cursing a D.D. tank that had come in beam-on, blocking the gangway. On the other side, beyond the log in the surf, men were working to salvage tools from a wrecked equipment truck. The laughing went on. He kept his ears clear of the wind, and felt his spine creep. He didn't like people laughing at him without even being here. He spun round, but the surf was empty, bringing nothing more than flotsam to the beach.

A mortar bomb plummeted down near the salvage gang, and they ducked under the wreck. He put one hand up to shield his face, and when the noise was over he heard the laughing again. He began to sweat. He was hearing things. Going off his loaf, he was. He shouted: "Shuddup, will yer?" He hadn't meant to shout anything; it was his nerves. It did not stop. It was a faint slow laugh, rising and dying on the wind.

"Cut it out, will yer?" His hands were shaking. He started off again, determined not to hurry. He'd got shell-shock, that was it. It made you think things. People said that if you——

He spun round again, clenching his fist, because the wind had brought the laughing very close; it was not in his head; it was somewhere here. He was looking at the log. The water had moved it, drawing a soft veil of it out at one side. It was dark brown fishing-mesh, with corks along the edge. The log-shape had broken up. It was a fishing-net, and it had collected rubbish and flotsam, and a man. It was the man who was laughing.

Corporal Pike put his concertina down carefully and

went through the foam, kicking it up with his boots. The man was lying on his back, one arm entangled in the net.

"Flip me," Pike said, "what you doin' 'ere, Neptune?"

The man had stopped laughing. His face was a good colour and his eyes were open, looking sanely at the corporal. There were pips on the shoulder of his battle-blouse. He said:

"Don't you know any more?"

"Any more what, sir?"

"Tunes."

"Eh?"

"Tunes to play."

Pike remembered the concertina. He swung his knife up on its lanyard and pulled the blade open. "Is that what you was laughin' about?"

"Yes. It doesn't quite seem the time to organize a concert." As Pike bent over him he added: "You can't get that out. It's broken."

"I know. I'm goin' to cut the net." He began work with the knife. " 'Ow long you bin 'ere, sir?"

"Not long. I was knocked out cold, and when I came to, there was your concertina playing. The first thing that came back to me was my sense of humour." He bit off the last word and Pike said:

"It's goin' to give you gyp, when I move this arm."

"You're telling me, Corporal."

The knife went through the last strand of fibre, and the arm was free. "You want me to straighten it, sir?"

After a moment the officer said: "Yes, if you will. When I say 'now'—all right?"

"Okay. When you're ready." He stood over him. The waves lapped past them, and seaweed caught against the net, flowing as dark as hair along the man's legs, shining as the light flashed through the foam.

"Now."

Pike jerked his hands and got the arm straight while the officer gave a shout like a gunshot and then began wheezing as saliva collected. His face went slowly white and he shut his eyes. A man was coming over from the salvage gang; he had heard the shout. Pike straightened up, feeling sick. He told the man: "I've got to get back to my tank, mate. Can you look after this officer?"

"Can do." He was an enormous Geordie, a gold-haired gorilla. He stood with his arms akimbo and looked down at the officer, saying to Pike: "Is he bad?"

The eyes opened. The face was still white. Most of the words were steady. "If you don't get me out of this bloody sea I shall decompose."

As the Geordie bent down to lift him, Pike warned him: "Mind 'is left arm. It's bust."

"I'll mind, laddy."

"Corporal."

"Sir?"

"Thank you for your help."

"That's a pleasure, sir." He put up a cheerful salute and walked away through the shallows, trudging on to the dry beach and finding his concertina. The explosions of mortar-bombs, falling near, had covered it with sand, but he brushed it off carefully as he made his way back to the tank.

II

THE bottleneck at number five beach exit cleared soon after 09.00 hours and the leading troops of 'C' Squadron moved on to the lateral road. Of the Squadron's original eighteen tanks, seven had been knocked out; the crews of three were dead.

Lieutenant Pope took Bloody Mary through the gap in the sea-wall; the tracks clattered across the assault bridge; the pennant was taut in a whirling dust storm sent out from the leading armour. Trooper Dove had his goggles on, and drove with the vision-slit open. Beside him,

Steiner sat listening to the great rush of the engine, and in his mind talked to his sister, saying that he was on his way to Germany, and that he would remember their father and their mother and the way they had died. In the turret Corporal Todd sat with his gun, watching its long dark finger pointing through the dust, turning to look at O'Hagan as he began thumping his wireless and fiddling it back on to net. Above them, Pope was standing with his head and shoulders slowly whitening as the dust covered them. His goggles were filming inside, and dust was filtering down past the handkerchief-mask he had tied across his face; but he was happy. To his youthful mind the most important objective of his life was to become experienced in war; and already he was four hours old.

In the wake of the leader rolled Moby Dick. Sergeant Goodall, too, was happy. Ten years older than his Troop-commander, he had for his objective the wish to fight on German soil. He was a regular, and he had fought in France, Africa, Sicily, Italy and Greece. Being in the Army as a professional soldier, his natural purpose was to fight in war, just as the natural purpose of a man in the City is to deal in finance, and that of a farmer is to grow crops. So that he was in his element here; and that is nine-tenths of happiness. The white dust swirled over him, and he did not mind. In front of him, in the driving compartment, Taffy Adams minded very much. He would have liked better to drive his tank at a pillbox, or an armed strong-point, than through this dreadful dust, for you could not see, and you could not breathe; all you could do was sit and think about your three silly sisters and hope the Lord would look after them, and perhaps one fine day knock some sense into their silly heads.

Sam Cox heard the engine miss, and he swore, and every time it missed again he swore again, until after a mile of dust and a list of curses it ran sweet again, proving to him that, if you were a good engineer, even a few right words could be your tools. He listened to the engine, part of his mind crooning with its rhythm, until an apple came whizzing past his head. He picked it up, turned round and winked at Watty, and took the first bite, spit-

ting out the dust. Faintly they heard Woods trying out the
B set and getting an answer from Top Dog. Woods was
at home again, sitting with the head-phones on, at home
with his friends, the voices. It had been like this in his
small cramped bedroom, wandering round the world
through the short-wave amateur bands, losing touch with
his room and the house and the poky town. Now he had
lost touch with the war, with the guns and the dust and
the cold sour dread that would lap over him like chill
water as soon as he took these head-phones off and met
with the world again.

A new voice came through to him on the B set, from
Top Dog's commander. " 'Ow you feelin', Woody boy?"

"I'm all right, thank you, Corp."

"I got a drop more rum, when there's a chance to swig
it, don' forget."

"I think it did me good."

"I'll say it did you good. It warms the cockles, like I
told you."

They heard Sergeant Goodall cut in. "There'll be no
drinkin' on duty, Corporal Pike."

"You call this duty, Sergeant Goodall? Standin' 'ere
with a gobful of flippin' dust what you're chuckin' up
with that bit of ironmonger's 'eartbreak o' yours? Call it
flippin' duty?"

"Well, what would you call it?"

Pike told him. From his gun seat, Bob Weston looked
up at his tank commander, awed by his invective. Lance-
Corporal Munro sat with his wireless, waiting for Mr.
Pope to cut in and stop the nonsense; but he couldn't be
listening, because Sergeant Goodall and Corporal Pike
passed the next half-mile in a ding-dong duet of repartee
that searched every outpost of soldiering in England for a
riper word than the last.

Below and forward in the driving compartment Soaper
sat with his sick head and his sick heart, thinking of leave
and Blighty. There would be trouble with the wife, once
she found he wasn't reporting back from leave, but she'd
just have to see sense. If she wouldn't help him, then she
could do the other thing; there were plenty of places

where he could go and hide up, places a sight more cheerful than Percival Road. It wouldn't do to have a woman round him when he was keeping low, especially a woman like Doris. She'd go and yap the odds across the next-door fence, just for the sake of the drama; and he'd be in the glasshouse like a shot.

He sat rocking to the roll of the tank. Beside him, on the driving clutches, Luff kept Top Dog as straight as he could along the cratered road, and turned once, to grin at poor old Soapy. "Why don't you get out an' have a good puke?"

Soaper went on staring through the dust. The driving compartment filled suddenly with frightening sound as something went screaming past. Crews looked up, startled, at their commanders. O'Hagan said: "What in the hell was that?"

"The M.E.," said Pike.

"The what?"

"Messerschmitt." He squinted through the dust. The aircraft had been hit, aft. The tail unit was flapping about like a dislocated knuckle as the machine streaked at tree-height across the dunes, vanishing in a burst of flame. "That'll learn yer," said Pike, and turned his head forward again.

Battalion orders came through on the A sets, and the commanders checked their maps. Two Troop was to leave the lateral road at the next crossing, and approach St. Marle, a hamlet three miles due inland across the marshes. Infantry of the East Yorks were to be shot forward to assault the strongly defended ridge a mile beyond. The orders were acknowledged. At the crossroads, where two scissor-bridges lay over craters, Bloody Mary, Moby Dick and Top Dog turned south, and their dust-cloud drew slowly away from the lateral road and went bannering over the marsh.

The remnant of 'C' Squadron was breaking up, to tackle three close objectives before re-forming and finding harbour. They were leaving the sea. Behind them the beaches lay under a fog of dust, sand and battle-smoke that even the wind could not disperse, for it gathered more strongly with each minute as shells flew down and the mortar-fire from the east flank of the sector kept up its bombardment, seeking out the fresh assault-crews as the boats came in.

The dark smoke of burning oil was twisting across the sand from the crashed Messerschmitt; it rested, bridging a crater, its flames slowly revealing its skeleton; and soon its shape was lost and it ceased to be an aeroplane. It was a blackened carcass, another rubbish-heap in the arena of the shore. Farther down, someone had thrown blankets over the men from Balham Belle, so that they too had lost their shape and their identity. Lieutenant Ashton and Troopers Burrage, Levy and Scott were gold-painted names on a board, and with them was Thompson, the unrecognisable framework of burned bone in the cooling shell of the tank.

There was a blanket, too, over the military policeman who had been caught by the crush of traffic; but the German boy lay uncovered, at the bottom of the sandy ridge where Sergeant Goodall had left him. His comrade had gone, perhaps crawled to a medical post with his bared nerves and his smashed mouth and his conscience. The big armoured recovery vehicle stood gutted, near number three exit, hauled to one side to clear the way. The third tank of One Troop, Steamboat Bill, was abandoned now, with its ammunition racks emptied and the crew gone. Later, its wrecked track would be repaired, and it would get a fresh crew; for the moment it was an obstacle, and cursed by all.

A new beach-marker wind-sock had been hoisted, and was a clear target for the Spandaus. Below it lay the body of the man who had erected it, his own frail monument. He lay among litter; nowhere in the sector could a man lie dead with any seemliness, for the rubbish was gathering, much of it thrown up by the sea, more of it on fire and adding to the smoke, some of it lapped by the waves as they drove in with the tide, higher across the littered sand. Tanks and soft vehicles stood on smashed tracks and shattered wheels or lay humped over on their sides, burned out or blown apart; the sea came in and swirled

among them, leaving seaweed festooned across their car-
casses. Wrecked boats were in the shallows and on the
narrowing strip of sand, holed by obstacles or ripped
open by a mine. Salvage crews were at work. The field
dressing-stations were full, and round them waited the
men with wounds and cigarettes, waiting to be taken in or
to be taken home, or to be taken anywhere, anywhere far
from this smoke-black outpost of hell where they had
wandered without luck. Past them they watched the prisoners go, as each pillbox and dug-out and sniper's post
was winkled out and won; they were grey men, grey of
face, with eyes sunk deep into their heads, eyes that could
look at nothing now without a flinch, not at a helping arm
nor an offered cigarette nor a cheerful face, nothing,
without a flinch, because they had been here in the long
night and at the explosion of the dawn, and their nerves
were jangling on, as mad as bell-wires jerking in the
crumbled ruin of a house. They walked like drunk men,
feeling the way with their hands along the insubstantial
drifts of smoke, moved back into their group by the
enemy, helped along by him, picked up by him, hurried
onwards through this inescapable maze of sand and pain
and smoke. *Kamerad,* they had said, men appealing to
other men, saying that they were comrades now, because
they could fight no more; the word might have been better said at the beginning, and not at the end, of this new
war. In their faces, and in the limp of their feet through
the littered filth, was the aspect that war has when the
mask is off. In these places, far from the seats of the
Governments, the speeches have been forgotten and
the clarion calls have died away; the ideologies have foundered at sea and the arguments have lost their point along
the alien shore; man fights man, forgetting the reason,
vesting himself in bestial acts alone. He goes forward, his
high heart turning to pulp as the bullet rends it, his war-
cry fading to a whimper as he falls on his face in the
muck, trying in the last instant to wonder why, and failing
even to ask. The shine is dulled on the once-bright
phrases; their shape now is the shape of a ripped boot
with a smashed foot in it. The gloss is gone from nobility;

it is a burned hand, the fingers groping for the lost comfort of the gun. The glamour of mere drama is shrivelled away beneath the sting of shot; it was very big to wave good-bye and hoist the flag and storm the enemy, but it is very small, this hollow on the shore, with the cold face stiffening against the blood-soaked sand, the left leg a withering stump, the heart's beat dying away as the last of the life drips out, over the minutes and the weeks . . . they've sent me a telegram, the War Office have; the last of the life drips out. . . . Mary's been asking me again, 'Where's Dad gone?' and I don't know what to tell her; the life drips out. . . . Susan's not stopped crying since she heard, and I can't get her to eat, or say a word; drips out . . . we'll have to change his room round, before Mother gets here, it'll only remind her if she goes in there; drips out over the hours and the days while the telegram goes and she shuts her eyes and they move the furniture round. There is the silence of the house; a head turns, in the bar of the pub, questioning, and the name is said again, and the name is really Charlie, with his tankard up there on the hook and his darts there on the shelf; the letter comes, in answer, stiff and embarrassed, 'Thank you for letting me know, I'm ever so sorry'; and the man has become a ghost, at last.

The prisoners went by, shuffling through the smoke; the wounded watched them, sitting victorious with a tourniquet for the limb and a cigarette for the nerves; and in the dust there was no field-grey and no khaki; they were men dressed in the one fashionable colour, a blend of dried sweat, and dried blood, and dirt. In the dug-out, under the big red cross that was spread on the sand, the doctors worked, isolated and silent, their trained senses anæsthetised against revulsion. Their material came in, and some of it was saved; men were sent out to wait for transport, cheerful men, unconscious men, patched men, all alive, some with a future, others without eyes, without hands, without nerves strong enough to raise them ever again from the slough of an idiot's existence.

Sometimes, in one of those strange intervals of calm

when every gun is reloading and every shell is down, they heard the sound of the sea; it lapped round the tombstone obstacles, drifting under the débris, tenderly moving a corpse or in a rush of temper throwing it up and dropping it, taking away what chance of dignity it ever had in its decaying dumping-ground. The sea came in, coughing discreetly at the funeral.

In the quietness a man said: "You hear that?"

" 'Ear what?" The cigarette burned his fingers.

"The sea."

A smile cracked the stiff face. He let the cigarette fall. "The sea, is it?" He remembered the sea, and what it really meant. "Then where's the bucket an' spade, an' the Wallsie-man?"

"Shut up shop, mate. You're behind the times."

The sea drifted, dropping a wave, drawing it back, rushing softly along the shore. Another man, lying to face the sky, said: "Where's my concertina?"

"Your what, chum?"

"I had a concertina."

They looked at him.

"Did you, mate? We'll 'ave a look round for it, soon as we can."

He moved on the stretcher, and the bandaged stump of one arm fell out from beneath the blanket. They gently moved it back, and covered him.

"You warm enough, boy?"

"Yes, thank you. Where is it, then?"

They gave him another cigarette, and lit it for him. "We'll 'ave a look for it. Don't you worry."

The cigarette poked up like a thermometer. He did not draw on it; he didn't know it was there. He stared at the dark sky, watching the smoke drift across, and when the guns began again they drowned his voice; it piped thinly, unheard in the shuddering din.

"I dropped my concertina, somewhere. Somewhere."

They saw his lips moving; the cigarette wobbled. The guns hammered the sky, the sand, the sea.

"I've lost my concertina," he said bleakly, staring up at the smoke.

THE LAND

I

IN ST. MARLE there were twenty-six houses, a church, two cafés and a horse-trough. Only three of the houses were burning. Snipers were holding one café, and the proprietor was holding the other. He was neither a patriot nor a partisan; whether it were a German or a British soldier who first crossed this threshold, he would fetch buckshot. The proprietor had been a patriot in 1916, and had suffered a lost ear defending his café in the Marne area against a local attack by the Boche. In 1940 he had defended this café, this very café, against a group of Colonials who were bent on carousing in the bitter face of defeat; and he had suffered a cracked skull. He was now a neutral, a defender only of his faith; and as his faith was in the grape and in these bottles, here he was with his shot-gun. Men had drunk wine before wars were made, and in these bottles there was more steadfastness and greater worth than in any man's shiftless skin; because you could taste this wine and know it for what it was, whereas you could talk to a man who was a Fascist last year, a Bolshy this, and a Royalist next, and you wouldn't know what he was, and, unless you knew, there was the risk of saying something wrong and getting shot; and since you could never know, the bullet was yours for certain.

He had lost his faith in men together with his ear; his resistance to war had been cracked, together with his skull; and now he accepted war, and was his own general and his own troops; and this was his battleground. Since he was the proprietor of a café, people were expected to come in here for the purpose of drinking wine, eating food, and conversing in friendship. If, therefore, they came in here to throw hand-grenades at him, or set fire to his establishment, or smash the bottles of his wine, then he would shoot buckshot at them. That was only logical.

The glasses danced sometimes on the shelves as the guns went off. Two miles from the café, 'C' Squadron was approaching in support of an infantry brigade, on a brigade frontage of one thousand five hundred yards. Forward elements of the infantry had already passed this way; the rest were coming up more slowly, saving their wind for the assault on the ridge beyond. Along the ridge were three main strong-points; between it and the hamlet were two anti-tank ditches and a self-propelled gun. From the north the dust rose yellow, and advanced in a wave as opaque as water, so that it looked as if a tidal wave were moving inland from the sea.

On the ridge, two fifty-millimetre guns kept up an alternating fire. The long barrel of the S.P. gun swung up, nosing the air, sniffing the dust that was coming. The snipers in the first café moved higher among the tiny rooms above, and one climbed to the roof and lay prone along the guttering. In the second café the proprietor raised his bottle and drank again from it, partaking the steadfastness of the wine that was his faith. Outside, a sack of bones in the shape of a horse drank from the trough, and looking at it, the proprietor wavered in his strict neutrality. That was a mark of the invader, over there, the stark ribs under the mangy hide; the invader was German; it would perhaps be a more enjoyable thing if it were a German who came in here first.

The dust rose higher and fanned out, sweeping over the marshes until its shadow touched the first houses of the village and darkened them. Now the yellow dust merged with the blue of the timber smoke from the three burning houses, and within minutes the wandering self-propelled gun was choking in a green-tinged fog. The road was straight, from the coast to the village, and cut through it to provide its one street; so that the leading transports came in fast, driving in from the great cloud at a conqueror's pace.

The cloud followed as fast, with the straight north wind, and the snipers put an eye to the sights, and the proprietor took a final hasty swig at the wine and lifted his shot-gun and waited. A scout-car was the first vehicle to reach the main street of the village and it shot between the burning houses and ran on fifty yards before it hit the mine in the road and overturned, its metal-work skating along a low stone wall, its crew tumbling out and rolling in the dust as nimble as rubber bobbins. Two of them got up and helped the third, lifting him clear of the road as a swift half-track came swinging through, shuddering as it hit the hole in the road and cleared it with a drunken lurch towards the graveyard wall and away again, while the first tank, following, found less room for its greater width, and clouted the overturned scout-car and dragged it a little way before dropping it in the dust. The tanks and the troop transports and the Bren-carrier came through the main street of St. Marle with the velocity of bricks hurled up an alley. The earth trembled. Stones pattered against walls and windows, and glass crashed. The dust ran through like a river and went tiding upwards, blotting out the roofs. Something hit another stray mine and the dust exploded and then fragments of metal went whirling against the walls; a streak of flame drew out and was snuffed by the dust; a man cried out and was not answered; the wheels spun; the tracks rolled with their bright steel beribboning the haze; a tin-hat went clattering down and found its rim and went bowling through the fling of stones; bullets came whining through the din, flicking against metal and skating away to ricochet among the close angular confines of wall and juggernaut; the sniper, dropping from the roof, vanished in the dust, his going soundless; a grenade fell below the window of the second café and the glass came away in a brittle cascade, its slivers fluting inwards and tinkling sharply as a hail of buckshot sprang against the air, fired by accident as the proprietor's nerves shivered, jerking his hand.

The leading armour was out of the village and rolling south. The transports followed, with men swaying together and clinging on. Through the dust and the thunder faint voices went, following their course through the ether, flitting like echoes. . . . *Hello Charlie One Able.* . . . *We are through St. Marle and proceeding south.* . . . *No opposition.* . . . *Over.* . . .

A medical truck, last in the convoy, swerved and hit a wall, and smashed a mudguard, and righted itself and ploughed on through the pall of dust. Echoes ricocheted from building to building, weaving a sound-pattern that minute by minute died away; and the wind, fluttering through the street, drove the last of the dust before it; the houses emerged. A door hung on one hinge like a wooden flag; a dog yelped somewhere in a cellar; a bloodied bundle sagged between the wall and the road, below the roof where the sniper had been; a skein of clear blue smoke went straying down from one of the houses that still smouldered, and the wind took it; it swirled up, a light blowy veil, thinning away.

On the south road the armour and transports halted, to deploy for the attack on the ridge.

II

IN THE EVENING of the first day, columns of the Twelfth S.S. Panzer Division were reported by air reconnaissance to be moving west. It was clear that the enemy's ground was to be held, even as far east as the ridge beyond St. Marle, until support concentrations could be brought up. In accordance with this general plan, the defence of the ridge was prolonged to the point of exhaustion. A mixed force under the command of a colonel of the Hants, comprising elements of five regiments, made their first assault just after noon, in the wake of a preliminary bombardment lasting twenty minutes, sent up from two field batteries, a group of S.P. guns and 'C' Squadron's armament.

Of the Squadron's tanks, nine were left. Two Troop was still intact. The Troop-commander was positioned in a fold of land half a mile below the east slope of the ridge. A dozen yards behind was Moby Dick. To their right, buried in a copse, was Top Dog. Their intermittent fire, ordered by signal, was directed to cover the slow and painful advance of the infantry across the foot of the ridge.

A spotting plane was turning in low, wide circles, sometimes drifting down across the bocage area, sometimes lifting and going in close to the summit. Twice it had drawn serious fire from the enemy guns, but it had bobbed calmly among the flak-bursts, taking its time and choosing its path until Two Troop grew worried about it. The law of averages alone must bring it down before long. Sergeant Goodall stood with his field-glasses up, following the small plane's flight until it was lost behind a soft green wall of poplars to the west.

The three tanks were the only vehicles in a square of bocage that was bounded on three sides by pasture-land and by the road on the fourth. For two hours the guns of Bloody Mary, Top Dog and Moby Dick had been systematically pounding the ridge defence, picking on the strongpoints near the east slope. The tanks were pushed well into the foliage, leaving only the gun-barrels poking out; but there was not much point in camouflage; the guns marked their own position clearly enough. A certain amount of smoke had come across the foot of the ridge from the west, put out by 'A' and 'B' Squadrons as the infantry went up; but the northerly wind dispersed it, and now the terrain was under fair visibility. The crews of Two Troop were uncomfortable, motionless under the eyes of the enemy, exposed by their own guns. They were waiting to be picked on; and the waiting was hard.

The first shell struck ground a hundred yards to the right of the bocage and coughed up half a ton of earth that sailed high and then pattered down among the leaves.

" 'Ello-'ello!" said Corporal Pike.

A voice answered from the hatch. "What was that, then?"

"What you think, mate?" He fished for his tin-hat and put it on. The stink of the shell came slowly across on the wind. In the driver's seat, Luff said:

"Was it a stray, Corp?"

"It was Number One, mate." He stood on his platform, sniffing the air. The wind had died, or they were sheltered here by the trees to the north. The air was almost still, and only the highest leaves were on the move. There was cloud over all; above it there was the sun, casting down heat and a white glare, but leaving its gold light shielded. He looked down, hearing a rustle in the undergrowth. Sergeant Goodall was coming towards him from the half-buried hump of Moby Dick.

"What's your trouble, then, Sergeant Goodall?"

"You're my only trouble, Corporal Pike."

A voice rose from the turret of Top Dog. "When can we move on, Sarge?"

"When we get orders, boy." He stood below Corporal Pike. More quietly, and without looking up against the glare, he said: "We're goin' to get shot at, you know that, don't you?"

"We are," said Pike. He waited a bit and added: "The boys want to get out an' 'ave a skip round."

Goodall said: "One at a time, then."

Pike slapped the armour with the flat of his hand. "Luff!"

"Hallo, Corp?"

"Come out an' stretch yer trotters, mate!"

In half a minute, Soaper appeared.

"I said Luff, not you, Soaper."

"I feel sick, Corp." He blinked in the strong light, the sheen of sweat on his face. He looked ill and weary. The driving compartment had enclosed him for four hours, trapping the heat and the fumes and the sound of the engine and the guns. He would give a lot never to go back to it.

"What you got to feel sick about?"

Soaper waved a limp hand. "Christ!" he said.

"All right, you can stay outside five minutes, but don't go far away. We're bein' fired on."

"Fired on? That was a stray, wasn't it?"

"Yes, it was about as flippin' stray as a Guards R.S.M. on parade. You jus' keep near the Dog, see?"

"Okay, Corp." He sank down and lay flat on his back in the grass, drinking the air and the sweet smell. His eyes throbbed in their sockets. His feet throbbed in their boots. He pulled them off. They heard the second shell coming with a rush, and they ducked fast before it fell. It hit the saplings in the centre of the bocage square, sending a blast-wave against the flank of Moby Dick, the nearest tank. Splinters came humming, one fragment clouting Top Dog amidships, another whipping into the leaves where Pike and Goodall were crouched. Soaper had rolled over on to his face.

In Top Dog, Munro heard the Troop-commander on the air to Battalion. *Are being fired on, six-minute intervals, fifties or eighty-eights.* The stench was strong in the air, lying in warm drifts about the tanks. There was acknowledgment from Battalion, but no new orders. In Moby Dick, Watkins-Price sat with impatience.

"Why don't they tell us to hit back, for God's sake?"

"I s'ppose they know best," said Woods. His pinched boy's face was paler than before. He listened to anything he could that was going over the A set. As long as the voices kept up, it would be all right.

A big wing of dust was drawing across the trees on the west of the bocage as transports came down the road from St. Marle. Something blew up, and a patch of flame raddled the dust; after minutes, a column of smoke climbed and was caught by the wind and tilted slowly over. At its base the flames crackled; ammunition was going off.

"Reinforcements," said Goodall.

"Ay," said Pike. He looked down at Soaper, who was still lying on his stomach behind the tank. "All right, Soaper. Send Luff out."

He sat up and pulled his boots on, breathing hard, as if he had been running. "We ought to get out of this."

"You better buzz the Colonel, an' let 'im know."

Soaper got back into the tank and Luff came out as the third shell arrived dead on the six minutes and crashed down immediately in front of the Troop-leader's tank. The explosive contact of metal to metal, fragments to armour, banged like a bell. Sergeant Goodall ran that way, dodging and jumping the undergrowth. Lieutenant Pope was getting his driver and co-driver out. Dove dropped from the tank and stood with his head in his hands, sobbing. Steiner dropped beside him, ashen-faced but quiet. Pope had his brandy-flask out and tried to make Dove drink from it, but he leaned against him with his shoulder and would not take his hands away from his head; the sobbing went on, monotonously. Pope didn't seem to know what to do, so Goodall took the flask and drew the man's arm down, tilting his head back. It was as if Dove were a stiffly-articulated doll; his arm remained at the angle to which it was moved; his head remained tilted to face the sky; the tears made bright ruts through the dust film and the dirt, falling on to Goodall's hand as he tipped the flask little by little until by habit the man was drinking. The sergeant passed the brandy to Steiner, but the Jew shook his head. The shell had made a noise, that was all, in the driving compartment, a noise dreadful enough to choke a man with his own breath, but only a noise. They would have to do more to him than this before he needed brandy.

"Better have a drop, Steiner."

"No, Sergeant, thank you. I am all right."

Goodall gave the flask to the lieutenant, and led Dove away a few paces, behind the tank. His hands were up to his head again, and the sobbing went on.

"Sit down, Dove. We'll have a smoke while things are quiet." He glanced at his watch. Four minutes had gone since that last shell; there were two more minutes to go. He lit a cigarette and put it between Dove's lips. They were running with saliva. When Corporal Pike came up, Goodall said:

"He's all right. It was just the noise."

Pike nodded, watching the man. The cigarette had fallen from his loose, nerveless mouth. Goodall picked it up, held it for a moment, and then got to his feet, saying to Pike:

"Send Watty over, Corp."

"Ay, Sarge." He went across to Moby Dick. Goodall checked his watch. There was a minute left. He turned to Pope and said:

"They're puttin' a bracket on us, sir."

"I know, but I can't get orders to move or fire back or do any damn' thing except sit here begging for more."

Goodall nodded. "Shall I get the men out, sir?"

Pope's eyes were jumpy. He felt responsible. He ought to order the crews to safety, out of this square of trees that was soon going to become a graveyard; but they couldn't leave the tanks. Orders might come at any minute. He said:

"Out? How the devil can we?"

"I mean out of the tanks, sir." He turned his left wrist. There was half a minute left. "If we get a direct hit and there's fire, we'll lose good men."

The lieutenant hesitated. He would like to be rid of this problem and of this much responsibility. It had been different, storming along through the flying dust, leading the Troop into action; now this was action, the worst kind of all, when you need higher authority even to fire your guns at the enemy, and must sit motionless and exposed, under orders to do just that.

"Yes. Get them out. All except the wireless operators."

Goodall raised his voice, turning towards the turret rim of the lieutenant's tank. "C'p'l Todd!"

Todd's head appeared. "Sarge?"

"Out, quick!"

He came, dropping. The driver and co-driver were out already, and so was Mr. Pope. That left only O'Hagan inside, with his wireless. Todd asked: "What's the drill then, Sarge?"

Goodall was looking at his watch. The six minutes were up. He said: "Go an' sit down with Dove. Try an' help him. There's another one just coming, so watch out."

Watkins-Price was here. "You want me, Sergeant?"

"Go and sit there with Dove. He's got shock." As Watty dropped on to the grass, Goodall looked at Steiner. "How d'you feel?"

"I am all right, Sergeant." His eyes were burning with something, and he was listening. He had seen Goodall counting off the minutes.

"Get down, then. There's one———" The rush came in the air and their bowels tightened. They were frozen men in a tableau. The lieutenant was standing a yard from the tank. Goodall was below the turret, his back to it. Steiner was facing him, for they had just been talking. Watkins-Price and Todd were sitting one on each side of Dove; and Dove was sobbing. The shell burst on the other side of the tank, in the fourth corner of the square, flinging up earth and leaves and sending splinters rapping among the tanks.

When the last of the earth had pattered down, and it was quiet, the tableau broke up. Pope said:

"That's the fourth corner, Sergeant."

"Yes, sir. Next one in the middle."

"Get the rest of the men out."

The sergeant noticed that Dove had stopped sobbing. Probably he had used the last of his strength, even for that. His face was a blotchy white, the skin transparent; it would look like that when he was dead. The brandy had been useless, a cup of water poured into a conflagration. Goodall started off across the undergrowth, joining Corporal Pike, who said:

"This is a turn-up, this is."

"Get your blokes out, except Munro. We're going to take cover under the tanks." He reached Moby Dick and looked through the driver's slit. "Come on out, you pair of winkles."

Adams and Cox went squeezing through the hatch.

"Goin' to dig holes, are we, Sergeant?" Taffy asked.

"There's no time. Just crawl underneath." He started back towards the Troop-leader, picking his way over the roots and wading through the leaves. The next one would be in the centre. Moby Dick was nearest. He found Pope in his turret and said:

"Have we got permission to move, sir?"

"I'm still trying."

Goodall shielded his eyes against the glare. "My tank's too near the middle. If we could move that one, it'd be something, sir."

Pope's voice was impatient with worry.

"I am still trying, Sergeant." He repeated his request on the A set and waited. Goodall checked the minutes; there were three left. He watched Pike going over to Moby Dick.

Woods was on his seat, and didn't look up as the corporal came over the turret rim and dropped inside.

" 'Ello, boy. 'Ow's tricks?"

Vaguely Woods said: "Mr. Pope's asking for permission to move, Corp."

"That's the ticket." He sat on the commander's platform and lit a dog-end. "You don't smoke, do you, kid?"

"No, thank you."

Pike held the commander's head-phones to one ear and they sat listening.

We have one tank in the centre, where next shell is expected. Urgently request permission to move it. Over.

Pike sat cursing Battalion. If he was Mr. Pope, he'd have them out quick, never mind if they were spotted on the move. Battalion could do what it liked; it wasn't sitting out here under fire.

Hello, Charlie One Able. It is vital to general plan you stay put. Use what protection you can.

The smoke from Corporal Pike's cigarette drifted up through the open turret. He hung up the head-phones. Woods was staring at the dials. Sweat was gathering on his forehead and his hands could not keep still. Every five seconds he swallowed saliva. Pike said:

"The sarge says you're a wizard at that thing. Were you at it before you joined?"

Woods nodded, without looking at him.

"They're like a flippin' jig-saw puzzle to me. Our set got broke once back 'ome, an' I repaired it myself, 'cause it was a Sund'y an' we couldn't fetch no 'elp, see, an' there was a programme what my mum wanted to 'ear. So I got a screwdriver an' opened everythin' up." He nipped his dog-end out and slipped it away. "Time I got everythin' back, I 'ad 'alf a yard o' gut left over an' the place was full o' flippin' smoke. Soon as I turned the knob on, there was a flash o' sparks, an' my brother George slung a kettle o' water over it, 'fore the 'ole 'ouse wen' up in flames."

Woods nodded, but did not look at him. His small body seemed to be shrinking on the seat. When he could, he said:

"Corp." He tried to steady his breathing.

"Yes, kid?"

"You ought to get out."

Pike put his head on one side. "Oh? 'Ow's that, then?"

"We're goin' to be hit, Mr. Pope says." His whole body was quivering, so that his breath became a flutter.

"Mr. Pope don't know everythin', boy."

With sudden thin anger, Woods said: "Why don't you get out?"

Corporal Pike was having to steady his own breathing now. He possessed no watch, and he couldn't see Woods's, and couldn't ask the kid to show him. It must be about a minute to go. He said confidentially, leaning forward with elbows on knees: It's too chancy outside, see? In 'ere, you've got somethin' over your 'ead." He leaned back again. "If you feel sick, though, you go an' nip out an' take cover. I'll look after this lot."

"No." Woods had flinched away, putting a hand up to the head-phones. As long as there were voices, it would be all right.

Pike shrugged. "You know what I done? I went an' left our drop o' navy rum in Top Dog. We could've 'ad a nice little flippin' party in 'ere. What a sufferin' clot, eh?"

The boy's breath was scraping in and out of a dry

throat, embarrassingly loud in the confines of the turret. He pressed the head-phones close against his ears, listening to the faint scratching of voices as signals passed among the Squadron. Pike could not hear them. He sat listening to the tick of metal as the big engine cooled, its components contracting slowly by fine degrees. The same tension was present in himself and in the boy; it was drawing their nerves out. It must be time now. Six minutes.

The metal of the engine ticked. Woods's breathing was harsh; the sound of it made things worse. Pike was trying to think of something else to say, to fill the waiting. He was angry with himself. He had come here to calm Woods and to help him, because he'd been in this position plenty of times and Woods hadn't, ever. But it didn't make any difference. A man could sit like this a dozen times a day and never learn to do it right, because the danger was as bad. You might have struck lucky a hundred times, but there was always a next time for death; and you knew it; and you sat there, and you couldn't do anything or say anything or think anything.

Through the open turret he could hear the distorted thud of the guns and the rattle of machine-shot, rippling sharply like a stick along railings; and there were mortars pounding. One of those heavier thuds would be the gun that would send the shell in. There was no way of telling which.

Woods moved the tuning-dial, centering the signal. He appeared to be listening; his eyes were blank. His face was wet now; he looked to Pike like a new-born drowned mouse. Pike fished out his dog-end, lighting it, hating it, tasting only rancid nicotine. He blew the smoke out and heard the shell coming. The rising rush of it was trapped in the mouth of the turret and the sound circled there so that they were certain it would come into the turret, right into the turret, here, and burst.

It hit the ground outside. The tank heaved on its springs in the blast of the explosion and then the splinters struck, driving through the blast-wave and hitting the plates with a rattle that rang through their heads so that their mouths fell open to let the sound come out before it split their skulls from the inside. Woods was coughing. Pike looked down and saw his dog-end smouldering where it had dropped. Carefully he put his boot on it and pressed it out. Fumes came in through the turret; the silence was strange.

The corporal stood up. He felt as if he had been sick, and was better for it. There was another six minutes now. That was a whole lifetime, after those last few seconds.

"I'll nip out an' see what's cookin', Woody."

"All right, Corp." As Pike reached the rim of the turret, Woods said: "That was close, wasn't it?" His voice was normal; he too felt the heady relief. Pike looked over the turret rim at the shell-hole outside. He said:

"Ay. We could've pee'd on it from 'ere, without strainin' ourselves."

He dropped to the ground. Sergeant Goodall broke his run.

"What the bloody hell are you doin' in my tank, Alf?"

"Just visitin', Sarge."

"Is Woods all right?"

" 'Course 'e is. Down there playin' with 'is crystal set."

The reek of cordite stung their throats. Pike asked: " 'Ow's the boys?"

Goodall stood with his hands in his pockets, watching Lieutenant Pope, who was down by his tank, bending over Dove. He said to Pike: "I think we've had Dove."

"Isn't 'e any better?"

"Would you be, with this lot on?"

"Is 'e 'urt?"

"He's shocked. You wouldn't get him back inside a tank unless you slugged him and threw him in."

"What's Mr. Pope goin' to do, then?"

"Leave him behind, I reckon. He's no more use."

Woods put his head over the turret rim of Moby Dick.

"Orders to get smoke out, Sarge."

"Smoke?" He shinned up to the turret while the cor-

poral turned and ran towards Top Dog. Munro was waiting for him. In the Troop-leader's tank Corporal Todd
was picking the bombs from the racks.

They were put due north, against the wind. The smoke
came drifting thickly, fanning out across the leaves of the
undergrowth and through the saplings until only their
frail tops were visible; then they were lost, and the sky
darkened, and the men were enveloped as they climbed
into their tanks. From the outside world signals were
coming through. Two Troop was to move off east, under
smoke cover, and harbour in the valley this side of Pont
Perigne.

Sergeant Goodall was on the B set, asking the Troop-
commander about Dove. Lieutenant Pope answered:
"We're dropping him off in the lane, outside the bocage.
There's a field post a mile up north. He can get transport
from there to H.Q."

"Can he look after himself, sir?"

"The point has occurred to me, Sergeant."

"Yes, sir."

Goodall cleared the air. The lieutenant had changed
for the worse, under the effects of action. On the sea-
crossing he had worried himself about the men; now he
was shedding responsibility with every mile. When a crisis
came to Two Troop, its commander would be as useless
as Dove. Thank God for Corporal Pike and the others
like him.

The tanks moved through the smoke, turning east and
pushing blindly through the leaves, breaking the saplings
down and lurching on, putting out more smoke as they
advanced. A shell landed, precisely at the next sixth
minute, falling wide and making no more than a dull
cough above the drum of the engines.

Goodall heard another sound, coming so faintly in the
drifting fog that he dismissed it as the after-effect of shell-
burst in the ears; but as Top Dog kept pace, moving
parallel to windward of Moby Dick, the sound was
carried, tantalising as a will-o'-the-wisp echo, across the
smoking air; and the sergeant recognised it at last. It was
a concertina.

SINGING DRUNK

I

AN HOUR AGO, before midnight, the last tank had come up into harbour. For a few minutes the engine had run on; voices had called across the hedgerows; sharp sounds had tapped at the silence, a hatch closing, a boot scraping, a tin-hat falling; then the noise of the engine had died away, and soon the voices grew quiet. The silence now was over all, as men slept exhausted, or lay spread-eagled under the night sky, eyes open, thinking, or trying not to think, trying to sleep or just forget.

Flares were dropping, five or six miles away, as enemy bombers searched out targets across the forward line; the tremble of anti-aircraft guns was in the ground, here in the quiet harbour; and the glow of the flares touched upon leaves and faces and equipment, brightening the track of a tank, picking out its silhouette in the shape of a shaggy elephant as it stood entangled in its camouflage.

Of those men who were awake, some had slept last night, dropping exhausted after the day's grinding work; others were kept from sleep by their nerves or the tumult of their minds; they leaned with their backs to a tank or a tree bole, with a cigarette, silent or murmuring together. In the new dug-out two men were brewing up, and their friends came and went, fetching more tea and sitting with the mugs cupped in their hands, leaving it to grow cold, comforted merely by its presence.

The echelon lorries had not yet come; in most of the tanks the fuel was low, and some of the Besas were without ammunition. Food was short, but no one was hungry, and there was tea. An army could sleep on that, or march on it, or fight on it; it was the prime munition.

One man, propped against a rolled-up bivouac, was

writing a letter. He could not post it yet, but would tuck it away with the others he had written, each numbered so that she could read them in the right order. This was number six, on the seventh day; for there had been a day when there had been no time to write, nor even to remember home.

Someone was cleaning his equipment, too worn out to sleep and too afraid to think; his hands worked at this habitual discipline, so that slowly he became refreshed in his half-stunned mind and, with the clean blancoed webbing in his hands, dared again to think about tomorrow.

A man snored. Another murmured in his sleep, turning and moving his fingers, fighting his day again alone. In the earth shivered the far shock of the guns; on the leaves fell the light of the flares. Trooper Cox said quietly:

"What day is it?"

His voice was intimate in the close air.

"The Thirteenth." Watkins-Price lay with his legs crossed, shoulders propped against a track of Moby Dick, his respirator for a cushion.

"We've been a week, then, over here."

"Yes."

There were gaps in their low talk; between comment and answer passed a minute's thought, circling and returning.

"Seems like a year."

Bombs went down under the bright flares.

"Like ten."

And England a million miles. If there were bombs going down over there, too, she would be at the window watching. God, make her come away from the window. He had thought of it so often, imagining her calm face cut by the flying glass, that it was as if it had really happened; often, when he saw her face over here, it was like that, scarred and bleeding.

"Did you hear what Goodall said?"

Sam Cox moved his head, easing the angle of his neck.

"What about?"

"That we're half a mile from Jerry, here."

"Oh, that. You think it's true?"

"He wouldn't've said it."

"Then they're pretty quiet, Watty."

"So are we."

"The stuff won't be brought up if we're as close as that."

"It'll have to be, or we're sitters."

Then they stopped talking about it, switching it off, each suddenly aware that it was someone else's job to get the echelons up here, and worry about Jerry being so close. They were here to orders; when they moved, it would be to orders, backwards or forwards, towards the fighting or away from it. There were a million thoughts a day, in action, that ran through the mind empty-handed, giving nothing, taking nothing, changing nothing. Orders would over-ride them. The enemy is here, is there; you will move, you will stay; the Squadron is attacking, is withdrawing. This was the way the war went, in accordance with the orders of the day.

"How's your mug, Sam?"

"M'm? Empty."

"You want some more?"

"I'm not bothered. You going for some?"

"It's not worth it."

They sat again in silence, watching the night, secure in the company of each other and of the men about them. Across the valley where the Orne ran, the bombers had gone, leaving a quick leap of flame, an orange flutter in the distant dark. The drone diminished, deepening the silence here.

Watty was thinking of Dove, and the way he had sobbed, sitting on the ground with the helplessness of paralysis, his eyes wide open, dropping their tears, understanding nothing that they saw as his head moved, lolling from side to side while the sobbing went on as without words he tried to tell them that he was still alive and could not stand it. He had come to pieces: the limbs moved of their own accord, shook and lay still and jerked to movement again; the head turned from side to side, a waxen sailor's head in a side-show, worked by strings and understanding nothing; the eyes, the tears, the hurrying panicked breath—they were symptoms quite apart; they were pieces of what he had been a few minutes before: a man.

Sam said quietly: "Poor bastard."

"Who?"

"Jim Dove."

Perhaps it was telepathy or perhaps there was a common source of their thought-streams somewhere near: the sight or the sound of something that had reminded them of Dove—a white face in the gloom, or a man's breathing.

"He's for Blighty," said Sam. "That's certain."

"We all are, one day, dead or alive."

"Well, that's a cheerful thought, that is."

Their talking fell away as they listened to aircraft flying in from the north. It was an Allied bomber group, its sound and number too heavy to be German. The slow crescendo built against the ear remorselessly, until it became malevolent. A sound like this, bloated with so much potential destruction, loses its nationality, and every man hates it in his heart.

When the bombs fell, the earth shook to them and the sky glared; the night gaped; the dark receded, shot with crimson and slashed with light-blades that seared through the hills' curves until the whole world was awake, watching and listening, waiting for the nightmare to leave it alone and let it sleep again.

Half an hour had passed before the silence came back, here among the herd of tanks; but the leaves were still red with the hue of the far light, where fire burned below bright cloud, east towards Caen.

"Proper pasting," Sam said, glad that it was over.

"Less work for us tomorrow."

Minutes passed, with no word between them. They watched the flicker of light across the hills; it reached their own faces, glinting in their eyes. The wind, what little there was, blew from the west, carrying the sound of

the conflagration the other way, leaving it silent here until
Sam roused himself.

"Listen."

Watty moved his head to look at him.

"Listen to what?"

Sam waited. "There," he said.

In another minute: "Someone shouting."

Sam said: "Singing."

"Singing, then."

They listened. The wind moved, taking away the man's
voice, bringing it back. Sam said: "Christ, listen!"

"He's drunk."

Near them Corporal Todd awoke. "What bloody clot is
that?"

Watty said: "There's a drunk, Corp. Wandering
about."

Todd's voice was still thick with sleep. "He'll get shot,
the stupid bastard."

The song softened, loudened as the wind moved. It had
no clear words; it was a maudlin, reeling song, burdened
with sentiment.

"Who's that stu-pid ba-stard?" asked Corporal
Todd.

"I dunno, Corp."

The wind moved; or it was the man moving; the song
grew louder, softer as he turned in this direction or
away.

Watty said: "He's up there, forward."

"He'll walk into Jerry."

The corporal said: "Let 'im bloody well walk, then."
He lay down again.

Watkins-Price stood up, stretching his arms.

"What are you on, then?"

He looked down at Sam. "I'm going to find out where
he is."

Sam eased himself upright. "He's up near Jerry, you
fool. Leave him alone. He's drunk."

Watty stood listening. Quite a few of the boys had got
drunk yesterday, when there was an hour's rest. They'd
been given wine, bottles of it, by French people as they

passed through the villages. Corporal Todd had had to throw water over two of them before they could move off. He was fed up with drunks by now.

Sam Cox said: "Let him rip, Watty."

"It might be one of our lot." He stood facing the direction of the song. It broke, then burst forth anew, its tune sagging and rallying on the low wind.

"For God's sake, leave him alone," Cox said. "If Jerry don't shoot him, one of our chaps will before he lets the whole Wehrmacht know we're here."

"Exactly." Watkins-Price fished out a Bren from the turret.

"Watty, don't be a prize bloody dope."

Watkins-Price went round the back of the tank and along the hedgerow, making his way quietly, hearing a question here and there from men half sleeping; he did not answer. Beyond the hedge was pasture-land, a great open space under the sky. Starting across it, he heard Sam behind him and turned.

"Sam, it doesn't need two of us."

Cox said: "If you're goin' out there, someone'll have to bring back the body."

"Look, I'd be much happier if you'd quietly bugger off and leave this to me."

The song lifted, cracked, and began again. The man was somewhere in the middle of the open meadow, between here and the enemy dug-outs. Neither Cox nor Watkins-Price said anything more. They went forward slowly, resenting each other's presence. Watty shouldn't be sticking his stupid neck out like this for a drunk. Sam shouldn't have come; it didn't need two of them.

They went towards the song that was reeling its way through the dark, blowing in the wind, flying up and falling and lurching on.

Sam said, his hand on Watty's arm: "Someone said this stretch was mined. I've just remembered."

Watty stood with his feet together. "Then you'd better go back, Sam. We don't want two of us traipsing through a minefield."

Patiently Sam said: "Listen. If this stretch is mined,

that drunk's going to find one, any minute. Even if we get
to him before he's blown apart, we shan't get him back
without someone being killed. Now why don't you see
sense?"

Matching Sam's patience, Watty's tone was reasonable.
"If someone doesn't fetch him in, he'll blow himself up,
or get shot by Jerry or one of our own mob. All I want to
do is have a crack at saving him. Whether I do it or not
isn't so important; I just don't feel like sitting on my arse
while that poor bastard dies. He's one of us and he's had
a skinful. Now for God's sake shove off and leave me in
peace."

He went forward slowly, crouching over to study the
grass in front of him at every step. The ruddled light of
the fires lay across it; there were small hummocks, mole-
hills with their shadows making a darker blob. He must
avoid every visible irregularity in the ground, and his
sixth sense would have to save him from any charge that
was buried beneath the turf in perfect concealment. He
didn't think about the big mines, the anti-tanks; when he
stepped on one of those he wouldn't know anything about
it: perhaps just a half-second in which to regret coming
out here, to see the image of his mother's face, quick as a
flashlight, then nothing. He was more worried about the
small stuff, the miniature charges that had no more than a
few ounces of explosive in them, just enough to blow a
man's foot off. He must not think about those things at
all.

"Watty."

He said: "Oh, my God, are you still here?"

Sam was up abreast of him, ten paces on his right.
"There's another bloke looking for the drunk."

"That's fine. Let's have the whole Squadron out here in
the middle of a minefield." He took another step, watching the ground. His mouth had begun drying. It was a
mounting strain to watch the ground, to study the lie of
the grass so meticulously that every tuft became suspect
to him, every shadow the sign of a small buried murderer.
He would have preferred walking through a snake-
infested swamp.

"There's two others," Sam said. His voice was fainter:
he was still abreast of Watty, but farther still to the right.
Ahead of them they could see a figure, a slowly-shifting
scarecrow. It had stopped singing. Others spoke. There
were five or six of them out here. The drunk was one of
them, and he'd had a skinful. The whole thing was very
logical. Watty called softly to Sam.

"Pass it along: this stretch is mined."

He moved round a light patch of grass, as small and
flat as an upturned saucer. The nerves in his feet were
tingling; they crept across the thin ice of his imaginings;
he walked with his boots full of pins and needles. At
intervals he looked up at the shadow that swayed ahead
of him, perhaps a dozen yards ahead now, silhouetted
against the skyline where the smudged red clouds touched
the earth.

The wind came across the field in soft warm waves,
dying and rising, bringing the faintest hint of smoke from
the last village behind the lines, where buildings smouldered. Except for the wind's soft rush against the ears,
there was a local peace, isolated from the far thud of the
guns. It was an unnerving peace, allowing you to hear the
brush of your boot over the grass and your unsteady
breathing. In this much silence, the mine would shatter
the whole world and the whole sky when its noise
came.

Watkins-Price moved again; a faint voice called, from
the far edge of the meadow; then the drunk began singing
again, lifting his voice and pitching it across the wind; the
raw sound echoed against the nerves, startling the men
who crept towards it, making them call out to him:

"Turn it up, you bloody clot."

"This way, chum, over 'ere, come on, then."

"Shut your gob, for Chris' sake."

"Come on, mate, let's 'ave you."

Their voices, calling from many quarters of the field,
cursed him, coaxed him as he swayed, legs apart and
head back, singing.

A bullet came.

"Watty?"

"Yes?"

"That's Jerry." Sam moved nearer him.

Watty stood still, getting his breath. He had been moving at a yard a minute, but he was panting. Across to his right someone had begun hurrying, his dim figure bent forward over the grass. He said to Sam:

"This is going to be bloody murder."

"I told you."

"I didn't expect half the Squadron to turn out." He felt very angry with the drunk. 'C' Squadron, after seven days' hard fighting through the German defences, looked like being wiped out at one blow, searching for a drunk in a minefield. The Colonel would be charmed.

The drunk sang with abandon. Watty brought up his Bren and loosed a burst high, to the left of the man and above his head.

"Christ!" said Sam Cox, his nerves riven by the gun's sound. But the drunk had stopped singing. Watty moved forward, trying to keep his anger down. If that bastard sang again, he'd fire at the feet, to hit.

"You men are to get back!"

They recognised Pope's voice, behind them.

"That's it, then," Sam said.

The others had stopped moving. Watty was a few yards forward of Sam, and could see the man. He was a dark hump, sitting down.

Sam called: "Watty, don't be a——"

"*You men are to get back!*" The lieutenant was furious. His young voice cracked with rage.

Watkins-Price reached the drunk and had to duck as a fusillade came over from the German lines. Voices rose, piping thinly in the wind. He waited, then took the last pace forward. The dark hump had a bright red face; the distant glow of the fires was shining on the sweat.

"Get up," said Watty.

The hump rocked, looking up at him. It said: *"Sie sind mein Freund. Wir sind alle Freunde."*

Watkins-Price moved his trigger finger on to the Bren. He was trying not to laugh. Half the Squadron in a minefield, and the drunk was a Boche. He said:

"*Kaputt*. Get up. Come with me." He poked the man's elbow with the gun, and he got to his feet. He was big, standing higher than Watkins-Price even with his frame slack with drink. "Now walk that way." He swung him round with the Bren. "March!"

The man lumbered off towards the British lines. Walking behind him, Watkins-Price asked: "Are there mines in this field? *Minen* here?"

"*Minen*?" He turned his head, half-falling as he tried to look round at Watty, who jabbed him with the muzzle and said very slowly and clearly:

"Are there mines laid here?"

The Boche shook his head. "*Hier sind keine Minen.*" Then he stopped, and swung round so heavily that Watty had to stand off with the Bren aimed at the stomach and ready to fire. "English," said the Boche, as if suddenly remembering. He stood uncertainly, worried by the gun. "I haf frients in Englant."

"Turn round and march."

"This war—" his big hands fell about, searching for the words—"finish now."

The gun jerked. "Turn round and march."

The man swung forward obediently, floundering across the grass so quickly that Watty had to break into a trot to keep up. Sam Cox joined them suddenly.

"A bloody Boche!"

"Yes." Their boots thudded over the turf. "We were wrong about the mines. He says there aren't any."

"*Ihr seid meine Freunde!*" shouted the man cheerfully. "*Wir sind alle Freunde!*" He ran with his legs threatening to pitch him headlong. Someone in front of them heard the German words and called:

"Halt!"

The man ran on. Watkins-Price shouted: "It's all right, he's covered!"

"*Halt!*"

"I am frient!" shouted the Boche in greeting. His arms were stretched out towards Lieutenant Pope. *Kamerad!* I wish to be prisoner!" He ran for another two paces and then stood still, the bullet-stream from Pope's Bren halting his body and tilting it upright. It swayed for seconds, already dead. Then the arms fell, and it crumpled like a sack.

"Who are you two men?"

The smell of cordite came, fouling the wind.

"Speak up!"

"Trooper Cox, sir."

"Watkins-Price."

"Follow me."

Cox moved. Watkins-Price stood for a moment looking down at the dark hump. One arm was thrown out; the head lay against the grass, on its side, as if he were pressing his ear to the earth, listening.

Watty left him, following the other two. Pope took them to the shallow dug-out behind his tank. A bivouac was rigged above one end of it. A hurricane lamp threw a pale light from beneath its hood. Lieutenant Pope was white-faced and his eyes were bright.

"You heard my order?"

They said nothing.

"Yes, sir," said Cox. Pope jerked his head to Watkins-Price.

"And you?"

"I heard it, sir."

"And flagrantly disobeyed it."

"No. We'd reached the prisoner by then."

"What prisoner?"

"The German you shot."

Pope leaned his shoulders against the earth-wall and folded his arms, taking his time before he spoke. "Do you happen to remember the correct way to address an officer?"

"Yes, sir."

"I'm glad. You say you had reached the German by the time I ordered you to come back." He moved his head. "Is that true, Cox?"

"Oh yes, sir." It was the 'Oh' that made it sound like a lie; it was over-quick.

"Of course you realise I can't actually disprove what you say."

They did not answer.

"You decided that since you had reached the German, you should bring him back with you as a prisoner?"

Watkins-Price said: "Yes, sir."

"At what point did he run amok?"

Carefully: "At no point, sir."

Pope allowed as careful a pause. "Oh? But he was running away from you, isn't that so? And when I ordered him to halt—twice ordered him, remember—he ran on, straight at me. I take it you don't deny that?"

Cox shifted one foot. Watkins-Price said:

"He wasn't running away from us, sir. He was hurrying towards our lines, under my orders, with my Bren at his back. We were keeping pace together." He allowed two seconds to pass. "There was no cause for panic."

The silence became hair-spring in the warm confines of the dug-out.

"Trooper Cox, dismiss."

"Sir."

He lost his footing, going over the edge of earth, and sent some of it crumbling down.

"Now look here, Price." And Watkins-Price knew that Pope was his. It didn't give him any feeling of triumph, his anger took on contempt. "We've been fighting pretty hard for a solid week, and we're due for a rest. Until we get it, we shall have to keep a watch on ourselves. When the nerves are put under constant strain, we're liable to make a lot of fuss about nothing. This is just a typical instance." He took a packet of cigarettes out of his tin hat, which was hanging by its strap from the wall. "You can stand easy." Watkins-Price kept his feet together. Pope offered him a cigarette.

"No, thank you, sir."

The lieutenant shrugged slightly, lighting one for himself, blowing out the smoke with elaborate care. "I'm going to accept it as a fact that when you heard my order to return, you were already with the German soldier, and that you felt that you wouldn't be flouting that order by bringing him back with you." His hand made a slow gesture, dismissing the point with modest generosity.

"Unhappily, your prisoner then ignored my two clear warnings to halt, and I was obliged to shoot. I've no doubt that if he'd been sober he would have halted, and so continued to live." His hand moved again, rounding off the unimportant post-mortem. "And there it all is. Since we're both in need of sleep, you can go now."

There was no question of a salute, as Watkins-Price was bareheaded. He half-turned to the wooden crate that served as a step, and climbed from the dug-out.

Sam Cox was standing by the tank when he got back. Sergeant Goodall was with him, and said:

"Are you in trouble?"

"No, Sergeant."

"Sure?"

"Yes."

"That's all I wanted to know. Try an' get some kip, before we have to move on."

He left them, vanishing into the gloom. Watkins-Price sat down.

"Did he tear you off a strip, Watty?"

"No."

"What happened, then?"

"Nothing." He leaned his head against the equipment stacked by the tank-track. "Have you got a fag, Sam?"

When they had lit up, Sam said: "You know, that bloke seems different, over here."

"What bloke?"

"Pope. Have you noticed?"

Fresh gunfire went poppling across the valley; its hard flash dappled the clouds.

"Yes."

"Back at Orford, he seemed the right sort."

Watkins-Price drew on his cigarette, listening to the guns.

"Well, he isn't," he said.

THE START-LINE

I

Two hurricane lamps hung from the rafter that ran down the middle of the cowshed. They sent a trellis-work of shadows against the high roof, and cast their light down wanly over the faces of the men. There were more than twenty of them, standing along the conference table, which was a plank on two ammunition boxes.

"This is a Corps attack."

The meagre light shone down on maps and aerial photographs that were spread along the plank. Major Knowles had a stick in his hand; he pointed at the maps, talking to his tank-commanders while the light burned steadily in the quietness. It showed weariness on these faces, and dirt, and stubble, and fortitude. The red rims of their eyes and the white of their skin gave them the masked look of made-up clowns.

The two shadows of the stick moved with it.

"This flank is still very much in the air. That doesn't affect us directly, but we'll have to remember that in the event of any big-scale repulse we can't expect support from that quarter."

A few of them had shaved, with dirty water and a blunt blade. Some had managed as much as an hour's sleep since the echelon trucks had been up to load the tanks; the others stood with their muscles locked, lest they should fall. The white of their faces made blobs against the background of timber and dark earth; they stood at angles, an elbow out with its hand on hip, a shoulder lifted as one peered over the shoulder of another to see the maps, a big back straight as a board with the legs apart and the head steady, and over there at the end of the table, a head nodding by tortuous degrees and then up with a jerk and a red-eyed blink in the light's glare.

"Our ultimate objective is the establishment of a bridgehead across the Odon, here. Once that objective is secured, we shall withdraw into Corps reserve. I take it nobody here has any objection to taking a rest."

Here and there a face stiffened into a smile; it hung there wearily, forgetting to go. Lieutenant Pope was not smiling; he was intent, impatient, his nerves poised on the edge of the crisis that was coming.

"In a few minutes, bombers will be going over." Major Knowles checked his watch. "The air programme is arranged for oh-three-thirty hours. That's roughly now."

Sergeant Goodall wore the stiff smile, because he liked Knowles, and trusted him as a man and a commander, and was ready to acknowledge any slight attempt to bring humour to this scene. But he was worried about Mr. Pope. There was no steadiness in him, and no reserve of any quality that a man must have, if he is to get through a war. He was draining his own courage, saving none of it for tomorrow, unaware that each man has so much, and when he has used that much he is finished, unless there is time to replenish it in sleep and peace of mind. When Pope reached a new day he let yesterday fall behind him, taking nothing from it, learning nothing. The fight was today, always today. He must push on, and push his men on, borne forward on the false premise that it is only the victor who can attack, and only the attacker who can be victorious. He must run towards the enemy; he must never stand and wait, or his nerve would go, even if the enemy were but one man, unarmed and crying *Kamerad! I wish to be prisoner!* When the nerve went, panic was in with a rush, bringing a consequence to fit the moment: the death of a single prisoner or the fate of a tank-troop of fifteen men. One day, Mr. Pope would not be in a position to run forward, dribbling his courage like a football at his feet; he would have to make a stand, and let the enemy come to him. Then he was going to break.

May God see to it that he broke alone, without imperilling his men. Sergeant Goodall looked away from the young feverish face and sought comfort in the Major's.

Knowles disliked panic. He also disliked men who panicked. He thought slowly, spoke slowly, quietly stripping a situation of its non-essentials and arriving ahead of the man who had worn himself out with the business of useless organisation. Goodall had been in the desert with Knowles, and in and out of hell on earth with him, and was ready to go again.

"The artillery will then take over, giving us a barrage on the start-line. Gapping-teams of assault engineers and flails will open up the ground, and we shall follow them through the first village, L'Haubeise, as soon as the mines are gapped this side of the hill. Our left flank is well protected along here. From the village we shall take this Class 40 route. If it's badly cratered, the ground on each side is firm."

The stick and its shadows moved. The ring on his finger caught the light, glinting. He waited, looking along the lines of faces: Williams, Bradlock, Goodall, Stevenson, their mouths set, Pike, Stacey, MacPherson, Marsh, their eyes driven into shadow by fatigue, Foster, Smith, Pope, Boxall, their heads at angles to watch the stick as it traced the maps, designing their day for them.

"Four and Five Troops will cross the stream here, over wooden bridges. Three Troop will cover them from this knoll of trees." The stick stopped. He looked up and said: "There go the bombers."

The drone was in the sky. They all raised their heads but could see only the dark cathedral timbers of the roof. They looked down, at one another, listening. With that high loudening drone their day had begun; it was part of them, they were part of it. Sergeant Verity looked at his watch. The air programme had been arranged for oh-three-thirty hours. It was now that time, precisely. He was aware of the size of this machine that was running, and was humbled by the thought of his own microcosmic part in it.

"We shall be up against very tough opposition."

Their heads turned back to watch him again while the drone went on above.

"The Panzer Lehr and the Seventeenth S.S. Grenadiers are veterans, courageous to the point of suicidal fanaticism: we have already seen that. There are two strong forces, here and here, of Mark Fours and Fives, and a loosely-deployed support force of fast S.P. guns with armour-piercing shell. Beyond the Class 40 route the terrain is difficult, and will be heavily mined. We have been in hard action now for more than a month, with no rest to speak of. The last week has been especially trying, although we've suffered very few casualties. This is going to be a tough grind, and it's better to realise it now than to discover it half-way to the goal."

He let the stick fall across the maps and put his hands in his pockets. "Personally I prefer a job like this to the type of campaign that goes off at half-cock with everyone darting about like blue-arsed flies and beating the air for inspiration. I think most of you feel the same; and that's what gives me so much confidence in you and in our ability to crack this nut wide open. Who's got a cigarette?"

Someone gave him one. Most of them lit up, and put their questions to him, tapping a finger on the maps, tracing the query, getting his answer. Most of them were satisfied; those who were not would never be, with any plan or commander or campaign. They were the doubters, hesitaters, men without faith in themselves or anyone else. But they could command a tank, and fight with it; they were strong enough to form the weakest link in the unending chain, or they would not be here.

The drone had faded. Before long, the earth began to shake, and the slap of the big sound-wind hit the shed. The lamps were set swinging gently, and the shadows of the men moved against the walls, back and forth, distorted and shuffling, each man's ghost standing behind him, waiting to follow him out there under the dawn sky and go with him as far as the pin-point on these paper maps where the bullet would come to meet them.

"We'll be on our way, then."

He dropped his cigarette. Their boots passed over it as they followed him outside. It was not yet dawn, but in the east, where the bombers were, the sky was red.

II

THE SQUADRON was on the start-line thirty minutes before zero with their engines warm and the wireless on net with Battalion. The bombers had gone back, and this time the commanders could see them, high up, a slow grey swarm moving among the cloud-weed. The day's first light was touching them; down here it was still dark. They waited for the guns.

The guns opened up before the bombers had returned to base. Again the earth shivered. Overhead the shells flew low, their flight crackling whip-sharp through the air. They landed east, between the start-line and the distant fires. After ten minutes there was a brief lull; then another battery joined the rest, and the barrage was re-mounted.

Six rounds of air-burst exploded within a hundred yards of the start-line and Major Knowles got the signal out to take cover. Another six rounds fell short, filling the dark with a blinding light, before he got through to the artillery commander via his O. P. tank: *Air-burst falling short. We are in shrapnel zone. Have we in some way offended you?*

Fragments clattered among the tanks; a piece took away Moby Dick's aerial and young Woods fished out the spare and mounted it while Corporal Pike in Top Dog crouched under his tin-hat and swore at the gunners, going from A to Z and back again, telling those festerin' sufferin' whoresons of 'am-fisted soft-'eaded barstids to stuffin'-well turn it up.

A signal came through to the Squadron commander: *Error corrected. In no way offended. Sincere apologies.*

The air-burst had lifted; they could see it flashing below the hill. Pike came out of his turret and looked across at Mr. Pope, alongside.

"If they do that again, sir, can we 'ave orders to fire back?"

Mr. Pope did not answer. He was watching the east through his field-glasses, impatient for zero.

"You gettin' windy, then, Corporal Pike?"

"Windy, Sergeant Goodall, me? 'Ere now, lissern!"

"I bet when they got you to the font for your christenin' you hollered out for a lifebelt!"

"Well, stuff me sideways, Sergeant——"

"I haven't got time——"

"You wouldn't know 'ow——"

"An' it's lucky for you——"

"Stop that talking!" The field-glasses were down. The thin voice cracked, unable to support its temper.

Corporal Pike deliberately turned his back, and Goodall saw it, and was sorry. With some of the men, Lieutenant Pope had lost his authority; with others, his claim to their loyalty. Among the N.C.O.s he had lost respect. It had come about in small ways, with a word or an action, most of them forgotten until another came, reminding them. No one disliked him; to be disliked, a man must have a character of a kind; in Pope, even that was lacking.

He raised his field-glasses again, to watch the crack of light that was breaking the earth from the sky. It was nearly dawn. The barrage ran on. He was feverish to go, get moving. It was galling to wait here, listening to the clap of shells and to the stupid badinage between his tank-commanders. There was a Corps attack going forward against a strong fanatical enemy, yet all his N.C.O.s could do was lark about. Didn't they realise? After their long battle experience, didn't they know what this meant? Or didn't they care? Dear God, to have their blessed ignorance!

He watched the crack of the dawn spread gold above the red of the fires where the bombs had gone down. The colours were of autumn sunshine on dying leaves, a subject for Turner; yet it was summer and the leaves were young still, and the sun had yet to rise. This was just a warscape, red and gold, the colours of bygone uniforms.

The beauty of it ached against his eyes. The raiment of war was exquisite, right until its end, even to the stark black and white of the beetle and the bone.

The shells fluttered along their airy streets, to plummet down against the hill and the village. There was no answering fire. The Wehrmacht was short of fuel and ammunition; its dumps and factories had been laid waste by Allied bombers; their shells were precious, and their gunners' efficiency keyed to this condition. The blessing was subtly mixed.

Cloud was forming, low in the west; the air had rain in it. To the east, the gold was curdling already as the cloud-fringe sagged along the horizon. A dark haze drifted beyond the hill, where the smoke of the fires hung in the moist atmosphere. Nearer, the trees were touched with light at their tips, poplars standing as still as dark candles waiting to be lit.

The barrage died. Lesser sounds became audible: the far crackle of small-arms fire, northwards; the voices of a crew manhandling a gun, a hundred yards behind the start-line; a cuckoo calling in the wood by the hill. Over the wirelesses:

Start up.

The morning light grew slowly to a flood; waves of it drew across the hill and the trees and reached the group of tanks, lighting their turrets and the long slender guns, defining their shapes. Their engines ran steadily. The crews were aboard and their commanders mounted.

In Moby Dick, Goodall stood with his legs trembling. There was nothing he could do about it. It had always happened, on a big start-line. He was long past trying to stop it, or reason it out. He felt afraid, because he was going into action and might die today; but not so afraid that he should shiver. It must be that his body was aware, with a primitive animal sense of its own, that there was a risk of appalling pain, and mutilation, and death at the end of it; and so it trembled. There was nothing he could do, except make sure that others didn't see.

He glanced down at Woods. He sat crouched in his head-phones, listening. His thin hands touched the set, caressing it; they were perfectly steady. The voices crowded against his ears; he was not alone. In this much comfort there was no place for fear; he drew his courage from the air.

Advance.

The air crackled, filling the head-phones as the engines throttled-up, their suppressors absorbing nine-tenths of the ignition interference as the sixteen tanks moved forward from the start-line towards the hill. Ahead of them were mines going up, bursting with dull red flashes, flailed alive by the great Crabs as they started forward to clear their lanes.

The pennants shivered on the thin antennæ; the long guns craned forward, thin-necked and alert; the bright tracks rolled, cleaving the grass, furrowing through soft earth, tearing at surface roots and leaving their peeled white bones behind; and then the first rain came, gently from the grey sky, mottling the camouflage paint of the tanks and darkening the earth, shining among the grass and sweetening the air. The pennants grew limp; the gun-barrels shone; the tracks lost their brightness, stained brown as they churned through the mud film and left dark ruts in their wake.

In the driving compartments and the turrets the eighty men settled to their work. The Squadron was two tanks short of full complement; among them were seven new tanks and fresh crews from the Delivery Unit. Only two original Troops were here, intact, Four Troop with Dumbo, The Rocket and Daisy; Two Troop with Bloody Mary, Moby Dick and Top Dog. The men were crouched in their familiar homes at the clutches, the guns, the wireless sets, hemmed in by the thick steel walls and the stacked lumber of their equipment, cramped among their motley furniture of live shells and Besa belts, smoke-bombs, hand-grenades, Verey lights and the work gear of a soldier at his war: the tin-hat, billy-can, gas-cape and respirator, the packet of fags, tea-mug, irons and shining kit, each tank independent and each crew with a home of its own, with things of its own: in Top Dog, a stuffed toy pup that was its mascot, a portable chess set and a box of pin-up photographs, and the corporal's concertina; in Moby Dick, a pair of plaid slippers belonging to Watkins-Price, a box of Camembert and an ash-plant walking-stick, and Sam Cox's diary with its elaborate lock; in Bloody Mary a gramophone, a cricket-ball, a bookshelf of Raymond Chandler paper-backs crammed between the 19 set and the ammo-racks, and the framed photograph of Dove's smiling wife. It had not been moved; he had gone back to her now, and wouldn't want it any more.

Taffy Adams sat with his tiller-bar, watching the tank ahead. His red eyes were narrowed and he blinked them often, fighting off sleep. He had refused to swallow fatigue tablets, for if the Lord couldn't keep him awake, then nothing could. When the big gun started to shout, he'd come alert again, for there'd be work to do and a man would need his wits sharp. The Lord would say to him, calling through the unholy din of the battle: "Taffy, there's work for you, man, so you'd better look quick about you." There was plenty of them who could do with a bit of God in their minds, only they didn't know how to ask, or didn't want to, like the sergeant with his legs all jelly just because there was a fight on, and Sam with his sad look and his heart in his silly mouth, thinking all the time about his silly wife, and little Bobbie Woods with no more blood in his body than would fill a thimble, and no more thought in his head but that he must listen all the time to his wireless set, never mind what else was going on, and Pike the corporal with his mind so full of blasphemy that there was not an inch of room for the Lord nor even for the toe of an angel, so heathen was he and not knowing that one fine day the Lord would send a thunderbolt right in his foul mouth and make him swallow it still hot.

Moby Dick rocked on the big springs, nosing through the rain, and Watkins-Price looked up as Goodall reached for his gas-cape and put it on, standing against the sky, giving a grin to Watty and mouthing an oath for the rain while he flapped about with the cape, catching it as the wind-stream played with it until it wanted another oath to set it right. The rain spat steadily on the armour-plating, its drops bouncing and merging, trickling away in rivulets; it was summer rain, warm and slow and bountiful, the kind of rain that used to go on till the end of the holidays and would now go on till the end of the war, so unhurried was it.

Two Troop crossed a waste of shrub in arrow-head formation, passing a Churchill Crab with a wrecked flail; its crew were out of it, grouped round the jib; they turned to give a shout to the fighting tanks, signalling the soldier's farewell with two fingers and a grin. One man was lying on the ground, half buried in the wet shrub, but Goodall could not see whether he was wounded or resting. An ambulance truck came past, swerving over the bumps and finding a thin clear line where the rain had begun puddling; water went up from the wheels as it sped along, vanishing. The Troop halted by a farm, waited five minutes and were sent forward again behind One Troop, which had skirted trees to avoid a crater. Above the drum of the engines came the pop of mines, and sometimes the pulse of a gun as the forward engineers forced the route open for the tanks behind.

Corporal Pike saw the first shell come down; it burst clear of the cross-roads where the Class 40 route began. Another followed within seconds, more accurate, hitting the barn by the cross-roads and flinging timber up; a third came, and a fourth, and a big group of half a dozen or more as the battery was joined by flank artillery. Half the barn was down; the other half was burning, as hay caught; then it exploded and sent its remaining timbers across the road, while animals ran to the open field, away from the other buildings as the bombardment set in and the shells came in groups, straddling the cross-roads and hitting an assault-tank, setting it on fire.

Signals were coming in, diverting the forward tanks and breaking up the Squadron into their pre-arranged groups, leaving them to choose their own immediate courses through the barrage. Two men had come out of the burning tank, one of them staggering blindly towards a crater, the other standing with his hands to his head, making no movement as the second chevron of 'C'

Squadron's tanks went past, swinging wide to clear the crater and reforming in line ahead down the wider road. Bloody Mary caught one track along the crumbled remnant of a wall and slewed, flinging out débris and straightening. Taffy Adams, following, worked on his tiller-bar and brought Moby to the other side of the road, keeping a good course and losing speed to keep his station.

Top Dog hit the débris of the wall and scattered it, bucking on the springs, shuddering as a shell ploughed up earth and plastered the turret, sending Pike below for his tin-hat. The rain had grown heavier, cutting visibility down to a few hundred yards along the route. Three craters, equally spaced, had broken the road for a quarter-mile, and One Troop was swinging off the route and plunging through a spindly nest of trees, regaining the route where a truck lay overturned, its crew gone, its petrol still flooding over the ground. Buildings were coming into view through the rain haze, a farm, a garage, a line of cottages where flame rushed flickering as the roofs were taken hold.

The village had not been badly hit; most of its buildings were untouched, but the steeple of the church was down, shot to a ragged stump by the guns of the forward tanks, a suspect observation-post. On the far side of the village people stood, French civilians in a bewildered group; they watched the tanks go through, oblivious of the rain and the shell-fire; they did not wave; they did not move; they stood silently, part of the history of their small village. Long ago tanks had come this way from Germany, and they had stood to watch them; now there were these from England, and they stood to watch them. This was history, not of the world or of France, but of their village, L'Haubeise, and they must witness it, and later tell of it.

As the Squadron swept onwards through the driving rain, its crew passed the crews of forward tanks which had been knocked out. Some of these men, driven as if from their homes, were walking along the roadside, back to L'Haubeise, carrying their kit or part of their kit, or carrying nothing but their uniform and their wounds, walking alone in single file or in groups that staggered along together, one man helping another. A stretcher came by, two rifles slung beneath a plank; a white face, a cigarette, a chevroned sleeve and the drip, drip, drip of crimson on the mud below. A man walked slowly, plucking a dead chicken; the feathers dropped through the rain, leaving his trail; there'd be a good scoff for him and his mates as soon as they could light some sort of fire; they'd gone in with a thirty-ton tank and come out with a chicken. The white feathers came fluttering away, to lie like petals on the mud.

NOT FAR TO WHERE?

I

THE SQUADRON had left the road. To have kept to the road would have been to offer itself blindly to obliteration. Four and Five Troops were heading towards the stream that was one of the river's sources. Two of the wooden bridges were still intact. If they were blown up before the tanks arrived, the stream could be bridged anew by the two A.V.R.E.s that were standing by near the knoll of trees, with their bridges ready for laying if the need should come. Three Troop followed the other two, veering for the trees according to plan. On the higher ground a German eighty-eight was being brought to bear on this area and was soon putting down a feeler shot at minute intervals on both banks of the stream.

The signal came for smoke, and it spread sluggishly on the damp air as Three Troop reached the trees and halted, starting a blind routine return of the enemy's fire. Of the six tanks put at the crossing, four reached the other side, leaving one with a shattered track, its forward horns buried among reeds. The other was on fire midway across the bridge, and the crew dropped from it blindly in the smoke, hitting the water and wading to the bank. Three Troop left the trees, but were held back by the smoke-screen, and signalled their position and situation while the main groups of the Squadron crossed the stream by the stone bridge half a mile along, meeting with heavy fire from mortars and an S.P. gun that had been sent up nearer the road.

There was rubbish now along the route of the attack: a farm-house burned fiercely, its walls crumbling in the downpour. A scout-car was upside down against a tree-bole, with no sign of its crew but a smashed leg poking out, the blood from it seeping into a puddle and diluting there. A signals truck stood heeled over at the gates of the farm, and some of the battle stragglers took shelter beneath it as a Spandau opened up from the higher ground. A stretcher-party, leaving the road, found itself among the smoke sent out by Three Troop, and wound its way through the trees, feeling less vulnerable: the enemy, with no ammunition to waste on chance targets, was shooting at what he could see. In the rain he could see very little. His main weight of defensive fire would lie in check until the attack closed on its objective, which was the Odon, three miles forward.

These three miles were of mud. The road, once tarmac, was now agape with craters, and the tanks had taken to the cornfields on both sides, churning their way through, leaving a waste of mud for those that followed. They wallowed, crawling, a herd of dinosaurs through the primeval mud, their thin necks probing the gloom, swinging as they sensed the enemy. They lumbered with a near-blind impotence, bogged down by their own weight, their great, slow shapes awash with the rain. A splash came as one of them floundered across a crater and spilled its water out, crawling away to leave a trail of slime; a scream of metal rose shrilly as a track scraped against stone, crushing it and lurching on; a group of animals, driven from the farm by fire and huddled in the rain, took sudden flight across the path of the dinosaurs and left them in dominion over their world of mud.

Those commanders who were still standing upright in their turrets were soaked limp, as exposed to the driving elements as a ship's captain on the bridge. They swayed to the movement of their tanks, calling their steering orders to the drivers over the intercom. Two had gone astray, floundering into a ditch. A group of A.R.V.s had gone forward with the flails and were now working constantly with steel cables and lifting-ramps to drag bogged vehicles clear. Two others had come abreast of a German S. P. gun entrenched behind a bank and were receiving tracer, turning to face the direction of fire with their heaviest armour towards it, then opening up with their own guns, firing blind through the rain haze at close range. A stray shell hit Top Dog across the spine, taking away the salvage gear and sending a shock-blast across the open turret where Pike had ducked to the shell's sound as it had come rushing. His head was grazed; he had gashed his shin; the shock-blast hit the breath out of him and for a minute he crouched double, bracing himself with his hands, nodding to Munro again and again, meaning that he was all right.

Within a mile of the river, forward gapping-teams were meeting intense fire from Spandaus and multi-barrelled mortars. In this area the mines were a deadly carpet; three Crabs had had their flails blown to shreds and were dug in to one side of number three lane, putting out close fire along the ridge of earth that was the last bastion before the river. A French S.P. gun stood burning, with its ammunition-racks going up and its own high explosive blasting it apart and sending fragments whirling through the rain. A Troop of Crocodiles had crossed the low earth ridge and were flaming a strong-point on this bank of the river, their tongues of fire licking a hundred yards long, blackening the concrete gun-post and shrivelling its crew alive, dealing out the worst death that modern warfare could devise. Their jets were quenched; they rolled forward against a concentration of eighty-eight-millimetre fire that blew the tracks off one of them and left it derelict and exposed to the mortaring while the flails drew past, their guns hammering, recoiling, reloading, hammering at the defences across the river.

By eleven hundred hours, the forward armour and three squadrons of fighting-tanks were making a stand within the final assault area, beaten to a halt by the rising force of the enemy's guns. Panzer armour, concentrating on the left flank, was digging in a hundred yards from the main bridge. Their fire, accurate at close range, was constant, murderous, and without mercy. The rain had not lessened; it hissed across the waterway, pressing down the smoke-screen that forward infantry had laid between 'C' Squadron's flank and the bridge; it filled the new craters along the road, flooding off the tarmac and puddling the earth, turning it to a morass where the tanks stood, their guns alone giving sign that they were still manned.

Signals were going to Battalion, confirming local situation and reporting the states of fuel and ammunition. A Red Cross post had been set up near the ridge, protected from cross-fire by the low earth rampart, but exposed to mortaring. Walking wounded were moving through the mud, their legs doubling, tripped by unseen obstacles that lay in their bewildering path: a wrecked apron-wire, a boulder, a fallen rifle, a man's body, a broken spade, a bundle of nameless reddened rag. Stretcher-parties, knowing the direction of the medical post, staggered with their burdens, calling to the walking wounded, guiding them straight, picking them up when they stumbled, leaving those who were dropped by the bullet-streams as a Spandau post put out a sweep of shot across the littered mud.

In the rear of the tanks, infantry were moving up from L'Haubeise in armoured transports, dropping off to dig in and wait their time. Two field batteries were setting up their guns in line with the main bridge; they began firing at noon. In the forward area there was no movement. The drivers sat in the tanks with their engines stopped, conserving fuel. The commanders, observing targets through the veil of rain, passed orders to the guns. The wireless operators coaxed their sets, losing contact, finding it, sifting the signals, plagued by interference from the rain and the racketing guns.

The leading tank of Two Troop was bogged down on the forward side of the ridge. Lieutenant Pope was crouched in the turret, willing his nerves to hold out against the onslaught of frustration and the knowledge that the attack was halted, its momentum dead. The rain fell on him, trickling past his bared back, hissing on the hot breech of the gun below him.

A dozen yards behind its leader, and to the left, Moby Dick stood flank-on to a matted hedge, its engine quiet. Sergeant Goodall's voice was patient. "Traverse right."

The turret swung, bringing the gun round slowly.

"Steady . . . Pillbox."

The gun searched the rain haze.

"On!"

It stopped, moved back a degree, and steadied.

"On, Sarge!"

The crew tensed for the shock.

"*Fire!*"

Their ears blocked, opened again. The shell-case hit the scoop and fell to the bag. Goodall had his field-glasses up. Flame was coming from the pillbox on the river-bank. The remains of its concrete were tumbling. He could see no more than this, for the rain was on his lenses, distorting vision. After five minutes there was still no fire from the gun. The flames had died away, but now the ruin of the pillbox blew apart as shells exploded inside. A blazing fragment sailed high, curving over and hitting the bridge.

"Okay, Sergeant?"

"It's okay, boy. You don't waste 'em much." He got down with a rush as a group of mortar-bombs burst along the hedge. They coughed up a whirlwind of leaves and earth. He could smell the sulphur in it.

"Sergeant!"

"Hello?"

Taffy's thin, wild face appeared in the driving-hatch. "What's happenin' to us?"

"Mortar-bombs."

"I mean what's our position, man?"

Goodall knocked earth from his tin-hat. "We've been halted."

"But I can see the river from here!"

"So can I."

"Then why don't we make an effort an' get across it for goodness' sake? We're close enough, look!"

The sergeant sat crouched in the turret, unwilling to stand up again until things were clearer outside. He looked at Taffy's face. It was the face of a man who would drive a tank across a bridge under close enemy fire, drive it through a burning house or a minefield and go on driving it until it blew up or burned out, killing him. He would do it because his was that kind of inspired confi-

dence that would take him through opposition strong
enough to wipe out a dozen like him, a dozen without his
faith. Goodall was not sure how much of Taffy's faith
was in the Lord and how much in his own powers. Taffy
was a man for boasting, but he backed it up. He would
never fail to try the thing he boasted he could do, though
he might fail to do it. There had been the wall, and the
new tank, and the visiting General, a few months ago in
Essex. The General was there to see what the new tank
would do. Goodall had left it to Taffy, saying: "He wants
to know if it'll get through that wall, Taff."

"I can get it through easy, man."

"You know how thick it is?"

"What's the difference how thick it is, when you're set
on doin' it?"

"That's all very well, but you don't want to go an'
make yourself look a clot. Colonel says to put on a good
show, but don't attempt the impossible."

"Well, either you tell me to do it or you tell me not to,
Sergeant, for I can't sit here dreamin' about it."

Goodall looked at the wall again, and said: "All right,
take it up and let it have a nibble."

The Mark 7 hit the wall with the left horn and then
came round slowly with its full weight going on to both,
and the sergeant could see that a wall this thick was too
strong for them, and that was that, and the General
would have to lump it. Taffy pulled the tank back a yard
and put it against the wall again with the right horn and
then began working with the tiller in a series of blows at
the wall, left horn, right horn and both, butting it like a
fighting bull and worrying it until the concrete began
breaking up between the bricks and the red dust came
flying through the driving-slit as Taffy pulled back and
smashed forward again, back and again forward with the
tracks rutting the ground and the bricks coming away in a
shower while the horns lunged among them, sending up a
long, raw shriek of metal and concrete that got on the
nerves of the men watching; but they stood with their
hands clenched, every one of them willing the tank to go
through the wall, the whole Squadron driving it and the

General too, until Taffy threw his clutches forward together and whipped up the engine until it moaned; and the wall went down and the tank went through in a scatter of flying bricks.

The men let up a cheer that came from their boots and went through their hearts, and the General was laughing his head off, and wanted to see the driver. Taffy had climbed out of the tank with his face a mask of red brickdust, all his cockiness gone now as the General shook hands with him, asking him how he had done it. Taffy had done what he said he would do, and it didn't always happen that way, so that when it did he was overcome by it.

"A fine tank, sir. Quite ran away with me, it did!"

He had backed away, trying to brush himself down and throw up a salute at the same time. Goodall remembered him for that. Taffy hadn't come swaggering out of his tank; he had come out humbled.

His face was framed in the hatchway now, questioning. Goodall said: "We cross the river when we get orders to. Now stop squawkin' an' learn to be patient."

"Patient, is it?" Taffy disappeared, shaking his head. Watkins-Price looked up at the sergeant and said:

"We're sitters, here."

"Now don't you start, Watty. You got any apples left?"

"A couple."

"Well, stuff one in." He straightened himself in the turret, pushing his head and shoulders into the rain. He could see the Troop-leader through the dull grey deluge; Bloody Mary looked closed down and derelict. Mr. Pope would be cooped up in there with his nerves worse than anyone's. The Squadron was making a stand.

A man appeared from the rain and slapped his hand on the plates to attract the sergeant's attention. It was Pike.

"You 'aving a nice time, Sergeant Goodall?"

"I was, Corporal Pike, till you came."

"Lissern. What are we goin' to do?"

Goodall was getting tired of questions. Any fool could

see the position they were in. Pike gazed up at him with
water running off his tin-hat. He was wearing a towel
round his neck. He said: "We got no tea, an' no 'opes.
The boys want to know if we got to dig in an' make
ourselves at 'ome."

A rattle of shot came flickering through the murk and
he turned his head and swore monotonously.

"Alf, get back in cover, you clot."

The corporal wandered away. Top Dog was ten yards
on the right, clear of the hedge. He walked through the
rain with his spirits low. The bruise on his head was
throbbing, and his shin was painful. His boots were full
of water and the towel round his neck was soaked. The
Squadron had stood here an hour, and he didn't like it.
Nobody liked it. The engines were silent. The tracks were
settling, minute by minute, into the mud. If they couldn't
move forward they ought to be digging in.

The enemy's fire was holding off again. Shells came
across the river at precise intervals, but the main barrage
was over. Sometimes a Spandau sighted a target and
picked on it with a short accurate burst, and a mortar
crew joined in, ordered by the same observer. In between,
the hiss of the rain was a background to voices as men
made their way through the area, wounded or going out
to help wounded, calling to each other, wading through
the waist-deep corn and trudging through mud, gathering
into groups and going back with their wet shoulders bent
under the weight of the stretchers.

Signals had gravitated to a few routine reports on fire
positions and states of readiness. A troop of armoured
recovery vehicles were wallowing among bogged tanks,
hauling them to firmer ground while R.E.M.E.s worked
with railway sleepers and steel girders, throwing them
under the tracks as they lifted, giving them support. By
these men, and by the medical parties, the enemy had
been forgotten; they had their work to do, and they bent
to it; and when a burst of Spandau fire broke the hiss of
the rain, or mortars coughed, it was accepted as a natural
sound, as unremarkable as a peal of thunder; but sometimes a man would drop, a group would go down as if to

a sudden wind, and the presence of the enemy grew real in these places and was remembered too late.

The tank crews felt themselves to be safer crouched within their armoured shells; but they had claustrophobia to deal with, the fear of being trapped and roasted by a stray shell. There was nothing for them to do. Ammunition was being conserved now as well as fuel; it might be that they would have to move off at any time, and keep on moving, fighting their way through the German defences until the one force or the other broke. The waiting was hard. Pope was not the only man who had to deal with the enemy inside, on the home ground of his heart, with patience at odds with frustration and the fear that they had stopped for ever, and would be here in the mud until they rotted here and rusted, turning to skeletons entombed in hulks. Those with ready imagination became their own most subtle torturers; others were subject to mere boredom, but it was as dangerous, for a man would leave his tank to stretch his legs or look at the scene, clearing his head of fumes and resting his eyes along the distances, until a bullet came and he fell dead of his own boredom.

Lieutenant Pope had left his tank and was walking towards the river-bank, alone, picking his way across the littered ground, leaning forward against the rain. Even the pointless movement of his feet, taking him towards the enemy, broke some of the dreadful tension that was rising in him. A man can control his nerves, in whatever way they tax him, up to a certain point, but not beyond; there has to be a giving-in at last, one fine degree before the point beyond which he will break. Pope did not know this, but all the same he was conditioned by this natural law. He was moving towards the enemy. The rain beat against him and he was unaware of it.

He was trying to understand himself, as often he had tried at home, at his school and at O.C.T.U. When he became a prefect (he had once realised) he would have arrived, arrived at the stage where he could feel good ground beneath him and look back without misgiving; but when he had become a prefect there was no stability in the ground; it was as shifting as it had always been. When he had passed from O.C.T.U., a full officer with men to command, he would have reached the real stage from which he could look back and get his past into perspective, and see it for what it was, and deal with it, and then at last forget it and turn his back on it; but his mother had been in the mirror, helping to fix the Sam Browne, her hands proud but her eyes reproachful still, because he was the son of his father; and he had looked back, through his mother in the mirror, and seen the vague shape of the man, swaying and dissolute, cheerful in his degradation, winking at the fine new uniform, patronising its meaning until it became just another cowboy outfit with the same silly gun.

Even then, as late in his young life as that, Pope had understood the wink in the mirror. Such a fine uniform, with its careful creases and perfect cut, and not a single spot of mud or good red blood to show there was a man inside. A soldier was only a uniform until he had fought in it. When he had been under fire he would find his firm ground at last, standing equal with other men, not proud of himself in any way, but whole, integrated, a man.

For a month he had been under fire, and had come as far as this beleaguered purgatory; and beneath his feet there was mud, the same mud, with new memories of his own inadequacy: his shortness with Goodall at times when a crisp word would have brought respect; his panic at the blundering approach of the German drunk, when a calm appraisal of the moment would have turned the whole occasion to a good story with a laugh in it, instead of a dead body and a taste in the mouth of every man who was there; his pathetic interview with Watkins-Price, who had left him feeling defeated, a nonentity in a trench, smoking a casual cigarette as a gesture to bravado.

Now he was too old in his young life to understand his father, to pull away the old worn scenery and find the real man, not drunk in his taxis, not slamming the front door on his wife's reproachful voice, not squinting above his cigarette at the dark girl across the bar, but the real man, standing out from his background with his salvaged qualities. What had they been? There were qualities in every man, in the very worst.

He stood in the mud and cursed his father for having denied him the common legacy, a man's knowledge of his roots. He had never known his father; his father had been the slam of a door, a cruel smile, a broken whisky glass, a silent telephone; and here stood the son of these things.

The river was so near that he could hear the hiss of the rain across its water. What did it divide him from, the river? His ambition to prove himself, to show people he was a man, even without a father? Who would care?

"Can't you bloody well help me?"

He was shocked by the nearness of the voice, and turned quickly and saw the man within a few feet of him. He was sitting in the mud with his legs out straight. Pope moved towards him, and saw his face, and turned away, dragging in a deep breath to stop nausea rising.

"Well, can't you?"

How could a human voice come out of such a face? Were there eyes in it to see him? The nausea mounted every time he made to turn back and help the man. He mustn't vomit. It was very important to the man that he shouldn't do that. He drew in his breath slowly and felt the almost physical invasion of his mind by the demands this man was suddenly making out of the mud and the rain.

"Help me, you bastard!"

The words were slurred, but the voice was strong, distorted only by the mouth. Pope turned towards him and knelt with one knee in the mud, looking at the man's arms and legs, laying a hand on the sodden khaki. "Where did you get it worst?"

"Head. I should think you could see, couldn't you?"

He was a sergeant of the East Yorks. He sat with a strange stiffness, as if at attention, but it was nothing to do with Pope's being an officer. This man had forgotten about officers and other ranks. He was crippled in the mud of his world, and another of his kind was with him, and must help.

"How long have you been here?" Pope asked. He could look at the face now.

"A long time.".

"I didn't see you just now."

"I was on me back, feelin' me face." He moved his hands. The rain slowly washed the blood from the fingers as he spread them out. "Come on, what's it look like?"

Pope studied it carefully for his benefit.

"It's repairable. What the hell are you beefing about?"

The hands dropped, cupping themselves on his lap with a resignation that Pope found unbearable to see.

"Repairable, is it?" The glint of his one eye stared into Pope. In the voice there was a whole winter's bitterness. "I fell on a mine. That's what they're for, blow off your foot or your face."

It was impossible to know what this man had ever looked like. It was as difficult to talk to him as it would have been to talk to a man in the pitch dark, or wearing a full mask. There was a nameless quality in their relationship that was macabre.

"You can't tell what the damage is like just by feeling your face. Are your legs all right?"

Machine-gun fire was wheeping across the corn behind them; the long stalks shivered to it.

"What the hell do I want legs for now?"

"To walk with. You're a walking case."

"I'm a case all right." The torn mouth flapped. Pope got out his field-dressing, breaking the strings and pulling the lint free. The man let him work. The rain soaked the lint before he could put bandaging across, and for one long dying moment he knew that hope had stopped, hope of all things, of an end to this war and rain and mud and his own inadequacy. This face was not for bandages, but for the dark. But he knelt watching his hands work, and slowly came to remember they were his own. He was fixing a safety-pin at the back of the man's head. He had even left a slit for the mouth and the eye.

"I used to look a smasher. All the girls."

Spots of blood were blown out by his breath; it soaked

into the wet lint beneath the mouth-slit. Pope put away what was left of his field-dressing kit and stood up.

"Try your legs."

The hands in the lap moved in a derisive shrug.

"A walking case, am I? Dear Christ."

"Come on, get up."

The sergeant raised his arms, and as Pope looked down at him, pity stung his eyes. He did not feel worthy to touch this man's hands, even to help him. All through these years he had nursed himself, a poor boy with no father; and here was a man with no face.

"Get me up, then, can't you?"

He touched the hands. The rain had washed the blood from them, and they were pink and clean; and then, as he pulled him up, he felt the great strength in them. They were hands that would reach out to anything, a rope, a straw, the grip of a moon-faced young college-boy officer, anything within their reach that might save his life; they would use what material there was in the world to keep himself alive in it.

The mud sucked at their boots and they swayed together for a moment as the sergeant got his balance; then he dropped his hands and stood quite still. There was giddiness rising, as quick and tangible as water, to engulf him, but he kept his feet still and stood in its wave, and only once lifted a hand to Pope to steady himself; but even before he could take it, the man drew it down again and moved his feet.

"Where do we go, then?"

"You'd better put an arm round my shoulder, Sergeant. The mud's tricky."

"I'm a walkin' case, you said." He turned his big square body away from the river, his one eye peering through the rain. They began walking together, picking their way towards a belt of corn still standing; there would be less mud there, and they would be better hidden from the machine-gun posts. When they reached the corn, wading through it and pushing away its coolness with their hands, he said: "It doesn't matter about my bloody face. I was thinkin' it did, but it doesn't."

Pope kept close to him, ready to catch him when he fell; because he was going to fall, some time, as soon as his body had to let him know that he was driving it too hard. They went through the soft wet corn, waist-deep in it as the low wind brushed across it in waves, bringing the rain to whisper among it, the sound as gentle as the rise and fall of surf along a beach.

"I can manage on me own now."

The big body was sloping forward, breasting the corn, the hands swimming through it, drawing it aside with each step. Once, when Pope fell behind him a little, he looked at him. The blood was starting to soak through the bandages, so that the sergeant looked as if he wore a crimson gag. Above the bandages his hair was matted with mud. In ways like this, thought Pope, the soldier came back from his war.

"I said I c'n manage."

"I'm taking you in."

"You won't get a medal f'r it, then." Something like a laugh came from the torn mouth.

"Sergeant, what's your name?"

They came to the fringe of the corn and began picking their way across bad ground where the mud was churned by tanks.

"Pierce."

Pope said nothing. He had just wanted to know. A name must do, instead of a face. Pierce.

They came to a huddled thing; it had been thrown down, riddled, and afterwards mantled with mud as vehicles had passed. A tin-hat was a foot from it, crushed as flat as a plate by a tank-track. The slit in the bandages spoke again. "You lie quiet, lad. You got glory, now."

They walked round the corpse and then the sergeant flung out his hands and Pope went for him, grabbing at his uniform; and again they swayed together in the mud, their feet shifting as the sergeant found his balance and Pope helped; but the sergeant didn't lift a hand to hold on to him.

"This is a rough enough road, this is."

"It's not far, now."

The sergeant turned to face him, and Pope made him-self stand and look at the slit where the eye was bright on him.

"Not far, eh? Not far to where?"

He walked on again, with a sudden swing of his shoul-ders. A stretcher-party on their left was climbing to the road, where smoke was moving across, the tag end of a screen drifting and drawing out on the wind. Pope put his hand on the man's arm and said: "This way. Over this way."

The stretcher-party had stopped, waiting for them. Pope reached an orderly with an arm-band, a mud cross on a mud background.

"Take this sergeant along with you."

"Right, sir."

"I don't want any takin', but you c'n show me the way, if you know it."

"Come on, then, Sarge, fall in."

They stood in the rain, half a dozen men with the stretcher-poles in their hands, patient as horses, and the three others who were beside the stretchers, helping by talking to the men who lay on them, by giving them another fag, another wink, another word when they could think of a word that wouldn't turn salt in the wound: because every word had a double meaning for these men. "You're okay now, chum, you'll be goin' home." But 'home' meant that she would watch him get out of the train, and pretend he was the same, that it didn't matter about the neatly-pinned sleeve. "They'll fix you up, mate, don't you worry." But 'fix' wore an antiseptic mask al-ready drenched in sweat, and used a hygienic-looking saw whose teeth were already blunted by the butcher's work, and once you'd been fixed you were like it for life, and lucky. "All you need's a good clean up, Jock, an' a bit o' shut-eye." But there was a lot to clean: the mud, the oozing blood, the pus, the waste matter of life, before the thing could be dressed with some lint and a prayer that the gangrene would not set in; and then 'shut-eye', for a few hours, a few days, or for ever.

Words had a double meaning for these men. They

picked each of them over, suspiciously, cynical about
even their tone, suspecting the worst of the best, rather
than give in to hope. Once they put their trust in hope,
and it let them down, there would be nothing left. They
must save it for the future, for emergencies.

The sergeant fell in, and they started off again. Pope
watched them, standing at the edge of the broken road.
Then the sergeant turned, still walking, and gave him a
salute. Pope did not answer it. There was nothing in that
last clear gesture but derision. It was a quick-mimed
satire on war, given to Pope for what it was worth. There
was a smartness about the swing of the right hand that
brought it close enough to the real thing to be a parody of
it; there was no doubting what it said. *You can stick your
war, lad, and stick your bloody commission along wi' my
bloody stripes. I done my bit an' I got no face, an' you
c'n finish the rest on your own.*

They were lost, one by one, in the tattered smoke; the
bearers, the stretchers and the man who had once been a
sergeant.

Pope turned back towards the river, and made his way
to the left, where the grey humps of the fighting-tanks
stood silently. Pierce. No face, just a name for the big
body and the angry heart. Gone, now, into the drifting
smoke. He might have been anyone; never mind his name
and rank and unit; they were words; forget the big square
body and the rich accent that, in a measure, placed the
man. He was still anonymous, just as Pope's father had
always been. If a man had no face, you can never meet
him, never know him. He can raise his hands to you, and
you can help him up; or you can refuse.

The two scenes in Pope's mind were locked together.
His father, coming out of the room, all those years and
half a war ago, had said: "I've bought a bit of trout gear.
Old Prothero's given me rights for a week on his
river."

Pope had said nothing.

"I thought it might interest you." He had a reel in his
hand, a new one. He tossed it easily like a cricket-ball.
"If you want to come along, we'll start tomorrow, early.

There's a good pub there. Comfortable beds and country beer." The new reel, rising and falling, had glinted in the light.

Stiffly, Pope had said: "Yes?"

"Tell you what. If you're interested, come along to my den this evening, and I'll show you the flies. That'll decide you. They're as gaudy as rainbows. Wait till you see 'em."

He had gone out through the French doors, still tossing the reel, in the same way that Pope had lit his cigarette in the dug-out, talking to Watkins-Price. In the evening, he had gone out, and had come home late. He did not know if his father had waited for him in his den, ready to show him the flies, gaudy as rainbows. The invitation had been tacitly turned down. But there had been other times—they crowded into his mind now; and they had been no better. His father had wanted to understand him, had wanted help; he had wanted himself understood. Young Pope had seen a face he could never recognise, and wouldn't go fishing with a stranger.

The other scene locked together with the first, different from it in every detail except one. Help had been asked. But the sergeant's plight required no thought to deal with it. He was hit, and down, and wanted to get up; and Pope was the nearest man. But what would have happened, in the years ago, if he had helped the other man? There might have started a slow alienation from his mother, as far as the point where he stood half-way between his parents, bewildered, having to judge for himself who was right. And who had ever taught him judgment, without giving it a selfish bias to suit their case? It had taken him this long to judge even himself. He was like the non-swimmer who floats within his depth, his hand or foot occasionally touching the sand to reassure himself—who can swim quite well, but only in this much security, until the time comes when he knows that he could float like this in fifty feet of water, and swim with ease, if he can do it in five. He has no more need of the shallows or the sand. He is free of them. The moment is serene.

A man did not have to know his roots to grow. They

were there, or he would not be here; that was all he had
to know. He had been denied love, affection, in his child-
hood; it had been mother's-love, certainly, and therefore
suffocating in its demands on him, but it had protected
him from worse influences. He had been denied any
knowledge of his father, but only because his parents had
made a bad marriage and had implanted him in soured
soil: neither of them had wished him anything but well.
What else could they have done for him? They could
have parted from each other, but their Victorian teaching had been that the child of a miserable marriage was
better off than an orphan, despite the agonies of bewilder-
ment that were his birthday presents, year after year during the long tearing-apart of loyalties. They could not
have been expected to pretend they loved each other,
when the loathing was made so obvious; the strain on
them would have been unbearable, and the shock much
worse for him when the day came to expose the ten-year-
old lie.

No man could follow his roots far down without finding the twists in them; and the knowledge would wither
him, if he let it. When they were above the surface,
twisted in front of his own ever-widening eyes, he had a
worse time of it by far; but he could turn inwards, and
find whatever security was there, inborn and unassailable.
Then there must come the turning again, this time out-
wards, breaking from the introvert shell.

It was a late time to be born again, in a mud-patch of
men's hate for other men, with death as the prize of the
day; but it was happening now, to the moon-faced young
college-boy officer who had helped the sergeant up. He
was not very clearly aware of it, for all the complex
contradictory thoughts that were jostling through his
mind. The sharpest of them was to do with Pierce. Whenever he, the man with no father, followed the burrowing
thread, it led him back to Pierce, the man with no face.
He must not think too much of this change in him; he
mustn't analyse his strengthening sense of renaissance;
this was no problem for the mind, but a change of the
heart; he should let it come, unquestioned. All he must

know was that he felt free of his past, and that whether his future would last him another minute before a bullet came, or many years if he were spared, it would be his own free future, unhampered by old misgivings and regrets, no longer cluttered with half-formed resolves too weak for testing by the new standards of growing up. Remember Pierce, and question nothing, and go on from here. Watch out that you don't die in this next minute, forgetting to duck. All that's happened is that you've found a man who wanted help more than any other man you've ever met, more help than you're likely ever to need yourself. It isn't just a feeling of consolation, because you've got a face. *'It doesn't matter about my bloody face. I was thinkin' it did, but it doesn't.'*

And the other thing that Pierce had said, that Pope would remember all his life. *'Not far to where?'*

The rain fell on him. He realised he was standing still, his feet cold in the mud, the low wind whipping against his ears. When he moved it was out of his own no-man's-land on to his own firm home ground. The tanks were still quiet, their engines off. It must have been a long time since he had walked down towards the river. Twenty-two years.

A gun, not far away, was firing west; he saw the orange explosion tinge the rain. It was one of the tanks, putting out a feeler-shot beyond the bridge. Then a sound began, slowly terrifying him with its nearing whine that loudened and rose to a drawn-out scream that hollowed out his heart and left him shuddering, hands to his head. The shell dropped among the corn, over to his right, a Moaning Minnie, designed to kill where it fell and to terrify those who stood clear of its blast. He made himself move again, remembering two of the men who had heard these things coming, yesterday, when the Squadron had been in harbour. Todd and O'Hagan had been sitting by their tank; he had been with them. The sound had started thinly in the sky, and they had recognised it at once. "A bloody Minnie. Listen."

O'Hagan had grunted out a laugh. They were committed to this hellish sound; they could not go anywhere, away from its rising howl; they could wait, and duck, and hope. They had done all they could about it by giving it a comic name, Minnie.

"Christ!" Todd had said. His hands were clamped to his ears. The scream lifted and reached a pitch where a man must run, or lie in a tight bundle, or shout out, taking his own way of dealing with the devil before it came for him. When the shell had fallen, the blast of it was a relief, almost a loved thing. The explosion was a rough big-minded enemy with a shape and size and risk about it that you could understand and cope with, a welcome thing compared with that thin rising scream that went riddling slowly through the nerves until they shrivelled and were raw.

Pope was still moving when the next one came, this time clear of the corn, bursting in the mud and sending a storm of filth through the air to bespatter him. He was running slowly now, with the intention of reaching his tank before the next onslaught to his nerves was mounted. It was better not to be alone with a sound like that; in most of a war's crises, the companionship of men was their best anodyne.

His feet went splashing through the mud; a tank's shape loomed and he broke his run. He stood panting.

"They're sendin' the Minnies in, sir."

Corporal Pike was looking down at him from the turret.

"Yes. But their bark's worse than their bite."

Pike shrugged under the towel round his neck. His face was pale. "All the same, sir, it's an 'ell of a bloody bark."

Lieutenant Pope was going to answer, and then waited, while the scream rose for the third time, filling the sky and the rain and the world until there was nothing left of any of them. The sky receded and the rain stopped and the world went shrivelling away, leaving only the scream in the universe. Then it burst. White light fanned against the tank, throwing Pope's shadow there. He felt his spine curve as he leaned forward, hands scraping down the metal, saving his face. The blast-wave drove hard, crushing him against the plates and bouncing, dragging him away and dropping him in a heap on the mud while the fragments sang above him and hit the tank and spun away, whining. The smell came, rasping into his lungs. Slowly the light died. Something fell near him with a thud, squelching into movement.

"You all right?"

He said: "Yes." There was mud in his mouth. He rose to his hands and knees, trying to throw off whatever it was that covered his head. Pike was tugging at him. He stood up, and tried to get his arms back; they were held forward, and his neck was bent beneath a soft hood. He heard the corporal laughing, and felt angry. "What the bloody hell?" he said.

Pike tugged again, and he was free.

"It's yer blouse, sir."

"It's what?"

He straightened up. His battledress had been torn forward over his back and head as tight as a straitjacket, and one of the bangs he heard against the tank must have been his tin-hat sailing off. Pike was holding it out to him, grinning through the mud on his face.

Pope knew, looking at the corporal, that Pike had enjoyed seeing his Troop commander like that, trussed like a duck in the mud. There was more than mere amusement in his face. This was how he thought of his commander, a useless enough kid with his hands tied by his own feebleness; and now he had seen him like that. You had to laugh when you could, in this lot, and be satisfied.

"You want to face the other way, you know. Never bend over, into the wind."

Pope took his tin-hat and put it on. The buckle of his blouse had been ripped off, but there was a button working.

"Back inside, Corporal, before the next one comes."

Pike turned and climbed to his turret. He looked down at Mr. Pope, with more colour in his face. The laugh had done him good when he had most needed it. He watched the lieutenant fumbling in his pockets.

"Corporal, have you got a cigarette?"

Pike vanished, then bobbed up again, leaning down from the turret, shielding the packet from the rain while Pope took one. His Tommy-lighter flared up at the first flick. He passed the packet back. "Thanks. Your chaps can have a smoke in there; but don't blow the ship up."

"Right, sir." The boys had lit their fags an hour ago, but it was nice to have it official.

Pope turned away and walked through the mud towards Bloody Mary, cupping his cigarette to keep it dry. From the turret of Moby Dick, Sergeant Goodall watched him. He said to Watkins-Price:

"What's the matter with our Mr. Pope? He's wanderin' about like a dick in a trance."

Watty spat the pips from his apple.

"He always does, doesn't he?"

"That's quite right," Goodall conceded.

The lieutenant reached his tank, and knocked the mud from his boots as best he could before climbing into the turret. His body was bruised from being flung against Top Dog when the shell had burst, and he was soaked to the skin; the slow drilling shock of the Minnies was still in his nerves, and his throat was parched with the smell of their explosion; but he felt strong. From below him, Corporal Todd said:

"What's it like outside, sir?"

Pope said: "It's raining."

MOONRISE

I

THE attack lasted two days more; the rain three. The bridge had gone down before the rearguard armour was across; but the infantry was already fighting its way into the bridgehead on the east bank of the river, and held its positions. The second night had been the worst; men had died in it, as yet uncountably. On this third day, flank elements were mopping-up towards the Gillarme Ridge, and battalions were counting their strength. There were gaps in the lists of men and tanks and guns that startled the jaded commanders. The action was won, but the price had made it a most wicked luxury.

Of 'C' Squadron, ten tanks were still on their tracks, but only four were fit to fight on. Three were missing. No one had seen them.

Major Knowles was in a dug-out a mile from the wreck of the bridge. It had contained a dozen German officers, ten of them dead, one dying and one crazed. They had been here under the bombardment of the British and Canadian guns and under the dawn attack, today, of a squadron of rocket-firing Typhoons that had made the breach for the ground forces.

But the field-telephone still worked. It had rung, an hour ago, and Knowles answered it. The caller asked him, in German, what the position was in that area. Knowles suggested to him, in English, that he come to see for himself. The line had closed abruptly.

He looked up at his second-in-command.

"Number Three, Two Troop?"

"Missing. Being looked for now."

"I hope so."

Captain Hallett said: "It's that bloody river. We know that two of them drove into it, in the rain." He waited for

the next question, his body aching to the point of collapse, his eyes squeezing water when he blinked their hot
red lids.

"You'd better go and fall down somewhere, Jim."

"I'm all right."

"You're half-dead. Too much benzedrine."

"Well, it got me this far."

"The main thing," Knowles said wearily, "is that a lot
of us have got this far. Enough of us to establish the
bridgehead they asked for." He dropped his hands on to
the lists of the present and the absent names. The paper
was wet, like everything else. It had been raining through
their bodies and into their souls for days on end. "At
least, I suppose it's the main thing." He sounded as if he
didn't care.

Hallett leaned his wet shoulders against the wet wall.

"We're passing into reserve, aren't we?"

"If they don't change their minds."

"But they haven't yet, as far as you know?"

"Not as far as I know."

"D'you think they're going to?"

Major Knowles got up. "Who the bloody hell knows?"
He lurched against the trestle-table. "The attack has been
successful. The bridgehead has been established. The infantry will hold it. Stores are coming across. So we're in
clover, aren't we?"

Hallett's pinched wet face was distorted by a grin.

"If this is clover, what's a nettle-bed like?"

"Bloody rough. Now for God's sake go and sleep. It
makes me feel like the tag-end of an air-raid just to look
at you."

"You seen yourself?"

Knowles sat down again, collapsing into the chair.
"I've got to carry on for a bit. You haven't. So just flit,
will you?"

Hallett stretched, shifting the ache in his muscles to
new areas. "There's still a bit I can do, Bob. If you want
me, I'll be somewhere handy."

He left the dug-out, worrying over the missing tanks. If
a tank was wrecked, it was a write-off and he could forget

it; but if it was missing, it might be anywhere, perhaps with a crew still aboard who needed help, desperately.

Sergeant Verity met him, red-eyed, mud-caked, halting smartly and standing rock-steady. "We've found two of 'em, sir. Mr. Jackson an' Sergeant Liefe."

The rain dripped from Hallett's tin-hat. He asked:

"What's their shape, Sergeant?"

"Mr. Jackson's bogged down at the foot of the ridge, sir. There's an A.R.V trying to pull 'im clear. Crew's okay."

The captain nodded. So the other one wasn't okay.

"What about the other one?"

"It's brewed-up, sir, half a mile down the river. None of 'em got out."

Hallett nodded again, remembering the Major's hands as they had dropped wearily across the lists. "That leaves Corporal Pike still missing."

"Yes, sir. We're still searchin'."

"When did you sleep last, Sergeant?"

"I don't remember, sir."

"Does it bother you?"

"Nothing special. We're goin' into reserve, aren't we, sir?"

"Don't bank on it. I've heard nothing definite, but I don't like the smell here. For a bridgehead this size, there doesn't seem much support yet."

"Oh, it'll get here. We're all right. I hear there's some mail comin' through."

"Mail?" It took time to remember what the word meant. The envelope, the stamp, her writing. My dearest Jim. "Good God!"

"Be all right, with a bit o' mail, eh, sir?"

"Yes. Those of us who——" he straightened himself, aware that his body had been sagging oddly. "Yes. May the Lord look sideways on the Army Post Office." The late-afternoon skyline was melting in front of his eyes, the light blinding him. He squeezed his eyes and opened them again; the horizon steadied.

"——Along the river, sir?"

"What?" He straightened his shoulders again. He felt like a fly sliding down a window.

"Shall I take some men and search along the river, sir?"

"The recovery unit's out. They'll pick them up sooner or later. You get your men easy, and let 'em sleep."

Sergeant Verity was still standing steady as a post. Hallett was annoyed with him for that. He turned away with a nod, trying to walk straight, trying to remember where he had to walk. He heard the sergeant squelching away through the mud. There shouldn't be men like Knowles and Verity. You couldn't let yourself break until they did; and they never would.

The raindrops hit his tin-hat with the noise of someone hammering rivets in. He walked as far as the nearest camouflage net, did not see it, walked slowly into it and used his last pinched reserves in trying to free himself from the mesh. Then he sagged on to it, face down, prone, thought the fly on the window had found a spider's web, and slept.

Evening came early, a slow seeping-away of the light from the sky. The river ran steel-grey through its banks, the water still rising, rushing more fiercely through the tangled wreckage of the bridge and collecting débris against it, running on smoothly below the big pontoon where the echelon trucks had crossed, minutes ago.

The garrison of the bridgehead was partly at rest, partly alert. Reports of the enemy were coming in quickly from observers and scout parties. The Panzers had drawn back to a ten-mile line that in places touched the river, enclosing the bridgehead in a rough arc, so that in places the British and Canadians slept exhausted within a few hundred yards of the exhausted and sleeping enemy.

A second telephone call had reached 'C' Squadron Headquarters before the Royal Signals had cut the line and re-connected it. The caller had said, in poor English: "You are being contained by vastly superior forces who are about to make an overwhelming attack and annihilate you to a man. You will be wise to surrender immediately, and save the lives of your troops." Major Knowles, stirring a mug of thick black coffee, had answered, in poor German: "You will please keep this line clear of unimportant messages, as we are busy organising a dance."

The evening was quiet, but there was tension. Patrols were out from both sides, and at intervals there came a rattle of gunfire or a mortar salvo, tinging the rain-scape with red and making the ground tremble. Tanks were on the move, finding a late harbour, or reconnoitring in small groups on roving commissions; and throughout the bridgehead armoured recovery vehicles and shifts of R.E.M.E.s were working hard, salvaging tanks that were bogged down, crippled or abandoned. In the lowering dark the work was difficult.

One British fighting-tank, still on the missing list, was ploughing slowly through the rain, driving almost blind with its wireless broken down. It had been moving for an hour, turning laboriously at tangents to the main direction, finding its way again and then losing it, bogging in the mud and struggling clear, with its commander and crew fighting nothing more deadly than exhaustion. Minute by minute it was beating them down, implacable and overwhelming. This tank was Top Dog.

The co-driver, Soaper, was asleep in the forward compartment, lolling with a doll's inertness against the head-plates. The driver, Luff, had stopped talking to him, seeing he was asleep, but felt no loss of companionship or support. Soaper was no help to anyone, awake or asleep; he was a dead weight in the tank, a bit of ballast. Nor was Luff disgusted with him. When the point came when he could no longer drive this tank through this godforsaken wilderness of blinding muck, there would be no one else aboard who could take over. He could out-work them all. He stared through the driving-slit at the rain, at the lift and fall of the ground and the ghosts of trees that swayed past him, coming out of the silence and losing their way, wandering back as the tank turned again, trying to find the river. Then the engine stopped. Luff tried to re-start it.

" 'Ave a look," said Pike briefly. Luff had a look at the engine.

"Timing-gears stripped."

Corporal Pike said after a moment: "That's our lot, then."

"Well, we can't move. It's a replacement job."

Pike nodded. Top Dog stood within fifty yards of a wood, facing east. There was good cover there, but they couldn't reach it. Behind him a crack of the sky was lightening, even as late as this.

Under the turret Lance-Corporal Munro was crouched on the occasional seat, head going down, jerking up, nodding again, lifting. His eyes came open as Pike said:

"Well, we got trouble, an' that's that."

The gunner, Weston, leaned against the breech, one fond arm draped over it. The metal was cold. The gun had not fired for three hours; the drops of rain fell without sound, without their *tiss—tiss—tiss* on the warm metal. He felt the loss. He did not like a cold gun. He said to the corporal:

"Is that all we got? Trouble?"

"We're lost," said Pike.

"No, honest?"

Pike sank down on to his little platform, dangling his legs, looking at Munro in the gloom. "Can't you get that wireless workin', Gutsy, fer Chri' sake?"

"Valves are duff." Munro's head had jerked up again; his answer was automatic; he had known the question would come, as soon as they stopped, and he had rehearsed the answer many times during the long dark grind.

"Ain't we got no spares?"

"I've used three. Others're bust."

"Well this is a turn-up, this is."

"I thought that's what it was," said Weston without spirit.

Gunfire began again, north of them. Small echoes were broken off by the turret-rim and rang inside the tank. Trooper Luff appeared again in the hatchway, jamming his shoulders there and looking at the three blurred faces among the familiar shadows. "You ask me," he said, "we're not safe here."

"What a shame," said Weston.

Their commander said: "Position is, we don't know where we are, we got no engine, an' no wireless."

Munro said: "Then for Chris' sake let's have a fag."

Weston gave him one, and the glare of the match dazzled them, lighting the confines of the turret with its blinding flame. The corporal said: "Why don't you send a festerin' rocket up, so Jerry knows where we are? Be brighter than a match."

"I'll send a rocket up in a minute," said Weston, "an' it won't have far to go." He gave Pike a cigarette, keeping the match going for him. When it went out they could see nothing but the three red spots of their cigarettes against the dark.

"You want a fag, Luffy?"

"Nope. Fresh air's what I want."

"Go an' get it then, boy."

Luff looked at the pale blur that was the corporal's face. "Okay, Corp?"

"Okay. Go careful, though."

They heard their driver drop to the grass. There was no mud here, for they were on a gentle slope that ran down to the east bank of the river, and nothing had passed this way to churn up the ground. Feeling the soft grass springy under his feet, Luff pulled his boots off, and his socks, and walked slowly round the tank, watching the trees, the gunfire, the widening crack of light in the west sky. He wanted to call out to the others, about how good his feet felt, cool on the soft wet grass. It was marvellous, he thought, how easy it was to find ecstasy in the midst of its opposite. You take your boots off, and suddenly feel like this, floating about with your heart free, just because of a bit of wet grass; it was marvellous.

He walked in wider circles, going directly away from Top Dog, his eyes half-shut, his feet nuzzling through the cool sweet miracle, his mind trying to pretend that the tank had gone, the war had gone, the battlefield agonies draining away and somewhere very far a bugle fading, leaving him alone here to wander where he liked, to lie flat with his face turned to the healing kiss of the grass, or sit against a tree and watch the light in the sky there in the west, and think of what he liked, or of nothing, letting the soft touch of the rain cool his body and soothe his eyes while he drew the slow air into his lungs, deep and deep, until its sweetness filled him and he fell asleep.

A close salvo from two mortars punched the wind and the bombs burst short, blossoming in the gloom. He turned his head. They had fired from the east; the bombs had burst in the west; he stood half-way along their trajectory, some quarter-mile from its path. The answer came from a tank-gun, west to east. He waited, worried, turning to catch the location of small-arms fire as a patrol opened up and was engaged. The smell was in the breeze, driving away the last hope of pretending that the war had passed beyond; it had everything, that raw metallic smell, to whip the memory up and send it spinning among the past, tripping on a friend's death, looking askance at men with mouths and bowels open to the half-second of fear before the obliteration and the blinding and the squirt of blood. Other smells, other memories: the kindly tang of tea, reminding of a snatched rest and a brew-up with your mates; the first pull at a fag, half an ear to a smutty joke, good for a laugh at any price; the heady scent of wild flowers, almost bewildering in its power to send you sailing away through the miles and weeks to the bit of a garden where the pears were nearly up, and the watering-can still leaked its homely piddle over the moss in the path—but this smell, this raw-gutted stink of cordite and phosphorus, made you sick in your memory. It was here now.

He swung round as a big gun banged, firing west from a tree-belt a mile down the slope. Firing west, from west of where he stood. He said aloud: "My Christ!"

Someone was moving about, near him.

"Luffy?"

"Hello?" He had cupped his hands, pitching his voice without shouting.

"See that, did you?" It was Weston.

When he came up, Luff said: "I told you, we're not safe here."

"We're right among bloody Jerry, eh?"

"Right there, mate. Does Alf know?"

"He'll've heard that gun. We better get back."

Luff said: "Take your boots off."

"Eh?"

"You don' know what it feels like. Better than havin' a woman."

Weston wanted to get back to the tank, but Luff was not hurrying, so he tugged at his boots and paddled about on the grass. "You're bloody right, boy. Cheaper, too."

"Pssst!"

They looked up. Corporal Pike was between them and the tank. "Stop shoutin' the bloody odds! We're up be'ind Jerry!"

They went towards him in the grey light. Above them the cap of cloud that had covered the sky for three days was drawing east, and the twilight was sharpening. Pike said softly: "Keep near the tank, ready to 'op in. You know where we are, eh?"

"Up a creek," said Luff.

"What you doin' with them boots off?"

"Paddlin'."

Pike creased his face up. "Now listen. You 'ear anythin', you report to me, see? Don't matter what it is—guns or shoutin' or transport, you come an' tell me. We got to get our bearin's, quick."

Munro was leaning with his back to the tank, smoking. He said: "We'll have to get out of here, Alf."

"Where to? It's better to stop 'ere with Top Dog than go walkin' straight into Jerry."

"Well, I'm willin' to take a chance."

Luff said: "Don't talk daft, Gutsy. At least we've got three guns an' some armour plate here. Corp's right."

"I'm not only right," said Pike reasonably, "I'm the geezer that gives the orders, too. Where's bloody Soaper?"

"Still inside, kippin'."

"Get 'im out an' give 'im some fresh air." He looked at Weston. "George, how's the ammo?"

"Five rounds in the gun, an' two Besa belts. An' a few grenades."

"By God, they won't get us far."

"They'll have to get us as far as we got to go."

Pike turned as Soaper came over the side and pitched on to the grass. "What's on, then, Corp?"

"We're on enemy territory. I don' 'ave to tell you more 'n that, do I?"

Soaper got up slowly, staring at the corporal. *"Enemy* territ'ry?"

"That's it."

"Oh God. Oh God." He said it softly.

" 'E won't 'elp, neither. 'E's got quite enough on 'is 'ands. Now get some air in your lungs." He dropped his dog-end and stamped on it, then put his head up, face to the sky. "You know what? It's stopped rainin'."

"Can't 'ave."

"Garn."

Pike lifted the palm of his hand, and then looked down, saying softly: "Look at that, then." He sounded awed, a witness to a miracle. "It's stopped. It's bloody stopped."

Weston stood in his drenched uniform, holding his drenched boots. "We're goin' to miss it, you know."

Munro shook his head. "I don't think I'm goin' to be able to stand it."

Half the sky now was clear, and half cloud still; but the cloud was drawing eastwards, leaving the first two stars.

"Why can't we go?" It was a whisper from Soaper. He was still staring at Pike. They looked at him. "We've got to get out of here." He was crouched a little; the tension in his body was visible. "Why can't we go?" He shut his mouth hard on the last word; they heard the tremor in his breath.

"We'll go, mate," said Pike, "when we're ready." It was kindly said, without a hint of contempt.

"They said they're not takin' prisoners, Corp. Corp."

"It ain't true. It's to scare us, see?"

Soaper jerked badly as another mortar salvo banged, and Luff gave a laugh. Pike looked at him and said: "Shuddup." He turned back to Soaper. "See what you c'n find in the way of camouflage nettin', kid, back on the racks. An' then start 'angin' it out. All right?"

It was embarrassing to hear the thin tone of fright in his voice. "But we can't stay here. We can't stay, Corp."

"You just get the scrim, an' put it up." He turned away before Soaper could say anything. "Munro, you an' Luff start diggin', under the rear, good and deep. And watch out you don't hit any metal with the spades. It's goner be a nice peaceful night, see?"

They moved, and Soaper moved with them, calmed by their easy obedience. Standing very close to Weston, the corporal said:

"Listen, George. I don't think much of our chances 'ere, but we got to stay. If Jerry comes, we fight it out. There's not much ammo, but it'll 'ave to do."

"What's going to happen in the morning, Alf?"

"For one thing, we shall 'ave 'ad some sleep. We need it, bad. And if we get a bit o' luck we can look after Top Dog till our lot take this area. I'm not 'andin' a good tank to bloody Jerry, for the sake of a crocked engine. Not Top Dog, any'ow."

Weston stubbed out his cigarette.

"Okay then, Alf."

"There's one more thing. Don't chivvy Soaper. 'E's crap-scared, we all know that, but don't go and make it worse for the lot of us."

"Okay."

"Now go an' check the guns, mate. We may want 'em."

Weston left him, climbing into the turret, careful with his boots. Inside, he found his gym shoes among the clutter, and put them on. He didn't have to check the guns. They were ready. He sat for a minute on Munro's seat, looking up at the sky through the turret, thinking how like a well it looked with the pale light shimmering

in its circle of dark. It was strange not to hear the rain.
Other sounds came, in the pauses of the gunfire. Outside,
Soaper was dragging some scrim over the gun barrel; he
sounded like a mouse trying to get in through the wains-
coting. And there was the soft thud of spades, behind the
tank, reminding him of the burial parties on the way from
the coast to here. This could be another, by the morning.

The rapid *pum-pum-pum* of mortaring filled the well of
the sky, beating against his ears, and the rim of the turret
reddened with light, seconds afterwards. He was suffering
an almost physical itch to use his guns, to bang a round
into his six-pounder and punch it out. He felt strong
when he was sitting there with an eye to the sights and a
fist on the tit, waiting for the order. It was when he loved
Top Dog most: when she barked. There might be a
chance tonight; it might even be their only chance of
staying alive. He had no thoughts about whether Jerry
would take prisoners or kill out of hand; his confidence
that Jerry could do neither was in his gun. When the
racks were empty, he might feel different; but that could
wait.

His head nodded, and he brought it up sharply, getting
off the seat. The air was stale in here, warm with the oil-
smell and the rough scent of the spent cases in the bag
behind the gun. It was a scent he loved; whenever he
smelt it, it was always from his own gun, to his mind. He
climbed on to the commander's platform, and looked out
over the rim. Nearly all the cloud had gone; there must
be a fast high wind up there, chasing east through the
night. Down here there was not much more than a breeze,
fresh with the wet grass and smelling of corn. It was a
lovers' night, star-eyed and timeless, false as Delilah, its
deceit exposed by the flicker of guns across the wood and
the slow throb of a spotter plane.

He could see Pike, standing some way from the tank,
alone. Pike would have to get them through this night; he
didn't envy him.

Soaper was struggling with the camouflage netting, and

Weston dropped to the grass and went to help him. Soaper said quietly: "Corp mus' be mad."

"No, mate."

"We won't have a chance, when they come."

"We got ammo, haven't we?"

"Five rounds? What's the use of that?"

"You can do a lot with five rounds. And there's the Besas."

"You're all mad, lettin' him get away with this."

Weston shut up, pulling at the scrim; it was heavy with rainwater, and badly torn. He heard the corporal coming across and climbing into the tank; in a minute he was out again, wandering over the grass towards the trees. Soaper's breathing was painfully audible in the patches of silence; he was dog-weary and afraid, but he was doing all he could to get the netting up.

Weston felt sorry for him, really sorry. He was not much afraid, himself, of the enemy. He had always been afraid of heights and of deep water, so that there had been times when this fear had risen in him badly enough to sicken him for days; once he had nearly drowned; twice he had forced himself to high places, challenged by his friends; so he knew what fear was. Soaper felt it in him now: this was his kind of terror, as natural as Weston's kind but different. It was no good just calling him a coward. A coward would run, and not stay here putting the camouflage up. It must take some doing.

"We'll be okay here," Weston said. "They won't see us till daylight, and by that time we'll have got our bearings and know which way to go."

Soaper did not answer at once. He must be thinking of a dozen answers; they all boiled down to the one. "I want to get out of here."

"We'll be okay."

The netting was sodden, chilling their fingers, filling their noses with its ship's rope smell. Weston heard a new sound, chipping into the silence, slow and rhythmic. He couldn't place it. It came from the wood, higher on the slope, a soft chipping noise.

Soaper said: "What's that?"

"I dunno."

After a while it stopped, and later Corporal Pike came back, dragging a great bush. Luff stopped digging and let the sweat run into his eyes, tired of trying to stop it.

"What's that, Alf? A bloody Christmas tree?"

Pike was panting hard. The bush was as big as himself. He passed the hatchet to Weston. "Take Soaper with you. Bring back all you can, big an' small." He took a deep breath. "There's goin' to be a moon afore midnight. We got to get Top Dog covered by then."

"Stone the crows!" said Munro. "We'll need a forest."

Pike pointed. "Don't take it all from one place, see? Dodge about a bit, an' when you leave bare wood, rub earth on it, darken it down—okay?"

"Okay, Alf." Weston took Soaper off.

" 'Ow's the trench, Gutsy?"

"Comin' on. What about a brew-up, to be gettin' on with?"

Pike stood with his hands on his hips, sweat shining on his face. "As soon as that trench is deep enough an' the tank's covered, we'll 'ave a brew-up."

"And what about kip?" Luff asked.

"We'll start shifts. I'm goin' to be first watch, for two hours. But get that trench dug."

They moved their spades again. Their clothes were drying on them, steaming. They thought of tea and sleep, lifting the spades, driving them in, pulling away the earth, thinking of hot sweet tea and the drowning delight of sleep as their spades bit, cutting through fibres, raising the cool earth smell, coming to chalk and bringing it up, crumbling and ghost-white in the glow of the stars, until Luff threw his spade down and let his body rock against the tank. He leaned there, shoulders to the cold metal, face to the sky, head throbbing.

"I'm done," he said. He said it to the sky and the night, more than to Munro.

"So's the trench." Munro dropped his spade.

"It's got to be covered yet." The corporal stood there, his body doubled, hands on knees as he took in slow, deep breaths. The silence lasted minutes.

Luff moved, falling away from the tank as if drunk.

"I'm going to start makin' the tea, Alf."

Corporal Pike straightened up, wiping a hand over his face. In front of his half-shut eyes, Luff and Munro wobbled. The ground dipped away and he swung his head, cursing in his mind, forcing it to work. "Get the trench covered first."

Luff said: "I'm beat."

"Then you're the only one. Even Soaper's still workin'." He picked up the hatchet. "Come on."

Munro moved, following him, picking up his feet and putting them at the slope, leaning forward so that his feet must move forward too. Pike turned his head.

"Luff," he said.

"I got to sleep." Luff had moved a pace and stood swaying.

"You're comin' with us, to 'elp us."

"I'm beat, you bastard."

Pike turned his head. Munro was still climbing the slope; his legs moved with a sleep-walker's rhythm. Pike looked back to Luff.

"I'm waitin'," he said.

Anger mounted through the fatigue in Luff's voice. "Even a God-almighty bloody corporal can't make a man work when he's— —"

Pike came towards him quickly and stood bunched against him in the faint light. "My stripes don' matter. You're goin' to 'elp us because you're one of us. If we're dead by mornin' it's not goin' to be because you backed out. Now jus' rake up your guts from somewhere an' come on."

"I've been drivin'— —" His voice broke, the anger gone.

"Now it's me who's drivin'. I got to get you lot through the night alive, so you got to 'elp."

Luff stood sagging. Pike put his arm round his shoulders and pulled him forward so that his feet had to shift. It was like walking a drunk, but as they went up the slope they got a rhythm to it, and when Pike took his arm away Luff came on with him, his breath grunting in and out to

the jog of his feet. They came to the wood. Leaves were
rustling where Munro was working. Soaper came out of
the trees farther along, dragging a bundle.

They worked for half an hour more, Pike staying with
the tank and making adjustments to his scheme of camouflage. He had raised three bushy saplings on top of the
tank, bracing their stumps with wire; the rest of the foliage was arranged as a base for them. Where a bush had
been growing upright, he stacked it upright; where a
branch had grown parallel with the ground, he fixed it in
that same way, so that Top Dog, before midnight, looked
like a clump of trees and bush, and not like an unlit
bonfire.

Weston, making his last trip down the hill with Luff,
stopped for a moment to look at the transformation. He
had not seen the tank, from this distance, since they had
started work; he had been too tired and too burdened.

"My God!" he said.

Luff stopped, head down, propping himself against his
bundle of leaves. "What?" he said.

"Well, jus' look. We're bloody good, you know. Who'd
ever think that was a tank down there?"

Luff felt himself falling, stopped himself, and moved
forward. He had not lifted his head to look at the tank; it
was too heavy. He dragged his bundle as if it were part of
his body, a broken limb that had to be drawn along.

Weston followed him, looking at the clump of saplings
and bush. In this light it was perfect. Any Jerry patrol
could walk right into that knoll of leaves and not know
what it was until they cracked their heads on the gun.

"You're good," he told Pike when he reached him. "I
hand it to you, boy."

Pike was wiping his face. A long bright graze was on
his arm, where a sharp end of wire had ripped the skin.
His voice was borne on one long breath, and he had to
take another to finish. "Soaper's got the billy on in the
trench. Don't waste water, we're short."

Weston stood back a few paces. "You're good, Alf.
Proper artist, you are."

They listened to small-arms fire, closer than a mile

away. The spotter plane droned, bee-like, under the stars.

Munro came round the leaves. "Tea's up, mates."

Pike said: "Where's Luffy?"

"I dunno."

They looked for him. He was lying on the grass, under the bower of leaves where the gun poked, supporting its camouflage. He was lying on his face where he had dropped.

Munro said: "I thought 'e was dyin' for a cup o' tea?"

Pike sat down, leaning against one of the boxes he had used to stand on. "He's doin' 'imself more good where 'e is." He folded his arms. There was satisfaction in him, because they had all worked hard and the job was done, and it was a good one; and this sense of achievement lulled his mind, so that he knew now how tired he was. The enemy was in here with him, despite all the camouflage: the need for sleep.

"Alf."

"Yeh?"

Weston crouched beside him. "We don't want a guard with this lot coverin' us. We can all get a kip."

"There's got to be a guard. We're goin' to take some wakin', once we're out."

"I'll do first shift, then."

"Now don't bloody argue. Go an' get your char. I'll 'ave you on guard soon enough, my son, so now's your chance."

Weston left him. He found Soaper in the trench, a mug in his hands. Soaper said: "Did you hear that gunfire?"

"Yes."

"Patrols. Nearer."

"Stuff 'em. Where's my char?"

The trench was warm with the heat of the Tommy stove; its fumes made his head reel. He spilt some tea over his hand and the pain roused him. The mug was jerked by the movement and more tea spilled, slopping on to the chalk.

"Can't you stop fidgeting, George?"

He waited until the first of the pain had gone; then, in the dark, he raised the mug to his mouth, tilting it by slow degrees until his head touched the earth wall, his lips expectant for the hot liquid, his hands ready to bring the mug down if it burned them. He went on tilting the mug, his breath hollow in it; and at last a drop ran against his lips, a single drop. The rest had been spilled. He lowered the empty mug and sat with his head against the earth, his body beginning to shake with the slow laughter that was rising in him. He listened to the sound of it, detached from it.

"What's funny?" Soaper's voice.

He went on laughing. There was little enough breath for it, but he couldn't stop. As it went on, its sound seemed to go farther away from him, and there was Soaper's voice again, far away too, and then the rattle of the mug as it fell from his hand; but it did not wake him.

Munro, feeling his way among the leaves, came to a patch of sky and saw Pike above him, perched on the turret. Softly he called: "Alf."

Softly: " 'Allo?"

"Here's your tea." He reached up with the mug.

"You're a china, you are."

When Munro had gone, the corporal sat watching the east horizon, drinking his tea slowly. The smell of the sap was in the air, rising from the hacked stems of the wood. He waited, alone, for the moon to come.

II

THE MOON CAME UP RED, through haze, beyond the villages where days ago the fighting had been hard. The battle dust, laid by the rain, was dry now and stirred by transports passing between the front line and rear positions. To the corporal who watched, it seemed natural that the moon was stained, like everything else, with the colour of war.

He had been thinking a lot about Sophie, remembering the last times they had had together before the war. She was very near to him now; perhaps nearer than she had ever been. A wicked little thing, Sophie, not much thicker than a whippet, born to the East End and thriving in its flinty element, dealing in its life with her own coin, and never in debt to the day. She was a clippie now, on the Aldgate run. She'd started the job since his last leave, and although he had never seen her there, he always thought of her now, swaying along at the back of her bus, clipping the tickets out. He liked to picture her that way. He had a dream about it, too. When this lot was finished, he'd be demobbed, and of course he'd have to let her know he was all right; but he wouldn't tell her when he was coming home. He'd be in his new demob suit, waiting at the bus-stop, and he'd jump on board and say: "Pitchford Road!" Then he'd watch her face. What would she do? It'd be a scene, all right. There'd be a few people on that route who'd get a free ride that day, and that was a fact. "Pitchford Road!" he'd say. He had said it many times in the last few months, but it still gave him a kick. He knew it was silly to keep on thinking about it; but no one else knew, and he could think what he liked.

The moon grew bright, losing its stain as it rose to clear atmosphere. Its light was sharp on the ground; it shone against the leaves here and washed over the grass. There was a stillness in just the sight of it, a distillation of its remoteness in the sky. In its milky glow the wink of gunfire on the dark earth was feeble and red-eyed.

The corporal no longer felt tired. His wits were far from alert, but the fatigue had lifted, soothed away by the knowledge that his tank was in good harbour and the crew sleeping. He even wondered if he had worked them too hard and to no purpose, for there was no sound of the enemy, apart from the clash of patrols now and then, and the sometime drone of the plane. He'd look a real clot in the morning, with Top Dog done up like a Christmas tree and no Jerry to come and look at it.

Leaves moved below him. He looked down. For a moment he resented the invasion of his solitude.

"Alf?"

"Up 'ere."

It was Luff. His face was pink in the moonlight, above the stubble of his chin. When he pulled himself up beside Pike, he sat for a moment with his hands together between his knees.

"I gave you a lot o' trouble, Alf."

"Eh?"

"Only I was that tired I thought I was goin' to flake right out, see."

Pike grunted. "I was tryin' to make you. It would've been all right if you'd only 'ad the grace to fall flat on your dial. You got no sense, you 'aven't. You don' know when to give in."

After a minute Luff said: "I think I did pretty bad."

"You did bloody miracles, so you can shut up about it. Look at that there moon, big as 'alf-crown, ain' it?"

"See any sign of them bastards, have you?"

"No. I told you, we're goin' to 'ave a peaceful night. What you doin' up 'ere?"

"Relievin' guard."

"I don't want no relievin'."

"You been up 'ere a good two hours, y' know."

Pike turned Luff's wrist and looked at his watch.

"So I 'ave. Where's the other blokes?"

"Both under the gun, spark-o."

Pike said: "Both? Who?"

"Gutsy an' George."

"Where's Soaper?"

"I don't think 'e's here."

"What you mean?"

"He's not in the trench, or anywhere."

"You bin lookin' for 'im?"

"I had a wander round."

The corporal watched the moon for a long time, and said: " 'E's 'ere somewhere, don't you worry."

Luff said: "That was a good drop o' tea he made. I'm goin' to brew-up again, that okay?"

Pike was thinking. He turned his head. "Eh? Yeh. Keep it quiet, though." As Luff began climbing down through the leaves, Pike said: "Why the 'ell can't you sleep, then?"

"Well, Christ, you can talk!"

He dropped to the grass, and took a step, and heard the engine. He stopped, listening. It was a tank engine. The low murmur of it rose and died on the wind, but each time it rose it had loudened.

"Alf."

"Don' worry. I'll watch it."

Luff moved again, going round to the mass of leaves over the trench and dropping into it. He could not hear the sound of the engine now, but with the Tommy-lighter in his hand he hesitated, and straightened up, so that his head was level with the top of the trench. The engine was still running. In the rhythm of it there were throttle variations, so that he knew it was a tank on the move. He put his lighter away and came out of the trench, crawling through the leaves until he could stand upright. The moving tank reminded him of a tractor in the next field at harvest-time in England.

"Alf."

"What now?"

"It's on the march."

"I know."

Luff climbed to join him on the turret. "See anything?"

"Not yet. I thought you was goin' to 'ave a brew-up?"

Luff could see a patch of moonlit grass through a gap in the leaves. He set himself to watch it. Unless he stood up, it was the only part of the ground he could see. "I didn't like showin' a light," he said.

"Down the trench? Safe as 'ouses, boy."

The big engine throbbed. He could no longer think of it as a tractor in a sunny field in England. The tank was moving through scrub at the top of the hill, its tracks breaking light timber that snapped, brittle-boned.

"Alf, what nationality's that bloody thing?"

"It's comin' from the west, ain't it?"

"But it could be one of ours. Lost, or something."

"Yeh. Or it might be a bus from Balham."

Timber crackled again, and Pike thought he saw the tops of saplings move at the edge of the wood; but it might be the wind or his nerves. Through the gap in the leaves he could see the hill brow, running from the wood to his left and out of sight. The tank would not come through the wood, because the grass was firm enough going. It would come over the horizon, over the brow there. He said:

"Go an' wake the boys."

Luff went down. Even in this dangerous moment he was aware of beauty as he loped forward, crouched, into the space under the camouflage where Munro and Weston were sleeping. The netting, festooned from the gun-barrel, was interwoven with the stems of brushwood and new leaves, forming an arbour in which a man could stand nearly upright. The leaves were thick, but there were gaps where the moon shone silver, dappling the grass. The two men were stretched out on a rucked tarpaulin.

"George." He pulled at his shoulder. "George."

Weston moved one leg, rolling over in his sleep. Luff got him by the wrists and heaved, so that he was jerked into a sitting position with his head lolling. He began mumbling.

"George." Luff dragged on him and he started to shout, reeling about with his legs jerking. "Quiet, George!" He had managed to get him upright, but his head still lolled and his eyes were still shut. He was asleep on his feet. Luff brought a hand across his face, trying not to make the slap too loud. Weston hit back at him, but he grabbed his wrist. "Listen, George. Jerry's here. Wake up."

Munro groaned, kicked into near consciousness as the other two swayed above him. "Gutsy," said Luff, "get up quick!"

"She's a bitch," Munro said, clearly and bitterly. "I tell you she's a bitch." He had rolled over and his face was against the tarpaulin. Weston said:

"What in Christ?" He leaned on Luff, arms slack. Luff gave him a light punch in the chest.

"Jerry's here. Jerry. German."

"Where?" He swung about, one arm flying. His hand hit the gun and he yelped.

"Bitch!" Munro said. Luff was sweating. He left Weston sucking his hand, bent down, lifted Munro by the belt and dropped him. The breath came out of him with a grunt and he got to his hands and knees, head down, coughing.

"Gutsy. The Germans are here." He went on coughing.

Weston said clearly: "Where, then? Where?"

"Listen. That's a tank. Panzer."

"Where's Alf?"

"Up top. Gutsy—*get up!*"

He stooped again, put his arms round Munro's waist, and heaved. Munro swung a fist. "Sod off!"

"Jerry's here. Jerry."

The leaves rustled as Corporal Pike came down, crouching into the arbour. Munro was up now, swaying, holding his face. They were all on their feet and awake.

Pike said: "George, up at the gun. Luffy, forward Besa." Munro swayed towards him.

"Where's Jerry?"

"Comin'. Get up there, quick. An' keep it quiet."

For a few seconds no one moved. Pike and Luff were listening, wanting to know if the tank were nearer. Weston wanted to get his bearings on its sound. Munro, for the first time, heard it. Then they all moved.

The throb of the engine was heavier by the time they were inside Top Dog, but there was no crackle of timber and there was nothing in sight as Pike stood on the top armour with the moon behind him. He called down: "Gutsy, we got smoke-bombs?"

He heard Munro shifting about in the darkness below. His eyes were watering as he stared at the thin line of the hill brow. He wanted badly to see the tank. Once he could see it he'd be all right. The noise alone was a mounting strain. He said quietly aloud: "Come on. Let's 'ave you, then. Come on, for Chris' sake." The throbbing loudened.

"I got 'em," Munro said.

"What?"

"Smoke."

"Right."

The throb was part of the night, a sound in the ears, in the imagination. There had never been a time when this sound was not here; and it would never go. "Come on, you bastard."

"Alf, can you see it?"

"No."

"Where the 'ell's it got to, then?"

"Shuddup."

The throb was so loud now that Pike cursed it and moved round on the armour-plate, pulling at the leaves and making new gaps. Through one of them he saw the tank come over the brow, well to the left. He was startled by its dark shape. In the same moment the throb died away to a murmur as the engine idled. He said, "It's a self-propelled gun."

Munro came up beside him.

"Stopped, has 'e?"

"Havin' a look this side of the hill." He could see moonlight flashing across a pair of field-glasses and the shape of the commander, a dark stump above the gun.

He spoke a little more loudly so that Luff could also hear. "Listen. 'E's two 'undred yards, ten o'clock. We can't move, an' we can't swing the turret."

"How can we fire, then, for God's sake?"

"We can't, that's what I'm tellin' you. Not till we can move, an' that'll be when they've seen us. We jus' got to sit 'ere, see? An' if anyone drops anything on metal, or 'its anythin' metal, they'll 'ear, an' we're goners. Don't forget that."

He straightened up slowly, turning his body to face the ten o'clock direction before he stood upright. The self-propelled gun had not moved. Munro murmured: "He's takin' a bloody good look."

"Don't make a noise. We're a Christmas tree."

Beyond the S.P. gun the sky flickered to a distant barrage, silhouetting it. Pike was quivering with frustration. If Top Dog were standing head-on to that Jerry, they could have blown it part with one six-pounder before he knew they were here. He was a perfect target, high on the hill, silhouetted against the light sky, motionless. But they could not move the turret. They were a Christmas tree.

Munro said: "It's very annoyin', isn't it?"

"An' the rest."

"If they cotton on to us, Alf, we've 'ad it."

"That's right."

"Better if we swung the gun on 'em before they can do anythin'."

"Don't be daft. Once we move, they shoot, an' that's an eighty-eight. We got to keep our 'air on."

Munro touched his arm as the S.P. began to move. It lumbered down from the brow of the hill, and stopped again. Now there was silence.

"He's switched off, Alf."

"Yeh."

They could hear the voice of the commander speaking into his wireless. Pike crouched, and put his head over the dark hole of the turret, speaking in a forced whisper. "George, he's got 'is engine off. We got to keep dead quiet. Tell Luffy."

"What's he doing?"

"I dunno. Tell Luffy."

Munro said: "The commander's got out. Havin' a walk round." Another man dropped. "An' there's the gunner or the wireless-op."

"Driver to come."

The German crew were out. There were four. They were lighting cigarettes. The commander was lifting his field-glasses again, looking this way, straight at Top Dog. Very quietly Munro said into Pike's ear: "If we could get 'em while they're all out . . ."

"It's no go, boy."

They did not move. Their faces must not catch the moonlight. The commander was studying them. The moonlight was on his glasses, glinting. He held them steadily. Pike began to sweat.

On his breath Munro said: "Je-sus. . . . "

One of the Germans laughed, walking a few paces on the soft grass, enjoying himself; his cigarette-end traced a winking pattern as it moved about. The commander had not lowered his glasses. They were trained on Top Dog. There was something he didn't like about this isolated clump of brush. Pike wondered vaguely what it could be: a bit of shine on the left track where the metal had polished on a stone, or a badly-placed bush, or his own face among the leaves. It was no good moving now. He listened to Munro's breathing.

The German laughed again, and then walked towards his commander, who turned, as if answering a question. The two of them stood facing this way across the slope, and the commander gave the other man his field-glasses and he raised them, and Pike waited again, Munro waited again. Munro was thinking that if those men suspected anything they'd go back into their S.P. and swing a shot across, to see what happened. And Top Dog would brew-up, first go, because its soft flank was exposed on the left forward quarter. Pike was thinking that if those men suspected anything Top Dog would have a fight on.

Below them a sound came, Weston or Luff moving about. Pike couldn't even turn his head. Facing the men with the field-glasses he spoke, using the left corner of his mouth.

"They're watching us. They're watching us."

The commander took his field-glasses back and raised them again. Under his breath, Munro said something to him in rich English. There was a feeling of shame in him, to have to stand here under that steady surveillance, like a chorus girl having to strip off and show her legs to get a new job.

Pike said in his throat: "Gutsy, there's goin' to be some action, mate."

"I'm ready."

"Goo' boy."

When the German commander lowered his glasses he

started to walk in this direction, the other man with him. They did not hurry. They had just decided to come and have a look.

Now that the field-glasses were down, Pike could move. He pulled Munro down with him. *"Inside, quick."*

Munro went first, sweating with the effort of moving with no noise in the dark confines. Pike felt for his Bren gun and brought it up slowly inside the turret-rim, clearing it with the barrel. He was whispering.

"Stand by on the coaxial. George, stand by on the gun."

He raised himself on his platform, finding a gap in the leaves. Using it as a sight, he moved his head until he could see the two Germans. They were walking steadily towards Top Dog. He could hear them talking. He ducked again, whispering.

"Stand by. They're comin'."

He straightened himself again, and had trouble remembering which gap in the leaves he had been looking through. It took him half a minute to find it, and the sweat was running from under his arms and his scalp pricked. They were half-way between here and their gun, still walking steadily. He got the Bren comfortable, steadied it, and sighted. Its metal was sticky in his hands. Its smell was under his nose, cold and exciting. Using the corner of his mouth he whispered:

"Any minute now. You got to be ready."

The Bren was heavy. His arms ached. He heard Munro's whisper from the dark below.

"We're ready, Corp."

He was calmer, at once. They were ready. He wasn't alone. But the sweat was a hazard, itching on him and sticking his hands on the gun. His left eye, closed for sighting, watered. The heat from his body touched his face. His scalp was a cap of needles. They were still walking. Then they stopped and the commander put his glasses up. The range was less than a hundred yards. Through the gap he could see the tops of their bodies and their heads.

The commander jerked the field-glasses down and hit the other man's arm and they turned to run back.

Pike fired.

"*Christ!*" The noise had shocked Munro, below.

Pike fired a second burst, moving the Bren in a close circle. The leaves ripped and fluttered down. The men were on the ground, one of them rolling.

"*Gunner traverse left!*"

The turret swung with it and the camouflage broke up as the gun came round, shedding the stacked bushes and tearing the leaves aside, exposing him. He crouched, his eyes an inch above the rim. The two Germans lay where they had dropped. Then Pike heard the S.P.'s engine start up.

"*Steady. . . .*"

The turret slowed.

"*On!*"

He waited for his gunner to find the target. The turret shifted another degree. He heard Weston's shout: "*On!*"

"*Fire!*"

The self-propelled gun was moving, turning quickly to face its enemy. The recoil of Top Dog's six-pounder shook more of the camouflage away. The shell hit low and ploughed into the earth so that for a moment the German was hidden by the dark flying wave of it. Munro, loading for his gunner, slammed another shell home. Pike called to Weston. Weston fired.

The first shell from the German eighty-eight cracked across Top Dog's back with the percussion of a thunder-clap and sent Pike dropping for cover. He heard the big shell burst somewhere in the wood.

Weston was shouting.

"*It's a smacker!*"

Pike took a look. Weston's shell had caught the S.P. square below the barrel at two hundred yards' range, buckling plate and leaving an eddy of smoke. He heard Munro putting another shell in.

"Hold it now!"

Luff was shouting, saying they'd got the bastard, they'd got the bastard. His voice was pitched thin and jubilant

above the engine. Pike waited. It looked like a knock-out.
The smoke cleared slowly. There was no sign of fire.
Weston said: "Finish him, Alf?"

"No." No sign of life, either. "Not yet." There were
only three shells left, and it was far from morning yet. "I
think 'e's finished already, boy."

Weston caressed the hot breech, itching to send another one. Pike breathed in the fumes that were rising,
relishing them. He said: "Keep on the target." He raised
himself a few more inches, using his field-glasses. The
S.P. looked derelict. He lowered the glasses. A popple of
flame ripped in the moonlight and he dropped, grazing his
arm as the machine-gun bullets fluted across the turret.
He squeezed his arm, sick with the agony. When he could
speak he said: "All right, Weston. *Fire.*"

The ears blocked. The fumes rose. The breech came
back. The shell-case hit the scoop and dropped. Munro
said:

"Alf, you hit?"

"No. Funny-bone." He pressed his feet down, sliding
his shoulders against the rim to raise himself. It was the
second direct hit. Luff shouted:

"It's a brew-up!"

Flame was fanning out of the S.P. Pike tried to use his
arm, failed, and forced himself out of the turret with his
other arm and both feet, dropping among the shambles of
the camouflage and landing soft. "Come on!"

They came after him. He ran across the grass, stopping
to look at the two Germans. They were riddled from neck
to rump. He went on, towards the S.P. It was well on fire.
Weston ran by his side. They could hear a voice, ahead
of them. Munro caught them up. The flames pinked their
faces. They heard the voice again. It was a scream now.
Suddenly Weston dropped back. Luff was coming up with
the Bren. Weston turned away from him and let him go
past, and when he had gone, dropped on to the grass and
cupped his ears with his hands as he heard the scream
again. He made a noise, inarticulate and tuneless, to
drown the other noise.

Pike stopped, as near to the burning S.P. as he could

get. There was no way in. The hatch was a chimney, furnace-red above its rim. Munro began going forward and Pike moved and grabbed him. When the scream came again, Luff cried out obscenities and brought the Bren up, firing through the torn gap in the plates, giving it a long steady burst, cutting the scream off.

Munro turned away, wiping an arm across his chin where sweat had gathered. His shadow danced on the grass in the flame-light. Luff was walking like a drunk, dangling the Bren. When they reached Weston he was vomiting; they passed him and Munro broke into a shambling trot, reaching the tank and climbing into the turret. When the others came up he was dropping out again, with a packet of cigarettes. They took them and lit them, and stood watching the S.P.

The petrol went up first, and then the ammunition. Their cigarettes were finished before the flames settled down to a flicker. The rose light died away across the grass, and the chill of the moon came back.

None of them felt triumphant. It was a big gun, an eighty-eight with a crew of four. Top Dog had knocked it out, and not even able to move her tracks. That was very good; but they did not feel triumphant. There were two men on the grass, and two human clinkers in the burnt-out shell. That was the way things had gone, and there was nothing else to think about it. In a little while Pike said quietly:

"George."

"M'm?"

"We've got two rounds left, eh?"

"Two, yes."

"We got a bit of ammo for the Besas, and grenades." He watched a scatter of sparks fall away from the S.P. When they had settled, he said: "That commander was callin' up his base, or some unit on the other side of the hill. 'E was tellin' them the ground looked clear, this side. Remember, 'e brought the gun down the hill a bit, to get it off the skyline, an' then switched off. 'E was waitin', see, an' while 'e was waitin' 'e thought 'e'd 'ave a dekko at our Christmas decorations. They didn't 'urry, remember. So that's 'ow it is."

Weston lit another cigarette. "You mean there's going to be more of 'em coming."

"Yeh. Infantry, p'r'aps, or tanks. We can't see our lot, from 'ere. We know there's a Jerry gun or two, west of us. It's natural for 'im to bring up support, as there's no opposition."

Munro gave a flat short laugh, looking at the red-hot shell of the S.P. "No opposition, isn't there?"

"Apart from us," Pike said.

Luff took a turn on the grass, cooling his feet. "So we're goin' to stick it out here, an' wait for 'em? That what you mean, Alf?"

"Yes."

He waited, not looking at any of them. Ash shifted in the wreck, and sparks went up. The soft wind took the smoke away, curling along the grass. After an age, Weston said:

"It's your orders, mate."

"I didn't want to make it an order. I want you to see for yourselves that it's what we got to do."

Again there was silence, until Luff said: "There's only two rounds for the gun, Corp. At best, we could only knock out two tanks."

Pike said: "That'd make three for the night. Wouldn't be s' dusty, would it?"

"That's at best," Luff said. "At worst, we wouldn't do any more than we've done already."

Munro said: "Let's cut our losses an' go."

Corporal Pike did not allow himself to be hurried in his argument. He meant to stay here, and use his tank till it foundered. He wanted these men with him, but not without their own faith in the rightness of it. He said:

"This is a crisis. We 'aven't got a tank that'll move. It's a case for balin' out. No one'd blame us if we left Top Dog 'ere an' took a chance on gettin' back to our lines on foot, before mornin'. So we needn't 'ave any conscience, see? But I'm tellin' you what I'm goin' to do, meself. I don't need a driver, nor a co-driver, because the engine's duff. I don't need a wireless op, because the wireless is duff too. That lets you out, Luffy, an' you, Gutsy. Soaper's took 'imself off already, an' good riddance. An' I don't need a gunner, because it's easy enough to work single-'anded, an' there's only two rounds left, any'ow."

"If we don't——"

"I 'aven't finished, quite. This is the bit that counts. I'm orderin' you three to bale out, an' try an' reach our lines as best you can. Now that's an order, but if you've got any objections, I'll listen."

He took a cigarette from Weston and lit up. Luff said angrily: "For Chris' sake, why don't you use your authority an' tell us to stay on? We can't disobey orders, can we?"

Pike said nothing. He cupped the cigarette, from habit, concealing its glow, though it was lost in the moonlight and a thousand times less bright than the embers of the S.P.'s wreckage.

"I've got to get some kip," Munro said, "before I fall over. You can't send me out in enemy territory on foot. It'd be bloody murder."

A ripple of ack-ack came from the sky. There was the drone of planes up somewhere. It was a remote and strangely peaceful sound.

Weston said: "I don't fancy walking into a bunch of those bastards and spendin' the rest of the war behind barbed wire."

Pike said reasonably: "It wouldn't be for long, mate. 'Itler's got 'is back to the wall, we know that."

"Well, I don't like your order, just the same. I think it stinks."

The anti-aircraft battery opened up again. There was a strong bomber force crossing the north horizon, and searchlights were up. Corporal Pike watched them as their beams moved over the sky, the long bright fingers fanning and touching, feeling the stars. Luff said, with less anger:

"I'm too dead-beat to think any more. All I want is some sleep. If I stay here, Alf, it doesn't mean I'd be much good to you."

"If you stay 'ere," said the corporal, "you'll 'ave to

work till you drop, an' maybe fight till you're dead, so don't make any mistake about that."

Luff sat down with his back to the tank.

"I want to stay."

"Oh? Why?"

"Because there's the gun an' two Besas. That's work for three men. An' the fourth can look after the smoke an' grenades. We're all in it."

The corporal said: "Munro?"

"Yes, mate."

"Weston?"

"Yes, Corp."

He dropped his fag and stubbed it out.

"Then God 'elp you."

III

PIKE had worked alone for an hour replacing the ragged camouflage. If he had lain down, he would not have slept; so he had worked. The gun was still traversed left, so that the shape under the massed leaves was a little different; but it still looked more like a crop of bush than a fighting tank.

Once he had sat down, and had said to himself: 'Alf, your number's comin' up, tonight. You're goin' to die.' But he had no deep feelings about this. Once a man was this deep in his war, his sense of drama was blunted. If this was one of his last few hours of life, there was nothing to be done about it. But he hoped that Top Dog would do well tonight. Then he could die happy.

He had thought, too, about Sophie. She was a long way off and now he seemed out of touch with her, and could not see her face so clearly or hear her voice. He had to stop thinking of her, because she was no part of this. The first she'd see of him again would be on the tailboard of the bus. "Pitchford Road!" he'd say. It could still happen. But it didn't do to think any more about that little dream. It was getting thin, wearing out. He tucked it away like a dog-eared snap-shot, and got up from the grass and climbed aboard Top Dog.

Switching on the tiny lamp he checked the instruments; then as he turned in the confined space his hand touched the concertina, one finger brushing along the bellows. He could remember the Angel, at the corner of Pitchford Road. He could almost taste the beer.

"Alf!"

He looked up. "What?"

"There's a lot of stuff movin'." Munro dropped into the turret. "Tanks, by the sound of it."

"All right, mate. The others still asleep, are they?"

He had the sudden thought that Munro's number was coming up tonight, too. And Luff's, and Weston's. Did they know, or weren't they letting themselves think about it?

"Yes," Munro said. "I'll go an' get 'em up."

Pike thought: He knows. It's in his voice.

Munro left him. Now he could hear the sound, from over the hill. It was trapped inside the turret. It was tanks, all right.

When Luff came, the corporal told him: "On the forward Besa, mate."

"Okay."

"Did you get any kip?"

"Eh? No." He went down forward. So he knew, too.

Weston came down with Munro. Pike said to them: "George, you're on the gun. Gutsy, unbolt that smoke-mortar and get it outside. It'll give me a bit o' room in the turret."

Munro got a spanner. "When shall I get the smoke out, then?"

"Soon as I give you the tip. You know where the wind is. But for Chris' sake don't let 'em off too early. We want them bastards to come in close." He slapped the breech of the gun. "Two knock-outs is top score. We ring the bell, we get the cigar."

Weston said: "We'll get the bloody cigar, all right." For the first time he had no confidence in his gun. He could kill a couple of tanks with it if they came close enough and he could see their weak spots; but there'd be more than two. There was a whole pack on the way. The third to go up would be Top Dog and the crew with it.

Soaper had got sense. He envied him. He despised himself for letting Pike talk him into this. They were going to die, the lot of them. How had it happened? What was he doing in here, trapped? His stomach was going sour on him as he listened to Pike's easy voice.

"Over you go, Gutsy."

Munro's boot scraped on the metal rung. He went over the turret rim with the two-inch mortar. Pike dropped a bag of smoke-shells after him. The noise of the tanks was rising. They would be nearer than they sounded, because the wind was towards the hill-brow, from the east. Munro stood outside the leaves, his body facing the direction in which he must send the smoke, his head turned to listen for the tanks and for Pike's order. He felt vulnerable, standing here in the open; on the other hand, he would not want to be inside the tank if it were hit. He could still remember the noise the German had made while he was being burned alive. Any man would make that noise— Pike, or the other two—if he was inside a burning tank and couldn't get out. He was glad to be here, vulnerable and unprotected, but not in a trap.

He listened to the tanks and his own breath. His breath was going in and out and making a noise like a man under an oxygen mask. He remembered the field hospital he had seen, three days ago, when he had taken some-one's belongings to him. The breath had gone in and out with a forced rhythmic desperation that was unnerving to hear. Now he was breathing in the same way. His body sensed it was in great danger, and was reaching out for more oxygen for its blood; and the heart was pumping faster, gearing the system to the pitch of readiness that was necessary if its life was to go on. He felt detached from his body; it was a separate animal with its own plans for survival, preparing its defences—the ears, hearing the danger coming, alerted the brain, and emotion was touched off, so that the fear should race the heart and fill the lungs and tune the senses finely. But the sum-total was a creature known as Lance-Corporal Munro, and he was the one who had to put out the smoke-screen. If he did it right, there might be a better chance for all of them. If he made a mistake, it might kill one of them or all of them. The best thing to do, before his knees gave way, was to concentrate on that.

He had never thought he was a coward. It was just this waiting.

The sound grew enormous, filling the night. There was half a squadron coming. He wanted to shin up to the turret and tell the corporal it wasn't going to be possible to do anything but die here, with so many of them com-ing. He was aware, as the noise rose, that he was saying the corporal's name, "Alf." Every few seconds, saying it aloud. "Alf." To try to tell him it was no good, there were too many. But he knew Alf couldn't hear. That was all that mattered, that no one heard. "*Alf.*" The name became a mere repetitive utterance, losing its connection with Corporal Pike. It had to be said, aloud, against the sound of the Panzers coming. It meant, sometimes, 'Christ', and sometimes 'Mother.'

The wind brushed his face, the sweetness of the rain still in it, and the smell of corn. It was a good wind for smoke; it would carry it well, perhaps save them all.

Someone inside Top Dog gave a shout.

The corporal answered. "You all know what to do." He stood in the turret, watching the moonlit grass through a hole in the leaves. The Bren gun was in his hands, its barrel resting on the turret rim. His stomach was filling with a slow delight. They would come, and pass the crop of bush and saplings, and then hear Top Dog's gun, and feel its shell. It would be a big shock for them, as good as the water-bucket on top of the school-room door, as funny as the snatched-away chair. Out of a bit of old bush, a six-pounder shell whistling at point-blank range. Number three tank, Two Troop, falling by magic into the middle of a Panzer squadron, invisible, a secret in the moonlight, a monster out of a fable. The delight warmed him. He was beyond the thought of death now. He had paid for this beautiful ice-cream and it was his.

He shouted again.

"We're goin' to knock 'em in the Ole Kent Road!"

Below him Weston sat with his gun. Alf had gone mad. Only a madman could have that joy in his voice at a time like this. He envied him the madness, as he had envied Soaper's sense. He should have run away or gone mad. To have to sit here, knowing what was going to happen, was a drawn-out torture that brought the sweat on him until he was limp; but his hand was braced on the gun lever, a tense, stiff-boned claw with the rigidity of death already in it. The worst fear in him was that he wouldn't be able to move it when the order came to fire.

Forward, away from the others, Luff sat at the Besa machine-gun. His thoughts were technical. In the moonlight it would be possible to make out the driver's slit if a tank came within fifty yards. A commander's head would be an easy target. If a man left his tank, he would die on his feet like the poor bastard Pope had shot.

What was the corporal shouting? It didn't sound like an order. The driving compartment was drumming with the sound of the tanks, exciting him. Impatience ran alive through his nerves. He had four 7.92 belts ready, and one in the gun. On the driving-seat, beside him, was his revolver. If Top Dog started to burn and he couldn't get out, the revolver would save him from the unthinkable.

Very faintly a voice rose through the din of the tanks. *"Here they come."*

It would be Alf's voice. He looked along the sights of the Besa, his impatience at explosion-point.

Pike had seen the first three tanks cross the line of the hill in arrow-head formation and at a fast pace. They would have heard the exchange of shots between Top Dog and the self-propelled gun, and would have seen the light of its fire. That they came at all, after this warning, was a sign of their numbers. Three more came over the skyline, clearing it at full throttle and spreading out over the slope, no longer silhouetted.

The leaders were Mark Fives, carrying long seventy-five-m.m. tank-killing guns. They were already below Top Dog, running on past the ambush without giving it attention. The second wave was nearer, with the flank man a few score yards' distant, but again there was no sign that the ambush was suspected. The leading tank of the second wave was opened up, its commander visible above the turret rim, swaying easily to the motion of its passage across the ridges and mole-hills towards the base of the slope. He saw the ambush and looked away, deceived.

Corporal Pike was bewildered. The camouflage was too good. They were going past in a bunch, certain of their ground. The whole of the Wehrmacht could go past here and Top Dog would be missed.

The third wave rose on the hill brow and came over, running into the mud that the leaders' tracks had left, bruising the west turf and churning it up, streaking the moonlit slope with dark earth stripes. Half a squadron over, and more coming. Top Dog was watching a parade.

Pike became afraid that the whole unit would go past, with no time for engagement. He stood with the taint of exhaust gas in his nose; a drift of it was in the wind, gathering away more thickly towards the hill brow so that the rear tanks came driving into the light blue haze of it.

He bent down.

"George. The next wave. The nearest one."

Weston's face turned pale in the gloom. He nodded and moved his head down, sighting. Pike straightened, looked through the leaves, saw the next three top the hill, and crouched again.

"Swing 'er, George!"

Straightening again he rocked to the movement as Weston put the turret in traverse, swinging the six-pounder to fix on the nearest tank. Then he traversed back, keeping on his target while the range came down from a hundred yards to fifty as the enemy Mark Five swung heavily down the slope with its turret open and commander mounted. Its flank was fully exposed.

Pike hit Weston's shoulder.

"Fire!"

Weston delayed two seconds after the order to make certain he was aimed at the turret. Then he fired.

Pike had stood upright to watch. The German commander was turned in this direction, perhaps attracted by the movement of Top Dog's camouflage as the gun had traversed, disturbing it. The commander was raising his field-glasses. Then Pike could not see him because the shell hit the turret at the rim, obliterating the commander and bursting against the raised armoured hatch. It smothered the tank under a shock of light. Below Pike, Weston was reloading with his last shell, taking his time. The fumes rose from the breech. Leaves fell away in front of the corporal as the recoil displaced the camouflage. He watched, absorbed. The tank had stopped. The turret didn't swing. The commander was dead and the crew shocked, dazed, perhaps the gunner and wireless operator dead too from shell-splinters. The driver would be without orders.

Beyond the crippled tank, two others were turning to face the ambush and their turrets came round.

Pike leaned over and shouted to Munro.

"Smoke! Gutsy! Smoke!"

He saw Munro move, then dropped inside the turret, to find Weston sighting. " 'Old it! Wait!" He slammed the hatch down. Weston saw his sights blank out as the smoke came past, enveloping Top Dog and drifting towards the enemy. Into the air, Pike said: "Save that last one, mate. Save it."

Weston sat with his shoulders hunched, watching the moonlight go out as the smoke billowed and brought total night. It muffled the sound of the enemy's engines; they had the remoteness of a noise outside a closed window.

Top Dog had become isolated. She was as alone as a submarine moving through the dark of enemy waters, as imperilled as an underwater target that is known to be there, that must be searched out and killed.

A shell came with a whip-crack sharpness, flighting through the smoke and bursting low, its blast hitting the tank like the flat of a spade. Others came, and when they came, Weston bobbed his shoulders and sucked in another breath. It would be the next one . . . the next one . . . this one, now—*wheeep*—and beyond, not that one but the next . . . going into the breech now and the lever closing . . . the German voice and then the slam of the air shock—*this one*—oh, Christ, oh, Christ—*wheeep!*—and still alive . . . dear God, make it be the next one, I can't stand this—*make* it come! The smoke and the dark and the engines, Pike in here, blast his bloody eyes for keeping us here to die, a little Cockney bastard, a God-almighty corporal who thought he—*wheeep!*—oh, Christ, Christ, bring it, make it come—make it be the next one . . . the next one . . . this one, now . . .

He sat with his mouth open, his back to the dark that was the armour-plate, staring at the dark that was the floor, his body alive with the last-minute terror of the bird over the gun, the rabbit under the snake, his body a thin-skinned vessel of frail veins and singing nerves, the heart itself trapped in it and quivering for escape. He was spread-eagled for the kill. It wouldn't come.

Wheeep!

Pike was laughing, shouting something about Jerry and bad shots, and his gunner sat hating him for this. Pike had sentenced them all to death, and was laughing. Weston got a sound into his open mouth, but heard nothing but the ghastly cackle of Pike above him in the dark.

A machine-gun began rattling, and the bullets came picking at the dark with the sound of their soft flight suddenly nearing until the gun's aim crossed Top Dog and they struck, hammering on the iron. The enemy was locating his target. Now the turrets would swing, and the long barrels fix on the line that the little gun had drawn for them.

Pike shouted again: *"Traverse right!"*

Weston moved by habit, finding the lever with a blind man's certainty in his familiar room. The turret swung. Pike hit his shoulder. He had watched the tracer coming and took his aim from it. *"You're on. Fire!"*

Weston dragged his hand. Their heads exploded with the gun's sound. The recoil came. Pike eased past him and shouted:

Luff! Luff!"

There was a faint answer. He shouted again:

"Bale out! We're gettin' out!"

Weston tried to stand but crumpled, gashing his cheek on metal. Pike knocked into him, grabbing at his arm. *"Come on!"*

The fumes thickened, creeping from the breech and the spent case in the bag.

Luff came aft, calling something that was cut off by the crash of a shell that hit Top Dog in the left track. Weston began sobbing. Blood from his cheek gathered; a string of it drew across his mouth as Pike shook him and his head jerked. The hatch was open and Pike was above him, yelling for him to get out. Grey light was in the turret, seeping through thinning smoke. Pike dragged at his shoulders. He could smell the wind. His hands clawed at Pike. They went over the turret rim.

A shell hit Top Dog's flank and ripped the armour. The tank heaved on the springs. Pike, on the lee side, threw Weston against the leaves of the camouflage and climbed to the turret. The white of flame dazzled him and its heat struck his face. He could see Luff, a moving thing with one arm up. He reached him, blinded now by the flame and working in the red of blank shut eye-lids, feeling his way through nightmare, shouting to Luff. They were together when the third shell came. It burst in the heart of the fire.

The smoke to windward of Top Dog thickened. Munro had fired two more shells. He clawed his way back through the leaves, stupid with terror, and brought his hands up as the heat struck him across the face. Something tugged at his leg and he kicked out, trying to fling himself back through the leaves, but the hand still clung

to his ankle and he fell, and saw a face in the red light. It
was Weston's face, and he was shouting silently. Munro
caught at him and began dragging. His ankle was free and
Weston was crawling with him. The thin stems of the
camouflage broke and scraped at their faces and their
hands. They cleared them and Munro stood up and began
running. Weston dragged him down.

"Don't leave me!"

Munro staggered, frustrated by Weston as by a broken
limb that he must drag after him. The smoke filled their
lungs.

"Don't leave me!"

Half Weston's face was bright blood, shining in the
glare of the burning tank. Munro heaved on his arms,
enraged.

"Get up, then! Get up, sod you!"

Weston lurched to his feet, sobbing. Munro pulled him
through the smoke, his feet tripping on the rough ground.
They came to the source of the smoke, and went forward
beyond it into the clear moonlight. It was like finding
land from a wild sea.

Ammunition went up in Top Dog. The Besa belts had
caught.

"Oh, God! Oh, God!"

"Shuddup," Munro said. He was over his terror now
and ashamed of it. He stopped and looked back at the
drift of smoke. The blaze was in its midst. He said between heaving breaths: "Alf's gone. Alf an' Luffy." He
seemed to shout it at the red smoke-cloud. "They've
gone!"

Weston swayed on his feet. He said:

"Serves him right!" His voice was pitched to a childish
temper. "He asked for it!"

Munro grabbed him again. "Who?"

"Pike." Weston's head swung against his shoulder.
"Corporal bloody Pike!"

Munro hit him and he fell, crying out. Bullets rattled
inside the tank, and sparks flew up. Munro turned his
back on it and began walking to the wood. He could hear
Weston still crying out, the voice growing fainter behind

him. At last it was lost in the drum of engines as the Panzers rolled down the hill.

He reached the edge of the trees and fell forward among them, his feet bearing him along and sometimes pitching him against the stems, bruising him. When he sank down and lay with his face upon brambles, he opened his eyes and looked at the dying glow of the flames that coloured the smoke with rose.

He had blood in his mouth. There was no wound that he could feel in his body, but he could taste the salt. "Top Dog," he said. "Top Dog."

PEACE

I

WEST OF FALAISE, at the end of July, 'C' Squadron was withdrawn from the fighting. Units went forward, passing through the village where they rested; the war was leaving them behind. They were not sorry.

They rested for ten days. During this time the Tank Delivery Unit brought replacements with new crews, so that the Squadron was up to full strength again. The only Troop still intact was Four Troop. Dumbo, Daisy and The Rocket had missed every mine on the road from the coast to here, had dodged every shell, cleared every trap and driven untouched through battle and barrage, bringing their crews of fifteen men to this quiet village, safe. These men, therefore, had been more strained and more shocked than any other group in the Squadron; they had been the first to drop and drown in the peace of this calm backwater, sleeping for days, floating in Lethe, awakening slowly to the sunshine of warm mornings with their memory healing and their spirit salved.

Five miles away was a stream, and two trucks ran a daily shuttle service, taking the men to swim there and lie in the grass under willow shade while they listened to the stream running by, and to the soft stir of the leaves above their closed-eyed faces when a breeze came full of the meadows' scent and the wild-wood summer smells. In the village, whose name was Brisaille-les-Champs, French families still lived and went about their work, at first resentful of these new foreigners who had driven the others out, then accepting them, not as conquering liberators, but as passing guests. Pity had moved a few of the narrow village minds, bringing them to recognise that there was a world outside these fields where men fought bitterly, and that Brisaille, by virtue of its French soil, had been ordained an ally of these Englishmen when at the distant conference tables it had been decided which way the blood should run.

The young girls of Brisaille accepted the occasion with no complication in their thoughts. It was summer-time and the fields were lush, and there was no brutality in these Northern men who had thundered in here with their tanks, driving the blond ones out. It was summer and the fields were soft, and twilight lasted half the night among the woods where they walked with the men and lay with them, tumbling in brief love and exploring the strange world of a new language, laughing at mere sounds and teaching each other their names and how to pronounce them rightly, getting it wrong and laughing again or lying silent for a while, rehearsing the lies they must tell their parents and the priest when morning came.

The men rested, and swam, and played with the girls, some lying as silent as they for a while, with the letters from home in their pockets trying to break their hearts, the name of a loved wife on the thin paper, almost touching the thigh of the girl beside them, a foreign girl, a total stranger with her body intimately known, but the rest a mystery behind the language barrier and the lack of time to prove it. It would have to be enough for their conscience that they had come near death a dozen times to be here, and would go near death again and maybe meet with it. This might be the last time, the last woman; they must make the most of it.

A few of the men did not go with the girls, and theirs, in their own way, was the deepest pleasure, taken without any thoughts of smug nobility. They wanted a woman; women were here for them; and they refused, and felt the better for it. The bachelors were not among these few. The bachelors had nothing to lose and all to gain; they became competitors in lusty mischief and compiled score-boards and talked of trophies, their beds in the billets empty by night, and sleep heavy on them through the warm days, with nothing to rouse them but an occasional fatigue or a summoning to drill.

Mail arrived steadily, hardening their morale and

bringing them a breath of England and a glimpse of
home. The letters were disjoined and difficult to read in
their right order; but they were edited, and treasured, and
put away within easy reach to be read again, more
slowly. Grace Cox had written in one of her twenty-three
letters:

You remember you wrote to me, weeks before you
went? You knew you were leaving soon, and couldn't
tell me, so you put the letter behind the mirror in our
room, meaning to write from France and tell me where
to look for it. But I found it long before you went, and
had to pretend I hadn't, when you came home on your
last leave. It was very difficult for me, because it was a
wonderful letter, darling, and I so wanted to thank you
for it and say I understood everything you meant about
us, and our future, and what I must do if anything
happened to you over there. But nothing is going to
happen, so I don't have to think about it. And darling,
you don't have to worry about the window. I never go
near it when you're not there with me on leave. It was
only when you were there in the room, safe with me. I
stood at the window to watch the raids, and the war
going on outside, knowing that if it touched me it
would touch us both. It was a wonderful feeling, hearing you there, with your dear funny voice nagging at
me to come away while the bombs fell. I could have
picked them up and thrown them back into the sky. Is
that understandable, or haven't I said what I mean?
It's difficult, in a letter.

Sam Cox said to Watkins-Price, who was sitting beside
him on the grass: "Women are very peculiar."

Watty was filling a pipe that a French girl had given
him. He was growing fond of it, and of the girl. "In what
sort of way?"

"Oh, I dunno. There's always something going on underneath."

"It's their feet moving as they walk along."

"Don't be a clot. I mean they think thoughts, quite a

lot of deep thoughts, while all you think they're doing is washing up or watching an air-raid. They're——" he squinted at the blue sky, lost for the word. "What are they?"

"Oh, my God, that's really quite a question. Just leave it at 'peculiar'."

"But they're a lot of other things as well."

"A hell of a lot," said Watty. He lit his pipe. "How's Grace?"

"Oh, fine. How's your mother?"

"Running an emergency canteen in Stepney, for God's sake."

"What's wrong with that?"

"Nothing much; but as she happens to live in St. John's Wood, it means she's got to cross half London under the flying-bombs alone."

"From what I've heard of your mother, she'll cope all right."

"Oh, she'll cope."

"And, anyway, we shan't be long now. The war's winding up."

Watty said: "Is it?"

"Well, isn't it? We're back in France, this time with Russia and the Yanks on our side."

Watkins-Price shrugged. "Jerry's making a stand at Falaise. After we've beaten him there, we might see the war winding up. But he's going to be a fanatical bastard when he's really pushed."

Sam Cox said: "Who've you been talking to?"

"No one specially." He lit his pipe again. Sam Cox said nothing more about the war. Watty was deep, with a good education, and he might have a better picture in his mind of the war and the way it was going than a lot of the others. But the future didn't look bad. In comparison with the Army's position when it had been here last—at Dunkirk—the present campaign was all right, and Sam was satisfied.

He said in a moment or two: "They're fascinating."

"What are?"

"Women."

Major Knowles had set up his H.Q. in the cellar of a cottage. There was a hole in the wall for a window and a shell crater just outside. It looked, Knowles thought, a place more fitting to the business of a tank squadron's headquarters than one of the other houses, where families were trying to live as if in peace. He was under no obligation, here, to civilians. This was his den; it had been dug out for him by the enemy; he felt comfortable in it.

On one of these calm evenings, when the men were coming back from the stream, and playing cricket against a tree, and wandering through the woods in the name of love, Sergeant Verity came to the commander.

"There's one of our men back, sir."

Knowles was sitting alone, caught at the end of his day by the stealing in of twilight that filled the hole in his wall with a dreaming mauve. Verity's arrival, which was in his normal parade-ground style, gave the Major the impression that someone had hurled a rock in here through the hole in the wall.

"What?"

"There's one of our men back, sir." The dust settled round Verity's boots.

"Oh!" Knowles eased himself more upright in his chair. "Who?"

"Trooper Soaper, sir."

"Soaper." He ran the name through his memory. "He was in Top Dog."

"Number three, Two Troop, sir." The formal echoes died.

"Isn't that Top Dog?"

"Yes, sir."

Knowles looked at the hole in the wall. When they had overrun the ridge east of the Odon three weeks ago, he had inspected Top Dog himself. It was a burned-out shell, cold and dark among the grey ash of leaves and branches. There had been two bodies inside, identifiable by their fireproof tags as the commander and driver, Corporal Pike and Trooper Luff. There had been no sign of Lance-Corporal Munro, Trooper Soaper or Trooper Weston. The tank had obviously been fighting when it died. There were no makeshift graves on the hill-side, nor any other bodies except those of the German crews. The repulse by 'B' Squadron had turned the Panzers northwards along the river directly Top Dog's gun and the answering fire had been heard from the bridge-head, so that there had been no time for the enemy to bury his dead. Munro, Soaper and Weston were posted as missing, presumed prisoners. Now one of them was back.

"Where is he, Sergeant?"

"Outside, sir."

"Bring him in."

"Sir."

There were three lanterns in the cellar, and the Major lighted them carefully, and let down the black-out canvas against the hole in the wall. Before he had finished, Soaper and Sergeant Verity were standing at attention behind him, their shadows black on the bricks.

"All right, Sar'nt Verity."

"Sir." He booted the echoes awake, dismissing them and himself.

Major Knowles put out his hand to Soaper. "It's very good to see you back." This man had never been of much use to the Squadron, he remembered; but if he had fought in Top Dog on that hill, he was welcome here. "We thought you were behind the wire."

"I nearly was, sir, but I managed to dodge 'em." There was no grip in his hand-shake and he did not meet Knowles's eyes.

"Congratulations. Get that chair and sit down."

He studied Soaper as he pulled the chair over, and reserved his judgment on the man's bearing. "Now where have you been all this time?"

"Field hospital, sir. St. Marle. They said it was nerves, sir. Couldn't make me out. I suppose I'd had a bit too much of it."

"Ye-es. You've been sent straight from there, have you?"

"Yes, sir." He put some papers on the desk, half rising from the chair, awkwardly. Knowles moved the papers an inch, but did not look at them. He was looking at Soaper's face.

"You've written your report, Soaper?"

"It's there, sir, with the clearance."

"I shall be interested to read it tonight." He leaned back, shifting his head to let his eyes escape the glare of the nearest lamp. "Top Dog's become a legend, you know, in the Squadron. It was pretty clear she went down fighting. What happened?"

"We got lost in the rain, sir." He looked at the papers. "It's all in there, sir."

"Yes, I expect so." It would be a very careful report, he was sure. There was guilt all over this man; his voice was half stifled with it. "You got lost in the rain. What happened then?"

"Then the engine conked out, sir, with a stripped timing-gear." He glanced at the papers again. It was all in there. He didn't want to say it. It was all down in the report. The light of the lanterns hurt his eyes and he could not get them steady.

"That was on the hill, where the tank brewed-up?"

"Yes, sir." Sod you. "Yes, sir."

"And what about your wireless?"

"That was broke too, sir. So we put up camouflage an' stayed with the tank."

"Was that Corporal Pike's decision?"

"Yes, sir."

A crowd of men were going by, along the village street. Soaper looked at the canvas across the hole in the wall, wishing to be with them. Their voices faded. One of them laughed. He envied them all, and hated them.

"Then what happened?"

He looked back at the Major, whose round face was in shadow. "A Jerry S.P. gun came up, sir, an' we knocked him out."

"You did well."

"We got a direct hit, sir." He had seen it from his funk-hole in the woods.

"What happened to the crew?"

"Crew, sir?"

"The men in the S.P."

"Two of 'em got shot, sir. Corporal Pike had the Bren in the turret." He had heard the Bren and seen the Germans drop. The camouflage had hidden the man in the turret, but it was probably Pike. No one could prove anything now. He didn't want to tell this story. He was being made to. It was in the report. Word for word, he was having to remember what he had written. The lamps' light pricked his eyes. "The others must have"—he moved a hand—"roasted."

Knowles paused. It was not a pleasant word to choose, even for the enemy. A man in a burning tank was in hell before he died. After the two in the S.P. gun, there had been Pike and Luff in Top Dog. The word wasn't a good one.

"What happened next?"

"The tanks come over, sir. We got one of them, an'——"

"How many tanks can you remember?"

"Half a squadron, sir, or more." He began anticipating the questions, so that some might perhaps be overlooked. "We got a direct hit on one of them, and then put smoke down, sir. Then we fired again, and——"

"Through smoke?"

Had it been? The report said it had. "Yes, sir. Then we got hit ourselves, sir." It sounded very heroic. He had been in Top Dog, a legend. He was a hero. The word sank through his mind, ashamed. He didn't want to be a false hero, just because he hadn't got the guts to be a real one. He wasn't like Sergeant Foster or Mr. Smith, shouting the odds and showing their fists when Jerry was miles away, and then nipping for cover the moment they caught a whiff of him. He didn't want medals or a mention in dispatches. He wanted to go home, get out of this bloody war and be left alone.

Major Knowles said: "The smoke was still down when you fired your last shell, was it?"

"Yes, sir."

"What did the gunner aim at, if he couldn't see the target?"

The tone of the question, for the first time, was openly doubtful. Soaper felt angry. It was the truth. He had seen the smoke-screen, and the tank had fired through it. How the hell should he know what they'd fired at? They'd fired, and it was the truth. Wasn't the truth good enough?

"I wasn't in the tank, sir."

The Major moved his head. The light played across one side of his face, brightening the eye.

"Where were you?"

"Outside, sir, puttin' out the smoke." From his shelter in the trees he had seen one of them come over the turret with the mortar.

"I see. And the others were all inside."

"Yes, sir." You bastard. "Yes, sir."

"And then?"

Soaper shifted in his chair and felt its hard rungs against his back. And then? Where had he got to? What did the report say?

"The tank brewed up, sir."

The Major put a hand out, touching his fingers along the edge of the papers. "Yes," he said absently. "We're very proud of Top Dog."

The silence went on until Soaper had to move his feeble mouth to break it. "Yes, sir." If they found out, what could they do? What would they call it? Deserting his post on the field. But they couldn't find out. He had seen the tank go up. Even the man outside with the mortar couldn't have lived through that lot. Pike had murdered them all, with his bloody heroics. And they'd been soft to let him.

"You were standing outside the tank, then, when it was hit. What did you do?"

"I couldn't get in, sir. There was fire, bad."

"What did you do?"

"I run, sir. I didn't mean Jerry to get me."

Major Knowles inclined his head.

"Naturally."

"It was all I could do, sir."

"To your knowledge, the rest of the crew were inside the tank, and were unable to escape."

"As far as I know, sir." He hadn't stopped to find out. Once the tank was hit, he had run like mad through the wood. People had said they weren't taking prisoners. He'd run for his life, and so would anyone with enough sense.

The Major got up. Soaper pushed his chair back. He could have cried out in relief. It was the end of his story. It was all they could expect of him. Now perhaps they'd let him alone.

"This report will go to the Colonel, of course. I've no doubt he'll want to thank you himself for your part in a very gallant action."

What would it feel like to stand here listening to these words deservingly? He must not let it matter to him. He must not care.

"Yes, sir."

Major Knowles was not holding out his hand. He stood half-turned to Soaper, head tilted, eyes watching the whitened archway of brick that supported the cellar's roof. "I may send for you later. Meanwhile, your friends will be waiting to welcome you back. You can go now, Soaper."

"Sir."

As he turned away, saluting, the Major was just picking up the papers, his clearance from the hospital and his report on his movements in the last three weeks. His boots were not loud, going out and up the steps; there was nothing of Sergeant Verity's confidence in his walk.

He stood outside the cottage and felt angry. They'd made him go into that bloody tank and they'd asked too much of him, and now they'd forced him to make out he was a bloody hero. And the Major knew. Well, he could do what the hell he liked about it.

"Stuff me, it's Soapy back!"

There were three of them: Corporal Todd, Taffy Adams, and Steiner. They stopped in front of him, shirts open to the evening warmth, hands in their pockets, surprised.

"What 'appened to you, then, Soaper?"

"We thought you was a prisoner, man!"

"Where you been, then, eh?"

He said as patiently as he could: "In hospital."

Lance-Corporal O'Hagan came up.

"Christ, where did you spring from, Soaper?"

They surrounded him. He could see others coming, attracted by the group. He was from Top Dog, and Top Dog had become a legend in the Squadron.

"What 'appened to you, mate? Tell us!"

He stood among them with his hands by his sides. He would have to tell them. He would have to tell them all today, tomorrow, the next day. They would ask him until they drove him mad with asking him; and every single time the story would have to be right.

II

'C' SQUADRON was beginning to forget the war. The sun was hot and the sky clear. The men went about naked to the waist. There had been more drill in the last two days, and they were wearing the tanks out with their cleaning-rags; but most of their time was idle.

Among the crews of the original tanks and those of the replacements, friendships sprang up. Sergeant Marsh, commander of The Rocket, Four Troop, came face to face one evening with the gunner of a new tank. He was Trooper Marsh, his own brother. Willy Saunders, a bumptious little co-driver from Five Troop, had a letter saying he'd become the father of twin girls, and he was pushed twice round the village on a stores trailer, pelted with wild flowers while he recited a speech of Nelson's he had learned at home, until, shouted down and still half seas over, he came off the trailer with a bang and was borne on a stretcher of crossed hands to the M.O. for stitching.

These small excitements had a felicity natural to the atmosphere of this becalmed backwater in the forgotten war; but now and then a reminder came when a line of dust would rise along the road from the east towards Falaise. Troops came back from the fighting on foot, in transports, in medical trucks and ambulances, their dust moving in a soft cloud towards the village of Brisaille-les-Champs. Soon the sunshine was dulled by it, and the stillness driven out by the bump of wheels as the column passed through to the deeper rear. Men swayed together on open trucks, their faces hollowed out by the fighting, their uniforms whitened by the dust. A few of them waved and sometimes managed to raise a cheer in answer to a greeting; but most stood silent, braced against the framework and against one another, with no strength left in them to lift a hand.

The men of 'C' Squadron felt the familiar guilt of the soldier who lives easy, watching the war go by. They remembered they had looked like this themselves, dead beat and fit to drop, along the painful road from the coast and the cursed sea; they had fought as hard as these men and had earned this rest; but the guilt was in their minds, eased only by the knowledge that soon they would look like this again.

When the dust had cleared, the sunshine was not the same. The swimming-party went off in the truck, for once without the light-hearted shout of hot men seeking cool water and the shade of willows by the stream. The dust was still in their minds, and their future haunted them.

Lieutenant Pope came out of Squadron Headquarters on the morning of the twelfth day and sent for Sergeant Goodall and Corporal Fraser, commanders of Numbers Two and Three tanks in his Troop. When they came to him he took them a little way into the field where men were idling at a game of cricket. The three of them sat beneath a tree, where there was shade.

"There's an 'O' group in about an hour," said Pope.

"But I can tell you right away that we've got orders to move."

Goodall sucked a grass stem, watching the cricketers. "That'll do me, then. They're gettin' bored."

"I know." Pope leaned on his elbow, looking once at Corporal Fraser. He was a new commander from the Delivery Squadron, with a new tank. He was here in the place of Corporal Pike. His tank was named Auld Reekie, and it was full of noisy Scots. "How does the news strike you, Fraser?"

"Me, sir?" He looked surprised. "Why, we're fit an' ready."

Sergeant Goodall liked the Scot. He was a small, thin, unsmiling man of twenty-five, with bright eyes that would never see enough of life however long he lived; they made their unceasing enquiries wherever they glanced, and looked at nothing without wanting to know more of it. He was almost the opposite of Pike; he never swore; his courage was geared to caution; he talked little, making no jokes among his friends; he addressed his crew by their surnames with quiet authority. The only fault that Goodall could find with him was that he was not Pike.

Mr. Pope lit another cigarette and said: "We shall be going forward as far as Moncielle. The Canadians have started cracking at Falaise. At the moment they've been halted by heavy opposition in the villages round Tilly-la-Campagne, which has changed hands several times." He blew smoke out. "The fighting has been described as constant, heavy and bitter."

Corporal Fraser gazed at the man across the field who held the cricket-bat. He was holding it badly. Fraser itched to shout and tell him.

Sergeant Goodall was watching Mr. Pope. Something had happened to him that Goodall could not understand, but he was glad of it. The boy was easier in his mind and more quiet of eye; his decisions were slowly bearing the true stamp of authority and judgment. The war was making a soldier of him; this was Goodall's explanation of the change, and he had watched its subtle development with affection, for he was an Army man with an Army mind, and was deeply satisfied to see a boy like this grow into a man at war.

"The big push is apparently on. We shall invest the western approaches to Falaise on a battalion front. The general indication is that once Falaise goes down, it'll finish the battle of Normandy and break the Wehrmacht's back."

Goodall pipped the grass stem out of his mouth and chose a new one. "Then we'd be for the frontier after that, would we, sir?"

"With their army broken, I don't see how they could stop us. Their navy and air force are gone." He shrugged. "But that's conjecture. The thing is, we're moving off."

The cricket-ball, a poor thing with a burst seam, went snicking against the tree bole and exploded, the soft white padding coming out of it like a puff of smoke. A derisive cheer went up.

Sergeant Goodall said: "I'll buy 'em a new one in Berlin."

Sam Cox had opened the elaborate lock in his diary and was sitting against a hedge, writing: *We're moving off in the morning to the front at Falaise. It has been perfect here, in the deep country sunshine, and most of us feel ready for anything again. The French people have suddenly become interested in us, probably because they're longing to have their village to themselves again, after all this time. I don't blame them.*

Taffy Adams came into the corner of the field where Sam Cox was writing and called something, waving his arm.

"What?"

"Special parade, ten minutes!"

Sam waved and nodded, and watched the man go.

Taffy is excited to be moving off again. He has been praying like an overworked priest all day, and climbing in and out of Moby Dick as if it was going to have a litter at any minute. Watty is seeing his girl tonight, I suppose for the last time. He does not say much, but I think it will be hard for him to leave her.

Voices shouted from over the hedge. He put his head back and lifted his face to the leaves and the dying sky, sad and afraid.

I shall remember Brisaille-les-Champs for a very long time.

He locked the book and got up.

Captain Hallett came out of Squadron H.Q. and climbed aboard the jeep. He was driven away, hidden in dust. A dispatch-rider was on the road from the rear; he swerved to a halt near a group of men; they pointed, calling to him above the throb of his engine; he swung away towards the cottage where the crater was.

Two N.C.O.s marched smartly along the street, turning their heads as an old Frenchwoman called a question; they smiled in answer but said nothing. Mr. Smith was waiting for them, a list in his hand. A five-tonner crawled past, going down to 'B' Echelon's field park.

The crews were falling-out from their special parade, quietly moving down to the cookhouse in the village hall, looking about them at the street and the cottages and the groups of French people as if they had just arrived here, and were curious. The engine of a tank started up and ran at full blast for minutes. Across the sky to the west, Typhoons flew in a bunch, rising from their base and turning north-east through the light evening cloud. As the sun went down, the horizon on the other side of the world took on a reddish glow that was not from the sun. It was from a village on fire, toward Falaise. The crews walked slowly down the street to the cookhouse with the sun dying against their eyes and the glow of the fire on their backs. The walls of the cottages were pinked by the glow in the sky.

The co-driver of Number One Tank, Two Troop, Josef Steiner, stood by himself at the edge of the street, looking towards the east. He had seen other fires, across Europe, bigger than that. His own town had lit the sky for three long nights, and he could remember the people running, and the dark official vans hounding their way through the streets, and the alarm-bells and the flag that had burned at the top of a building with its bright flames whipping to the wind before the blackened shreds of it fluttered away and left the wooden pole and a few red sparks to go floating across the roofs.

He stood neatly and alone, watching the sky. The dawn would come up tomorrow, as red as that, over Falaise.

In the tangled spinney where paths ran, a mile from the village, Thérèse was crying, her thin shoulders pressed against a tree. She had told him she would cry like this, on the last evening, and now she was; but the tears were real ones; her young heart was breaking.

Watty stood with his hand lightly on her arm, talking to her in his scholar's French that was formal for lack of idiom.

"You will feel better tomorrow."

Her dark head shook. "Never, never." Her slight body shook with the crying. "You won't ever come back to me."

"You will forget about me, Thérèse."

"I'll remember you all my life." She put her brow against his shoulder, wearily. He stroked her hair. The faint light of the sky came into the trees, purpling the ground and the shadows. She began crying again, so he said:

"I will come back, after the war."

"You don't mean that." But she had lifted her face.

"Yes, I mean it." And if he came back, she would not even remember his name. "I will come back."

"You'll take me away with you, to England?"

He stroked her hair slowly. "Yes, to England." He thought of her parents. She had told him she was seventeen, but she wasn't. They'd go mad if they knew the things she did in the woods, and he'd get the chopper. But if she hadn't done them with him, it would have been with someone else; and he had been careful with her. "Now I must go," he said.

"Promise, promise!"

"I will come back, after the war."

"And take me to England."

"And take you to England."

Her body was still trembling. She began kissing him, quickly and desperately, her thin arms going over his shoulders and her small hands strong. He made her pull them away. "I must go, Thérèse."

"You've promised, on your heart."

"Yes."

"And you will keep the present I gave you. The pipe."

He got it from his pocket.

"Yes, I will always keep it." He was touched by the absurdity of this lovers' token, and smiled; but she was serious.

"It won't smoke well, so you'll break it or throw it away."

"It will smoke very well, and I shall never throw it away. Now I am going." He kissed her gently, and began wanting her again, and so had to stand away from her and straighten the buckle of his battle-dress, and put the pipe back into the pocket, and look at her for the last time. She looked a child, and he felt guilty. But she would cry all night long, being a child, and would forget him the more quickly. "I will go with you as far as the village."

She said that she would stay here, to cry.

"You must not stay here alone." He took her hand. She pulled his hand quickly and pressed it over her hard breasts, watching him bright-eyed in the soft purple light; but he smiled and made her walk with him, and had to tell her patiently that it wasn't that he didn't want her any more, but simply that he had orders to go back to his billet by midnight, when there would be a special roll-call. She would not like him to be in trouble? Never. She would never do anything against him, and would love him always, and be waiting for him when the war was over; and he would take her to England with him.

He wondered, cynically, in a kitbag? Or stowed away among the salvage-gear on Moby Dick? When they came to the line of cottages, he had to say he would not kiss her good-bye until she stopped crying, and unless she

climbed straight into her window without making a
sound. She met these demands, and he stood at the edge
of the vegetable patch, watching her as she wobbled on
top of the wood-pile and then pulled herself to the window, which was so small that even she had to squeeze
through. She vanished, like a bird into a hole in a tree.
He lifted his arm, and turned away to step carefully
across the garden until he reached the field's edge. Looking back, he could see only the line of cottages with their
tumbled roofs and the dark patches that were windows.
He was not even sure which was hers.

Here the short peace ended, by a street of cottages he
would never see again, with the love of a girl for him that
would soon die. He could smell the sprig of wild berga-
mot that she had tucked in his battle-blouse, and he took
it out and let it fall, feeling unfaithful as he walked on
towards his billet.

THE BATTERING-RAM

I

THE day's march had brought the Battalion to a line of hamlets from which the French had gone. Falaise was five miles forward. The enemy, driven back from this sector, was entrenched on the fringe of the city, making a bastion for the defences of the garrison. This garrison had long been identified as the 12th S.S. Panzer Division, part of von Kluge's command.

The Canadians were still attacking from the north-west, up the long dangerous road that was slowly killing them in hundreds; but more came on. The enemy batteries were positioned as thickly as a castle's battlements, and in the hamlets and the woods, in shelters and buildings and natural lodgements there were gunposts and mortar crews, snipers' nests and self-propelled armour; and in each square mile of ground lay a thousand mines. Already, after weeks of fighting, the land was littered with dead. Falaise still stood.

'C' Squadron, on a battalion front west of the city, had not met with opposition until their fourth day out from Brisaille. There were snipers, and mines, and sometimes mortar-fire from hidden posts; but this was not opposition. They moved according to plan, nearing the objective on schedule, until they overran the remnant of an enemy holding-unit, and took Moncielle. There they harboured for three nights, burying their few dead and priming their stores.

A column of armour, going forward at dawn behind a creeping barrage, reached a village that was a suburb of the city; and there they were wiped out. They had come under the fire of a group of 105-m.m. guns that had been observing them, and waiting, and holding their fire until the range was short. Infantry that had been ordered to follow the armour through were drawn back and held in reserve behind a strong-point within a mile of the road. The road had not been shelled. It had been left open by the Germans, whose guns were trained on its three-mile stretch, waiting for the next column to advance. By night, dust drifted from the city and from the battlefield to the north of it, and the light of fires turned it orange, and tinged the smoke that crawled from the red horizon and spread across the sector, so that the waiting forces were choked and blinded by it.

There had been seven major attacks by bombers of American, Polish, British, Canadian and French squadrons in the last two days. It was not possible to watch the city from the battalion line and believe that men still lived in it. Falaise was burning, and as it burned, the bombers went in again, driving through heavy flak and dropping their loads into the conflagration. But on the long slope to the north, the Canadians were still running into murderous fire, and were driven back.

On August 13th, orders came for 'C' Squadron to work round to the south-west through Pinchau-le-Bas, a village in a fold of land below the hill. The enemy were holding it. It was to be captured. The Squadron commander briefed his crews an hour after midnight.

"This village is strongly defended. Behind it, along the main anti-tank ditch, there are self-propelled guns. You can see their present positions on this plan, and the indications are that they're dug in and not likely to move. There will be no preliminary barrage. We are expected to make a pounce-attack and break up the defences with the first blow. So the first blow has got to be a good one."

He watched the faces of his commanders. They were not tired men. Since Brisaille there had been very little to do, apart from skirmishes on the march. The Squadron was only one tank short of full strength, and the crews were fit. This time he was not standing by the map-table half-asleep, briefing red-eyed men who were nearing the limit of endurance before they began. This gave him a confidence that was clear in his voice and visible in his movements.

"We shall be in support of infantry fresh from the rear.
A unit of the Buffs has to be relieved, two miles west of
the village, here." His finger stabbed down. "Apart from
that, we have only the main job of blasting this objective
apart. To me, it looks like a good shoot." He passed his
tin of cigarettes round in the lamplight. "One last thing:
we've had rumours before that the enemy is not taking
any prisoners. This time we are to take it as a fact. From
the reports coming in, Falaise is going to hold out until
the garrison is dead, to the last man. The defence of this
village, Pinchau-le-Bas, will obviously follow the same
pattern. For our part we shall, according to the rules of
war, take prisoners." He paused for two seconds, three.
"When we can."

Sergeant Goodall glanced up sharply and Major
Knowles noticed it, but looked away.

The silence drew out. "I'm ready for questions."

They questioned him, but did not mention the matter
of prisoners. Those who had learned to read the tone of
orders in the field—the men from Africa and Sicily
among them—had suddenly a clearer picture of this coming action than the maps could give them. They were
going forward as a battering-ram and there might not be
time to remember the rules of war. To some it was an
uneasy thought, and by a degree it sapped their confidence and their belief that even in this bloody arena there
was humanity in man. Most of them were not worried.
The Major had not told them they must not take prisoners. They were to take them when they could. And if the
Boche were ready to shoot a man down, even with his
hands raised in surrender, then the Boche must be shot
down too. It was ludicrous to fight a war with boxing-
gloves against a knuckleduster.

But there was regret, in Sergeant Goodall, and in Corporal Fraser, and Taffy Adams. The British Army could
beat the German Army by what methods it chose, without borrowing the inhumanity they were here to conquer.
It was very simple to these men. The others, who were
unworried by this minor point in their commander's
briefing, were prepared to blast their way through the

objective and finish the job, neither giving nor asking for mercy. This too was simple enough to understand.

"The start-line is here." Knowles drew his finger along. "The attack will begin at 03.00 hours, in forty-five minutes from now. England expects this day that 'C' Squadron shall meet the enemy, and string him up by his guts."

The dust lay in a pink coud from north to south. Beyond it was the smoke of Falaise. The crews on the start-line could feel the movement in the ground under their tanks. The ground was hard, in many places cracked and fissured by the drought; and the earth-shock spreading from the Canadians' guns and from the German defences reached this far, and trembled underfoot and in the air. Against the pink cloud, the seventeen tanks stood in black silhouette, a cut-out frieze of war, sharply defined and without movement. Men coughed in the dust, looking about them at the nightmare scene, their ears pulsing with the guns' sound, their faces ruddled by the unnatural light.

A mile to their rear an artillery battery had opened fire, putting its shells into the burning city to provide sound-cover for the tanks. The barrage had run for ten minutes; it was to continue for another hour, by which time the Squadron would be engaged with the enemy in Pinchau-le-Bas. Fifteen minutes ago, infantry had gone forward in carriers and converted S.P. guns. On the start-line, commanders were mounted.

Lieutenant Pope had only the simplest thoughts in his mind. The village was ahead of them, somewhere in the smoke. It had to be captured. The Squadron was in good shape. They would be successful. Then Falaise. Then the long swan to the frontier, and Berlin, and finally London and home and peace. In the chalky orange smoke he saw all these things coming to pass.

Below his pedestal the big tank was warm and the crew lively though idle for the moment. Bloody Mary weighed thirty tons and her brake horsepower was 350; she had a 75-m.m. Q.S.P.A. gun and two 7.92 Besa machine-guns. The ground was hard: there would be no bogging-down on the road to Pinchau-le-Bas. This tank was one of seventeen, so that the armoured battering-ram weighed over five hundred tons and had just under six thousand horsepower to drive it. With good crews and hard roads and a sound-cover from the barrage to give them the advantage of surprise, what could stop them?

The guns, Goodall was thinking. The Jerry guns. They could stop anything. They were stopping the Canadians who were struggling with incredible courage up that murderous road from the north, into Falaise. This road, to Pinchau-le-Bas, was another like it, on a smaller scale. The Major hadn't put it that way for nothing. This action was to be to the death. His legs were trembling. He was more afraid than sometimes he had been before, on the start-line, but still not scared enough to make him tremble. It was just his legs again; he could forget them. The bloody things had a mind of their own, and were nothing to do with him.

In the creep of the red dust there was the smell of the dead, of dead men and dead cattle, men and cows and goats and dogs, with nothing to show the busy beetles which hump of rotting chemical pretended to a soul and to higher things than this determination to kill its own kind. In the fields here and along the sides of the roads there were lying the young and the noble, the gallant and the brave, and also those who had been driven there by the greater fear of being called a coward, and who had therefore suffered the worst and been braver than the rest, and also those whose lives had been squandered by mistaken orders or a bad decision, or by their own inability to obey. Along with the goats and the dogs, the beetles buried them. They were a stench on the air, offensive to the living, more repugnant than the smoke and the dust. It was a crude reminder that whatever nation won or lost, however the war would end, it had these little endings all along the way.

And after Pinchau-le-Bas the stench would be worse; and after Falaise worse still.

Start up.

The drivers moved their hands; the engines began running. Taffy Adams listened to the sound of his engine, trying to hear a fault. Beside him, Sam Cox was writing in his diary, and the Welshman would have liked to know what he was saying in that book. It was a good way of telling people what you were thinking, at a time when you could tell nobody and had so much to tell. It must be as good a way of fighting off the sense of loneliness as praying was, except that, like an argument, it took two to pray, you and God. He listened to his engine, and heard no fault in it.

Below the trembling legs of his commander, Watkins-Price sat at the gun, thinking of her thin shoulders and the way she had vanished into the small dark window, quiet as a bird. She had made love like a woman, and had cried like a child, and was gone. But her name remained, Thérèse, and he had only to think of it to remember all the rest. He should have got over her by now. He must get over her soon, or she'd become an obsession with him and he'd come back here after the war, and go to the cottage in Brisaille-les-Champs, and stand watching her face while she tried to remember his, and failed.

He looked at Woods, sitting with his beloved wireless. The kid was absorbed. The wireless was a mother to him, each voice in the head-phones a reassurance. But lately he had begun to find reassurance in things outside the head-phones. The mere companionship of men was a strength to him, and in Moby Dick he had companions who were his friends. The sergeant was a pillar to him, and in a way he worshipped him, because he was a man stronger than he could ever be, and yet not an arrogant man sure of his own invincibility. To Woods, that seemed to be his strength. He had told the crew, half an hour ago:

"That's the job, then. You've seen the maps an' you know what we've got to expect."

"A bloody riot," said Sam Cox.

"It'll be a riot, all right, but we'll be the ones to start it, see? The main thing is, you've all got to know what we're at. I shall be up there in the turret, an' I'll be the one to get it first, an' you'll have to take over. So it's going to make all the difference to Moby Dick if you get that right from the start. If you've any questions, I want 'em now."

Watkins-Price said, rubbing the bowl of his pipe, "What about this business of prisoners, Sergeant?"

"What business?" He needed a second to think.

"Do we take them, or don't we?"

"You heard the Major." By the same principles that put him in disagreement with the hinted order to shoot on sight, he must support that order, word for word. "We take them when we can."

Woods had asked no questions, about this or anything else. He'd be on the wireless, and Taffy driving, and Watty at the gun. That was the pattern, as clear as a Meccano set. There'd be no thinking to do, for him, once Moby Dick was away.

He sat with the drum of the barrage beating against the head-phones, and with him, inside the head-phones, there was more than the voices in the air. There was the sergeant's strength and the friendship of the others, and his growing reliance on their part with him in the tank. As he grew older in his war, the operator's seat was becoming less to him a refuge, and more his battle station.

The voices came, and he tuned the dials, waiting for the order, the one word. In the gloom was the dull shine from the pilot-lamps along the metal walls, and the presence of the dust that was falling through the open turret, and the smell of the smoke and the dead things in the fields. He took shallow breaths. Under the steel tracks the ground shuddered, all the time; and the engine trembled.

Advance.

The dust fell more thickly through the turrets as the Squadron moved from the start-line. It came drifting through the drivers' slits as the tracks crossed the hard ground and crumbled its surface where the fissures ran. The dark silhouettes were softened by the rising of the dust. The commanders wore masks across their mouths, a rag or scarf or handkerchief. A few of the drivers closed

their slits and steered by periscope, already cursing the
eye-strain that was to come.

The sound of their own engines was louder than that of
the barrage a mile behind them, a mile and a half, two
miles behind them as they drove through the blinding fog
of the dust that whirled about them, sent up by their own
headlong march and blowing against them as the big
springs dipped and rose and the commanders grew
hunched in their turrets, their goggles slowly smothered
and wiped clean again, smothered and wiped clean, with
nothing to see ahead of them but the great pink cloud of
dust.

This was not the first attack on the village of Pinchau-
le-Bas, for they came upon the left-overs of units in re-
treat. A big truck, burnt out and upside down, loomed
out of the dust and the leading tank of One Troop struck
it squarely and pushed it over, so that for a moment they
were like two big animals fighting in the dust, the one
rolling over, the other butting it and insisting on the death
before it passed beyond, leaving the mangled wreck
across the roadway, to be picked on by the others of the
herd, until the truck lost its truck's shape, and then even
its wreck's shape, and became flotsam spread out along
the dusty ground.

The first mines were reached and were blowing, their
explosions patching the battle-fog with orange and sear-
ing white as the herd floundered on, maimed in some of
its members as a tank reeled and halted and another
smashed a track; but the herd went on, leaving its
crippled, driving through the cloud—fifteen tanks keeping
station on their route and keeping schedule according to
plan, their dark shapes rocking through the dust, as lost
as ships at sea and souls in hell.

The enemy had heard the mines. The tanks were falling foul of them along the road; the infantry, massed in
the fields on each side of the road and through the bocage
on the flank, were finding the minefields and dying in
them man by man. The others went on. The weight of the
assault could carry it to the objective despite considerable
loss. That had been the policy of the plans. Days ago, the

special devices had gone down this road and through these fields, clearing lanes and blowing the mines and reaching the first house of the village. Their wreckage was there still. The lanes had been sown afresh with mines and booby-traps. The men who would fight in the village were those who would get through to it, by luck and by their position on the route. When a man blew up a mine, the men behind him were saved from it; so they pushed on, and when they found another, and blew it up, those behind them were saved from it; so they pushed on, and behind them came at last the men who would reach the village alive, and overwhelm it if they could; and if they could not, those behind them would. Their commanders were not concerned with losses, in this action. The alternative to throwing men and guns and tanks against this objective was that of holding back, and waiting, and wasting the enemy's strength together with their own, until after months the losses would be the same.

The Second Front had been bogged down overlong in Normandy. Now it was pushing out. The enemy had concentrated his forces in this area, the crack and the cream of them, machine-trained fanatics who would fight until they were dead. This, then, must be the killing-ground.

Fourteen tanks of 'C' Squadron, running in arrow-head groups towards the village, struck obstacles now that rose from the dust like islands in a driving sea. They were the special devices, the Crabs and Snakes and Bulls-horns that had ploughed their lanes through the minefields and then been smashed by the guns. The fighting-tanks met them blindly, swerving at the last second as a driver caught a glimpse of a rising shape, or running against them slantwise and slewing to a halt and steering back to round them and run on. Moby Dick hit a pile of junk where something had been blown apart, and the left track screamed, scraping at bared metal, lifting its great weight bodily and pitching the crew about as it ground through the wreckage and lumbered on.

Lieutenant Pope was a thin hooked figure sagging at the turret-rim with his ribs bruised and his eyes blinded by the mist inside his goggles and the dust outside; but he

saw a shape that neared him, and called up his driver;
and Bloody Mary swerved, glancing off the obstacle and
grazing the flank of Auld Reekie as Corporal Fraser altered his course to keep station with the troop. Both
tanks slowed. Behind them the others came on, and
found the obstacles, and ran into their own tanks, and
slowed with them, until the advance moved at a crawl
through the blinding wilderness.

The enemy had heard the mines going up, minutes ago,
and now they opened fire. It was an hour before dawn.
The attack was mounted on a two-mile front, with wing
units wheeling in from the west to relieve the Buffs who
were holding the fringe sector.

By dawn, two-thirds of the attacking force had reached
the objective, and Pinchau-le-Bas was under siege.

III

THE dawn came and no one saw it. The clear sun
mounted, and cast the first long shadows west of the hills
and the tufts of trees, glinting across a stream, warming a
pool of milky mist and slowly thinning it away, brightening the gold of corn, softening the air and conjuring up
the scents of field and wood and farmland. No one in this
patch of countryside was aware of the new morning. Falaise burned, a bloodying wound on the sweet earth
smothered in its own smoke and the dust of its mortal
conflict, while to the south its smoke was joined with the
smoke over Pinchau-le-Bas, so close that the shroud was
shared, and covered the feverish movement of vehicles
between the city and the villages as the German garrisons
sought to maintain communications and the supply of
arms.

British infantry were already in the village, jogging
with fixed bayonets through the dust, a company com-

mander positioned on a low wall, using his megaphone and waving them on. A platoon had broken through a weak point in the outer defences and swarmed against a barrier of machine-guns that ripped them down before they had a chance to dodge for cover. The company commander went pitching from his wall and bounced spread-eagled on to barbed wire. A Piat team was picking its way through the smoke, stealing into the alleyways between the cottages and setting up its weapon to command the main street. From the big guns, shells cracked over their heads and sailed north, bursting among the columns of armour that were nosing through the dust.

Before noon the assault had been halted, driven back and then re-mounted, driving in again as the defending fire was decoyed for an hour to the west, where Bren teams were rounding the village and opening a breach. The tanks, bristling out from their columns, went forward again, crawling to new positions and halting to bring their guns to bear on close targets. Many of the buildings were ablaze and their light flickered in the smoke cloud that sagged over the village and the fields beyond, with no wind to shift it.

Nine tanks of 'C' Squadron were still fighting, six of them untouched except by bullet-splash, the other three with a track wrecked, a turret jammed, a driver dead; but their guns were firing, covering the slow movement of the six that were crawling forward, halting, firing, crawling again through a trellis of withering fire that was coming from two Spandau posts and a Hotchkiss that was set up in a pillbox beside the main street.

Auld Reekie had caught a direct hit from an armour-piercing shell, minutes ago, but for a little time it was one of the three that could no longer move but could still use the gun. Then the gun ceased fire. A hundred yards forward, Bloody Mary was forcing a path between a cottage wall and a burning truck. Lieutenant Pope was in the turret, one sleeve crimson and the hand useless. He directed his driver on the intercom until the obstacle was cleared and they halted with the gun poking from the corner, trained on the main street. Beyond the pillbox that was now burning its Hotchkiss crew alive, Moby Dick was swinging to line up with the street, within sight of the Troop-leader. They were both alert to the shape that had stopped moving, half hidden in the smoke, behind a road block fifty yards up.

Sergeant Goodall stopped his driver.

"Gunner traverse left."

The barrel swung a degree. "Steady. . . . Hornet. On!"

Watkins-Price called back. In the drifting haze, the dark shape was lost again until an air wave brought its outline back.

"Fire!"

The A.P. shell left the gun. The scene trembled in front of Goodall's eyes, then steadied. Flame burst ahead. Then he ducked inside the turret as a machine-gun stream began pattering over the hull. The Hornet was brewing-up, but they were still under heavy fire from other quarters. A fragmentation-bomb hit the street and the pieces rained their music and percussion. The flames were leaping higher from the enemy tank. Bloody Mary had poked its gun another yard into the open and was halted again. Fire was being brought to bear on both of them.

In the drifting smoke the flames bannered between the walls of the cottages, setting one of them on fire, licking to the eaves and touching off the thatch. A shell hit the roadway, bursting, filling the confines with an instant of freezing light and deafening the crews.

Taffy Adams got the *Advance!* from Goodall and Moby Dick moved forward, scraping the corner and lumbering across the remains of a concrete block. A second shape was looming in the haze.

"Halt! Gunner keep steady. . . . "

Watty answered, the target in the sights. It was coming fast, darkening through the smoke and taking shape.

"Fire!"

The gun recoiled. The shape came on, an orange flash in its centre from the gun. The world exploded and Goodall was shouting for a long time, unable to hear his own shout, but feeling the breath push out of his throat

and aware of the words. He was saying they were hit.
Something fell against his legs and he got down. He could
hear nothing now. He slapped his ears but their deafness
was heavy as if stone blocks were pressed against his
head, crushing him into the dreadful silence. He could see
everything in the grey half-light. "Watty," he said,
"Watty."

A pale face came dodging up as Woods held his arm.
The kid's mouth was calling, but Goodall could not hear.
He felt sick, suddenly, and let his shoulder fall against the
plates. He leaned there, not moving, fighting the sickness
off. The smell of metal was in the fœtid air of the tank,
the after-fumes of the white-hot friction as the shell had
come in. It was a worse smell than cordite, or dead cows.
He opened his eyes, his sickness ebbing away. Woods was
calling to him, wondering why he did not answer. He
banged his ears, but the big cold stones were still there,
enveloping his head.

"What's happened in front?" His voice reverberated
inside his head, trapped there. Against his shoulder he
felt the vibration of bullets on the outside of the plates.
Woods was squeezing through the hatchway to the
driver's compartment. Against Goodall's legs, Watty was
moving. He was staring up at him, his face a white water-
lily in the gloom below. Very faintly Goodall heard a
crack, as light as the snapping of a twig, above him, and
he knew it was a shell going over, and that he wasn't
going to be deaf for the rest of his life.

"You all right, Watty?"

The pale face nodded, swam away and floated back as
the plates swerved and hit Goodall. He shuddered, and
tried to steady. He had fallen against them. The snicker
of machine-gun fire picked at his ear-drums. He could
even hear Woods's voice as he came back through the
hatchway, but could not hear what he was saying. He was
vomiting. Goodall told Watkins-Price to get out of his
way, and dropped down across Woods. He fumbled for
the medical kit and squeezed sideways into the driving
compartment.

The shell had come in here. It was difficult to make

out the details of the scene, because dust was falling
through the driving-slit in soft little waves as the air
movement pressed and sucked outside. The stench of the
burned metal was bad in here and his stomach jerked, but
he had to begin thinking hard, and forgot the nausea. He
tried to see in what position Taffy had fallen, and thought
at first that his neck must be broken because he could not
find his head. When he realised what had happened to
Taffy he turned to look at Sam Cox. He was muttering,
and Goodall felt a small relief among the terrible other
feelings that he was no longer deaf.

Sam's overalls had been ripped open and his intestines
were out. His face was withered, all of its blood gone. It
was a dead old man's face, muttering . . . "away fr' the
window . . . away, Grace. . . . " Goodall found his
needle and drew a whole capsule of morphine into it, to
make it quick for Sam. He put the needle in, and
squeezed, and drew it out carefully so as not to break it.
Something shook the tank and his ears blanked off again,
but only for a few seconds. He waited, pressed against
the edge of the hatchway, watching Sam until his head
rolled on the limp neck. But there was still a pulse and he
waited again, some clear part of his brain registering surprise that there was enough blood left in this body for the
heart to drive.

Dust fanned through the slit as a building collapsed.
Heat flowed in. He could see a mass of orange in the
oblong of the slit. Then, under his hand, the faint pulse
stopped, and he forced his way back through the hatch,
tucking the medical kit into his blouse. Woods was laughing; it was a thin cackling laugh that ran fast out of him
with hardly a pause for breath. Goodall slapped him
across the head. He saw Watty on the commander's pedestal, and said:

"We'll get out when we can."

The tank shivered as something hit it. Not a shell. It
had been rammed. It didn't matter. Watty said with ex-
traordinary calm: "Are they dead, in front?"

"Yes." He helped Woods to stand up. He had stopped
laughing. "We'll get out of here, kid, as soon as it's more

quiet, an' then we'll be all right." He kept one arm round him. It was like clutching a sparrow.

Watty poked his beret above the turret rim and it was whipped away by a bullet stream. He found some loose cigarettes on the racks and they lit up. Woods had never smoked one before and he seemed to be interested in it, holding it in front of his face and looking at it. Very slowly, Watkins-Price began pouring out obscenities against the enemy, thinking of Sam and Taffy, going on and on while Goodall said: "Yes. . . . Yes, Watty," as if he were answering the intonation of a priest reading a psalm.

Sparks went blowing across the turret from the fire that was running through the cottages. After a long time Watty said: "We'll have to get out soon, Sergeant."

"Yes." The heat was growing quickly. They couldn't breathe without consciously sucking the air in and blowing it out, snatching at what little oxygen was left.

"Try again," Goodall said.

Watty put an empty ration-box on top of the Bren and poked it over the rim. The fusillade was immediate and the box span away.

"Never mind, Watty. We'll give 'em a bit of time."

Woods began coughing and dropped his cigarette, stamping it out and looking up at Goodall and breaking his heart: "I don't like them."

The sweat was dripping from the kid's face. As the heat in the tank grew worse, the smell grew worse. Goodall had a rag pressed to his face. He listened to the crackle of timber as the cottages burned, making this tank a slow oven. They would have to get out soon, now, if only to breathe. He leaned close to Watty and said quietly: "Look after Woods." Then he took the Bren and went forward through the hatchway, shifting Sam's body from the co-driver's seat and putting the Bren down while he tried to see if the hull Besa would sight. The armour-piercing shell had missed the Besa and bored a perfectly round hole through the plates. Afterwards it had run amok in the compartment.

He cleared the dust film from the machine-gun sights

and took a look. The cottages burned on the left a few yards away. Ahead was the street: a haze of dust and smoke and flying sparks, with the forward half of Bloody Mary just in sight. He aimed at the confused shape of the road block, dead ahead, and gave it a burst. The paper belt ran through, breaking up. Answering fire came in a sudden hail that rang against the hull until the bullet stream found the driver's slit and he had to duck, sprawling across the wet red rubbish that had once been Sam's legs. He had to think of the other things, and not think about Sam, about this mess having once been Sam. He thought of the road block and the Spandau that was going to keep them in here until the heat killed them or drove them out to the fresh air and the bullet rattle, and he thought of his Troop-leader up there forward with his gun at the corner. He had faith in Pope, where there was none before. Moby Dick wasn't alone here, as Top Dog had been on the hill.

Bullets were slicing in and glancing, pattering down with their momentum lost. They made a wicked sound, a killing, riddling clatter as they flew ricocheting round him as he drew one more breath, and then another, sucking in the smell of the metal and cordite and Sam's blood while the bullets came, flickering in like metallic light, and he crouched with his hands behind his neck and his eyes shut so that they didn't have to see Sam. Then when the Spandau stopped he grew enraged and got back on to the co-driver's seat and hit the Besa, moving the gun without sighting, pumping out a burst that circled and dipped and rose down the unseen street to hit at whatever was there—and then a big gun banged, and high explosive burst somewhere forward and the fragments came whirling. That would be Bloody Mary. He could have cheered, but his stomach was too sick.

The dust came in, blown on the blast-wave. His eyes were full of it. He pumped the gun again, but it jammed and he cursed and fumbled for the Bren; but he could not see. His eyes were streaming, ridding themselves of the dust. The Spandau started up again and he had to sprawl for half a minute until it stopped. When he got up, blood was flowing down his neck and the light flickered in his head as the pain began, drilling with a strange, almost pleasant agony along the side of his scalp. The thought was in his mind: it can't be much or I'd be dead. He got a grip on the Bren and took it back with him through the hatchway, ripping his battle-blouse open as he squeezed through. He heard the medical kit fall.

"Christ!" someone said. He groped round for the kit. Woods was lying slumped under the coaxial gun. He kicked him and said:

"Get up, Woods!" The boy's eyes were open. "Get up, you bloody fool!" His head was flickering with light, but his eyes were clear again. He grabbed Woods by one arm and heaved, and he started to sob. Goodall said: "Get up there in the turret!" There would be more air.

Watty came down half pitching and helped him lift Woods past the pedestal. The heat was wet. Their lungs thirsted for air and they began imagining it, as a parched throat drives a man to think of water.

"Sergeant, I'm going out." It was Watty. No one but Watkins-Price would call him Sergeant at a time like this.

"You're stayin' here, understand?"

"I can't breathe."

"You're stayin' here. Get the kid's face near the rim." He bent down and searched for the medical kit again, and found it, and fell down again when he straightened. All he could think of was *this is no good, this is no good,* as he reached up a hand and tried to get hold of something. Watty grabbed it, and pulled, and he thought: *You'll get a bloody medal, my son, if we get out of this,* but he didn't think they'd get out, and after what seemed a long time, he found himself leaning against the hard edge of the pedestal feeling sad about poor Watty's medal he'd never got. Someone was shouting, and he jerked his head up. He was losing blood or it was the fumes. He mustn't go under.

"*—Getting out!*"

"Stay here. You understand?"

He dragged himself higher. Watty was holding Woods,

who was unconscious. It wasn't the fumes that had knocked this poor kid out, it was going down there and seeing Taffy like that. He put his hand up to the side of his head. The bullet had gouged through the scalp. He was lucky. "I'm dead lucky," he heard himself say.

"It's clear!"

He looked up, and his full consciousness came back for the first time in minutes. *"What?"*

"It's clear!" Watkins-Price was holding his arm above the turret, waving it about. There was no rattle of Spandau fire. That last shell must have found the nest. He pulled himself up, standing on the pedestal.

"Stay where you are," he said. He'd waved things before in the desert—a tin-hat, a piece of junk, and it had been all clear until he'd poked his head out. If the Spandau were still functioning, it was saving its shot for a kill. He got his head above the rim and almost felt the bullet spray that did not come. He pushed his shoulders out and said: "All right—out."

The street had gone. There was a wall of fire and a valley of smoke between it and the humped shapes on the other side. There were men moving, low on the ground, dragging something. He got out of the turret and stood on the hull, shocked by the inrush of the heady oxygen. It sent him drunk and he reeled, falling against the turret rim—"You manage 'im? Manage?"

Watty had got Woods over the rim. A mortar-bomb hit the ground and they flattened themselves. The wave went over them, stinking. Watty dangled the boy over the side and let him drop, going down after him. Goodall sagged against the turret for a long time, trying to move, to think, to keep his stomach down. *I'm drunk,* he said to himself, *I'm pissed.* There was something he had to do. He had to get the Bren.

Watkins-Price was sitting behind the tank, leeward of the flames' heat, with Woods's head pillowed on his knees. Goodall came dropping. He had the Bren, two revolvers and a bag of grenades.

"How's Woods?" He could speak clearly again. Suddenly it was all over, and they weren't burned alive and

the Spandau wasn't firing. He felt negative and depressed.
He didn't care how Woods was, but he had to ask.

"Poor little sod," Watty was saying. He was stroking
the pinched, white face. "Poor little sod."

"Is he all *right*?" Goodall asked impatiently.

"He's fine, Sergeant." He was looking at Goodall
calmly. Goodall could have hit him for being so bloody
calm. Why hit him? Hit Watty? Christ, what for? He
wished to God he could feel sober, or alive. It was the
fumes in there. Morbidity of the blood, sucking in toxins.
Watty was saying: "I'll see you as far as a field post."

"Me? What field post?" The street was an inferno.
Where were the fields? That was before the war. The
blood was stiff on his neck, a sharp starched collar.
"Christ, what's the matter with me?"

Watty's voice thinned above the crump of a shell that
burst among the flames on the other side of the road.
"You've got a head wound."

"Then where's your field dressing, man?"

"You want me to do it?"

"For Christ sake," Goodall said, fighting off the unreal
feeling that none of this was happening, "put some
bloody iodine on it an' let's get moving."

He sat quietly while Watty put a bandage round his
head. Woods rolled over suddenly and jerked his eyes
open. All he could see was the wall of flame, and perhaps
he thought they were still inside the tank and that the
tank was on fire, because he gave a thin child's scream
that scraped across their nerves.

"Christ," Watty said petulantly, "don't *do* that."

Woods had seen Goodall and was staring at him. The
boy's head was clear enough. He had wakened to the
dreadful sight and sound of the blazing cottages, and had
been terrified for a moment. Sergeant Goodall was here,
so it was all right. He said to the sergeant: "Did you
see?"

"See what, son?"

"Them. In the front."

Goodall said: "Yes. They're all right now."

Woods took his word for it. His young brain was defending itself against the onslaught of mental shock in this battlefield where the mind and the emotions were as imperilled as the body. His mind was dealing with its problems in its own way. You've seen a man with his head off? Forget it. He was your friend Taffy? There's no friend of yours called Taffy. Sergeant Goodall says it's all right, so it must be.

"Are you hurt, Sarge?"

Watty was pinning the bandage. Goodall said to Woods:

"No, boy."

Woods picked up one of the revolvers and checked the breech. "Can I have this?"

"You're getting out of here," Goodall said. He didn't want to talk, because little by little he was twisting his mind round straight and getting things into place.

Woods stood up. He looked ridiculous holding the revolver. It was too big for him. The light of the flames flickered against his face and was mirrored in his eyes. Watty finished the head bandage and picked up the Bren.

"That's mine," said Goodall.

"You ought to take it easy, Sergeant. You're a dead shot with a revolver, and I'm not."

"Don't give me any bull, Watkins-Price. If I can't lift a Bren, you can bury me."

He stood up, staggered, hit the tank, bounced off it and swayed, ripping out a long diminishing curse that came from his heart where Sam and Taffy lay dead. Watty made no attempt to help him. He was checking the Bren, moving off casually. Woods waited for Goodall, holding the other revolver for him. The sight of these two men did much for him, and he felt himself being almost physically straightened out. Three-fifths of the crew of Moby Dick were on their feet and had weapons ready; and all he could think of doing was to tell one of them to get out of this, and the other to give up the Bren. He must have been pretty far gone.

"Watty, pick up two of them grenades. And two for you, lad. I'll take the rest." He started walking, and felt that so long as he could walk steadily like this he would be all right, but if he had to throw himself down when the bullets came, he wouldn't get up again. He said when they had picked up the grenades: "We're goin' to work round to the back of Bloody Mary. I think they've been hit." They started off.

He was still having to deal with his predicament. How had he reckoned that his Troop-leader had been hit? Some part of his instinct, developed by long training, had let his eyes see the other tank and his brain consider it. Bloody Mary had not fired the gun for a long time, and the Besas were silent and the turret empty. Up there, his brain had been thinking with an absurd devotion to duty, it looks as if that tank's been hit. You'd better go and have a dekko.

Watty was walking beside him, half crouched with the Bren at the ready, his lop-sided face thick with the dust, the two grenades bobbing inside his battle-dress blouse like a woman's breasts, looking so like the clothed, soft flesh where a babe could suck and draw its sustenance; but the babe who would suck at these would get his vitals ripped and his face blown away in pulp.

They kept close to the wall of a house with their heads turned away from the heat. Along the wall, a sound came, a rising thunder that stopped them and made them stand looking at one another. The wall was a sounding-board for the lifting thunder and they could not tell where it came from.

"Christ!" Watty said. Goodall's eyes were narrowing as if by closing them he could shut out the sound.

"Building going down," he said, because he had to give this frightening noise a name, explain it away to his nerves.

Woods had his back to the wall, and felt it trembling. Something was coming, out of the sky or up from the ground, monstrous and unstoppable, coming to overwhelm them.

Watty was shouting, but they could not hear him above the big headlong thunder. It pinned them to the wall in the blood-red flickering light.

III

THE TANKS CAME THROUGH in line astern at a cracking pace that carried them past the wall of flame, their great beetle bodies lifting across the street's rubbish and driving onwards against the wreckage of the road block and the knocked-out German tank behind it. The leader hit it glancing, and slewed, and straightened, and ran on while the others followed at full throttle. Their commanders were mounted. Their thunder bellowed, battering past the line of buildings where Goodall and Woods and Watkins-Price stood pinned, deafened and blinded as the dust engulfed them. They slid down the wall and lay flat, waiting as prone as dead men and as deaf and as blind, with the joy inside them rising to their throats as they heard the tanks go through. Into this hell of half-light and flame and filth they had come suddenly, a long, linked battering-ram, and behind them were armoured-cars and Bren-carriers and a wave of infantry at the run, so that when the thunder faded and the dust eddied away there were the faces, voices, and the tramp of living feet bearing the strong arms along at a pace that nothing left in this burning citadel could stop.

Watty had been shouting for a long time. *"It's 'B' Squadron! 'B' Squadron and the bloody Yorkshires, look at em!"*

The tide of men went by. No face turned this way. These three were part of the rubbish of the first assault, dropped where they stood and swept aside. Goodall was yelling to them and waving them on, calling them beautiful bastards, calling them his sons, his bloody darlings as they ran by him in a dust-thick wave with their bayonets fixed and their tin-hats bobbing on their heads.

When he looked at Watty he saw he was crying, with tears going down through the film on his filthy face. He was watching the British go through, and couldn't stand it, because there was a ghastly beauty in this pack of dust-smothered running men who went in a fast brown tide along the street, men with dirt on them thick as muck, streaming down this filth-strewn drain with beauty on them enough to drown the heart.

Goodall was on his feet, dragging Woods up, and then helping Watty to find the Bren. The three of them began running, pitching like blind drunks in the wake of the infantry, tagging on to them and running with them, drawn into the tide of them and becoming part of them as the tanks drove through and cleared the way. Against them was no more than a drizzle of bullets from the Spandaus that gave a rattle in the throat of a dying garrison.

With the evening came the bitter-sweet smell of the dead, an overpowering malevolence that made the living pray for wind to come. Parties of men moved about with spades, and with the battle over, some of these died late, for the enemy had left booby-traps even wired to his own corpses, so that they had to be lassoed from a safe distance before they could be shifted. A mass grave was being dug by the few prisoners for their own comrades, following an argument between the second-in-command of the garrison and the colonel of the British battalion. For reasons of hygiene, the colonel ordered the grave to be dug. His own men were busy mopping up the fringe of resistance to the south, where there had been no orders to surrender, so that these prisoners must do the work. The victors were under no legal obligation to dispose of the enemy's dead in orderly graves; this, then, was offered as a privilege to the vanquished. Even a mass grave was better than the alternative of throwing the corpses bodily into the fires that still burned throughout the village. The German second-in-command conceded the point and set his men to work.

In some of the buildings, snipers were still active, and these were being dealt with by roving groups of infantry and tank crews who had bailed out. Of Two Troop, five

men were alive and helping with the work: Lieutenant
Pope, Sergeant Goodall, Troopers Steiner, Watkins-Price
and Woods. Pope's arm was in a sling; Goodall had re-
covered from the head wound sufficiently to keep on his
feet and join the searchers. With him were his own two
men from Moby Dick. Steiner had not been seen since
the second assault wave had driven into the havoc and
broken the enemy's resistance.

In the village of Pinchau-le-Bas a kind of peace had
come. Daylight was still over the horizon. Falaise burned
on, sending a light of its own across the ruins here. Twice
bombers had been heard in the north, feeding the fire of
Falaise and easing the work of the Canadians and British
units who were besieging it.

Ambulances had come into the village, overtaking the
rearguard of the infantry, and the wounded were going
back to medical centres west of the Falaise-Pinchau road.
Men lay among rubble, dying for want of help, the toxic
fluids of their wounds spreading quick poison through the
blood. Others lay unconscious, the mark on their forehead a sign that they had been found, and given
morphine, and would be fetched as soon as the stretcher-
parties could make their way through the shambles left by
the whirlwind.

Under a canopy of fallen beams and plaster, 343
Trooper Soaper, 'C' Squadron, lay without a wound but
with his last courage gone, knowing that he could not go
again into a fighting-tank, nor face another enemy nor
another morning in this war that was too big for him; so
with his revolver he shot off his thumb, and thought of
home.

Men lay sleeping where they could, along the field
below the village church, still as death or starting up in
sweat as the battle-dreams wakened them. Others joined
the burial parties, working because they could not sleep,
and buried an officer, a man, a stranger, a friend, waiting
for the padre to come, or doing his rites for him. *They
dug a hole and dropped me in, and put wild flowers in a
tin.* The spade, the earth, the blanket, a whole man or
half a man with a face or no face, undignified in death by

the spilt vomit and the cake of blood . . . *put him with his head to the enemy* . . . the kindness of the dark earth tumbling in, the silence of it and the mercy of it, hiding them for ever, leaving them to be remembered with their eyes clear and their faces smiling, the hair slicked back and the new uniform somehow comic on them, tragic on them in the proud prized photograph that would soon be put into a more expensive frame as a token of their immortality.

It was Watkins-Price who, going into a house where a sniper had been suspected, found the first of the hanged men in Pinchau-le-Bas. He was a German rifleman, swinging from the ceiling joist by his lanyard. There was a bullet-hole in one wrist, but he had died by strangling. Watkins-Price brought his sergeant up to see.

Goodall said nothing, but turned the corpse, inspecting it for other wounds; there were none. He said:

"The Lancs infantry found some of these in Morain-ville, farther back."

Watty turned away from the bloated face. "Did they?"

"I've got no ideas." Goodall went out of the room with him, climbing over the brass bedstead and the tumble of plaster on the stairs. "They don't do it themselves. A man can't string himself up like that."

"They wouldn't," Watty said, unpleasantly moved by the mystery. "They'd shoot themselves if they wanted to get out of it. That's a soldier's way."

They left the house. Later, Goodall reported the hanged man and then forgot him. As the light from the sky faded and the glow of Falaise cast the long night's sundown over the village, shells came in from the last S.P. gun that was holding the anti-tank ditch on the south, and infantry were sent out to silence it. With the infantry were stragglers, some of them tank men who were not tired of fighting, or who resented the sound of the German gun in the village that was theirs, or who could not sleep and would not join the burial parties because their stomachs would not let them; among these men was little Steiner, no longer neat in his uniform, but steady in his step and with his head quite clear of any shock. He lived in his past, here in the shattered village, and felt himself closer to his mother and father, almost believing that he had been born beneath a tumbled ceiling with the jack-boot ringing past the house and the swastika flying on the roof, born under the German law that made a Jew a criminal. He had been a young man before that had happened, but he could not remember a time when he had not hated the Hun. He went with the infantry, and before midnight the self-propelled gun was quiet. Only one man had refused to surrender at the last.

This man had come running with a gun in his hand, emptying its ammunition uselessly, a huge young man who ran like a stallion against the group of Yorkshiremen. *"Heil, Hitler!"* He came charging with his long legs flying under him—*"Heil, Hitler!"*—and they had to give him a burst with a Sten, because he would do damage even with an empty gun in this high-and-mighty mood of his. They saw the bullets riddle into him, but he came on, checking and then pitching forward with his feet still pounding. The Sten rattled again. His blood ran down his legs—*"Heil Hitler!"* He was still running. They were afraid of the miracle. A dead man could not run. The Sten put out a long burst that went into his body like the sharpened links of a steel chain, and he cried out, but the blood came into his throat and there was the *"Heil——"* and a liquid coughing as he ran three more paces and fell, the bullets as thick as acorns in him.

A man looked down at his big bloodied body. "God save the King is what we always say, lad."

They left him, forming up by their officer and going back to the village. The prisoners went in front of them. In the anti-tank ditch were the enemy dead, bundled in for the sake of tidiness, all except one, who was later found hanging from the barrel of the self-propelled gun.

In the light of the burning city, four miles north, the ambulances worked in the village, and parties were searching for wounded among the ruins, and bringing them out. There was no discrimination, at first, between friend and enemy; if a man wanted help he was given it whether he moaned or screamed in English or German when they moved him gently and sent the agony bursting against his eyes all over again. But later, when the searchers were tired and their hands raw from tugging rubble away from the living treasure and their stomachs touchy with the sight and smell and feel of grotesque distortion, they came upon German boys of seventeen and eighteen, the younger fanatics whose intense indoctrination had turned them into courageous, inspired ventriloquists' dolls.

"Filthy English!" they cried, and if they had a whole hand they hit out at their rescuers. "Do not touch me, swine!" There was a group of these youths half buried under the steeple of the church, the big gold cross sticking up from the rubbish and turned rose-red in the light of Falaise.

"Do not touch!" A sick-faced boy with his leg smashed was hitting out at the R.A.M.C. corporal.

"Turn it up, will you, Fritz? There's a good boy."

But some of the men who were having to drive themselves to keep on with the work grew tired of this, and began leaving the German boys to die.

"Filthy English sons of whores!" Their English was very good, for these were the élite, the educated.

A rescuer straightened up. "Have it your own way, mate."

The smoke drifted across the rubbish from Falaise. The men worked with ghostliness through the nightmare, dissolving in the smoke and reappearing, stalking the wounded.

Major Knowles, climbing painfully over the bricks and timber, still looking for Captain Hallett after four hours' ebbing of hope, said: "Orderly, there's one over there."

"Sir?"

"That one." He pointed.

"He won't let me touch 'im, sir. I'm filthy English."

"He's bleeding to death, man."

"He won't let me get at 'is wound, sir."

"Then shoot him." Knowles picked his way through the masonry.

"Sir?"

He turned his head. The smell of them was in his soul. "They shoot horses, don't they?"

The orderly moved on, red-eyed and with his stomach curdling, looking for others, wishing to get away from the bad dream within the bad dream, the stupid young Boche and his own mad officer.

An armoured bulldozer was butting at the débris at the end of the main street where the tanks had come through. A medical sergeant led his group after it, in case the shifting of the rubble should expose a man with life in him still. They followed the big machine with the patience of birds behind a plough.

"That tank there. Check inside."

Two men clambered into Moby Dick, but there was nothing for them to save. They joined the others. A man passed them, mumbling and staring-eyed, the battle-palsy shaking him as he jogged along, going nowhere. The sergeant said: "Get him." They took him with them as far as the regimental aid post, though there was not a scratch on his body. They could not search for the sane mind that was somewhere buried under the rubbish of Pinchau-le-Bas.

In the field below the church the earth tumbled softly in and they stood with their spades, Goodall and Watkins-Price, side by side, while Mr. Pope said with the quiet embarrassment of a layman: "You died in all honour. God rest your souls."

Turning away with him, Goodall said: "It came in through the front, so it was quick." In a small way this eased them more than the other words.

Falaise burned through the night, its rose light flickering and its smoke rolling softly across the meadows and the road. All night men moved about in the shattered village, and the stretcher-bearers worked with blisters in their boots and their hands torn, the canvas of their stretchers long ago dyed red.

Masonry fell, tumbling suddenly from the buildings' skeletons, making the work more difficult. The bulldozer turned, keeping the street clear for the ambulances. Stones fell, cascading. It turned again and tidied them. In the casualty clearing station outside the village the doctors worked, cutting the cost of the victory by a penny here, a shilling there. The men were brought to them, fully conscious or with the narcotics keeping their minds safe from the horrors of the body. Of those who could think clearly, there was the consolation that they had their passports to England with them now, a lost foot, a broken hip, a chest wound, a thumb shot off. They must wait patiently.

In the field not far from where the dead lay buried, the living slept or sat awake with a cup of compo tea and a cigarette. The golden cross, sticking from the rubbish in the street, caught the light of Falaise, and burned until dawn. Alone in a dip of grass, Steiner slept, with blond men dangling in his dreams. The bulldozer rumbled, driving its echoes through the broken walls.

Towards morning, a wind came and took the smoke eastwards, so that as the light strengthened, Pinchau-le-Bas was exposed minute by minute to the wide-eyed brutality of the sun.

In the truck, Mr. Pope sat near the tailboard, his arm out of the sling and his round college-boy's face looking ten years younger now that the sweat and muck and stubble was gone. Only the eyes retained their age. The truck stopped, waiting for a scout-car to lurch past in the dust and vanish towards the Falaise-Pinchau road. Then it jogged off again behind the convoy.

During the last two days the noise of Falaise had died down hour by hour. The bombers had gone in again this morning, but it was not a big raid. And now, in any case, the truck was taking them to the rear, so that the sound of the fighting would be lost on their journey. Sergeant Goodall watched the road go ribboning out behind. Up there, near the ridge, was the shattered village and Moby Dick. He felt lost, and felt he was going in the wrong direction, away from the tank and the fighting.

At noon when they were past the stream the convoy halted and there was a lot of shouting, and the dust went up from the road as a bunch of dispatch-riders swerved

their way among the trucks, calling to the drivers and the
officers who were asking them questions. The riders had
come from the east. The rear truck got the word before
the others. Pope looked down into the dust-filmed face;
the rider straddled his machine, grinning up, jumping his
foot on the kick-start as the engine stalled. He nodded
again as Pope shouted:

"Yes, sir!"

Goodall had not heard. "What's that?"

The motor-cycle revved up and swung away. When the
noise had faded, Pope said: "Falaise has gone."

After a few seconds the sergeant said: "It's ours?"

"Yes."

They bumped along, Pope, Goodall, Watkins-Price and
Woods, nudging together as the truck ran wild over the
ruts in the patched-up road.

"That's a bit of okay, isn't it, sir?"

"The last time I saw the Colonel, he told me that once
Jerry lost Falaise, it'd be his last hope gone of holding a
line in France. They'll be on the run now to the Rhine."

They sat with their thoughts. Should they be cheering,
now that Falaise was gone? They supposed they should.
The truck made them sore. The convoy was going full
belt across the Normandy plain. It was taking them the
wrong way. They were lost, without a tank, without a
home.

Goodall stared at the dust that went whirling along
behind, and said suddenly: "How the bloody hell are we
goin' to catch up with 'em, then?"

"They'll give us a tank soon enough." Pope watched
him, amused by the big man's impatience. Goodall
looked as wretched as a tortoise out of its shell. "Don't
worry, I'll see they fix us up."

Goodall looked at him and nodded seriously.

"You'll have to, sir. I mean, we got to have somewhere
to live."

THE DESTRUCTION
of DRESDEN . . by David Irving

"The destruction of Dresden remains a serious query against the conduct of Allied bombing."
— *Winston Churchill*

On February 13, 1945, in a series of three bombing raids, the beautiful city of Dresden, Germany, was obliterated. The reasoning behind the most successful and indiscriminate annihilation in human history —the devastating destruction of countless art treasures, 175,000 homes, and approximately 130,000 human lives (almost twice the toll at Hiroshima)— has never been clearly defined.

In "one of the finest and most memorable and valuable documentaries concerning the last war" (John Pudney—London *Evening Standard*), David Irving lifts the veil from what may well prove to be one of the most controversial episodes in the history of warfare.

> *"We should be grateful to Mr. Irving for having devoted long study to this question and for having now provided us with as accurate an account of what actually happened as we are likely to obtain . . ."*
> — *Sir Harold Nicholson*
> The London Observer

FULLY ILLUSTRATED WITH REMARKABLE PHOTOGRAPHS
U6026   75¢

BY THE AUTHOR OF ZORBA THE GREEK

FREEDOM OR DEATH

Nikos Kazantzakis' mighty novel of war and rebellion on the island of Crete.

"FREEDOM OR DEATH is the whole world. It is written from heart, mind, soul and entrails, written with power and pervasive humor. This is the work of a master."

—*Saturday Review*

U7027   95¢

To order by mail, send $1.00 (includes postage and handling charge) to Dept. CS, Ballantine Books, 101 Fifth Avenue, New York, N. Y. 10003.

Ballantine's War Book Series, comprising more than 60 titles by top German, Japanese, British and American authorities, provides the most complete coverage of the war available in paperbound books. In the list following are described some of the most recent titles:

U5016 DUEL FOR KILAMANJARO, Leonard Mosley 60¢
Africa 1914-18—The dramatic story of any unconventional war.

U6012 FULL CIRCLE, Group Captain J. E. Johnson   75¢
The tactics of air fighting—1914-1964.

**U7003 MOLLIE AND OTHER WAR PIECES,
         A. J. Leibling   95¢**
A collection by a brilliant war correspondent and critic.

U5019 THE LAST BLUE SEA, David Forrest   60¢
A novel of war against the Japanese in New Guinea.

U2815 U-BOATS AT WAR, Harald Busch   50¢
Complete account of German submarine actions and losses in World War II.

U2803 THE BATTLE OF THE BULGE, R. E. Merriam   50¢
(Original title: Dark December. **Abridged**)
Full, factual, exciting story of Hitler's last desperate gamble. With maps.

U2805 THE FIRST AND THE LAST, Adolf Galland   50¢
Rise and Fall of the Luftwaffe, by Germany's commander of fighter forces. Photos.

A SELECTION OF
BALLANTINE WAR BOOKS

LAST ACT: Barrie Pitt 75¢
A vivid and dramatic narrative describing the smashing finale of World War I.

LAST BLUE SEA: David Forrest 60¢
Novel of fighting men in jungle warfare of New Guinea.

GOD IS MY CO-PILOT:
General Robert L. Scott 50¢
The personal story of an outstanding World War II fighter pilot.

BATTLE OF THE BULGE: Robert Merriam 50¢
Hitler's last desperate gamble to win the war.

THE FIRST AND THE LAST: Adolf Galland 50¢
A history of the Luftwaffe.

SAMURAI!: Saburo Sakai, Fred Saito &
Martin Caidin 50¢
The greatest air battle of the Pacific from the Japanese side.

AMERICAN ACES: Edward H. Sims 50¢
Stories of the top surviving American Aces.

BEYOND COURAGE: Clay Blair Jr. 50¢
True tales of US Airmen down over Korea and their escape.

FIVE DOWN AND GLORY: Gene Gurney 50¢
The sweeping story of America's ace fighter pilots.

THE DAM BUSTERS: Paul Brickhill 50¢
The fantastic close-in bombing of the Eder Dam.

DESTRUCTION OF DRESDEN: David Irving 75¢
Most appalling air attack of W. W. II.

PANZER LEADER: Heinz Guderian 75¢
The most revealing personal account ever published of the war from the German side.